MARGARET FRAZER

The Squire's Tale

ROBERT HALE · LONDON

© Margaret Frazer 2000
First published in Great Britain 2002

ISBN 0 7090 7055 1

Robert Hale Limited
Clerkenwell House
Clerkenwell Green
London EC1R 0HT

2 4 6 8 10 9 7 5 3 1

Typeset in 10½/13pt Classical Garamond Roman
by Derek Doyle & Associates in Liverpool.
Printed in Great Britain by
St Edmundsbury Press Ltd, Bury St Edmunds, Suffolk.
Bound by Woolnough Bookbinding Limited.

FOR SARAH AND BILL

Most excellent friends and superlative people
who—for good measure—gave me an idea for the
next book

An housbonde I wol have, I wol nat lette,
Which shal be both my dettour and my thral . . .

—Chaucer, *The Wife of Bath's Tale*

Chapter 1

The spring evening was drawing in to blue darkness under the tatters of low black clouds streaming away to the east on a warm-edged wind that promised a fair dawn tomorrow.

A tomorrow he had almost not lived to see.

Robert felt at the edges of that thought while he stood watching the darkness come, his good hand cradling his hurt one against his chest. From here at the parlor's open window in the west tower he could see out over the garden's low turf wall into the orchard's gnarl of upper branches, barren yet this early in the spring. Their black shapes were darkening into the darkness now that the last fade of sunset light was gone but Robert went on watching, not ready yet for the room behind him, for the lamplight and talk and people who had not been almost dead today. Better the darkness for just now and thinking of other things, rather than trying to belong with them just yet.

It was the orchard that brought him back to Brinskep Manor early in every Lent, to be here when the bare black branches frothed out into a sea of creamy blossoms. It was something that every time joyed his heart to the core in much the same way that first sight of each of his children had. With the children the moment passed and never came again, succeeded by the other joys they gave – from sometimes no more than something as simple as Robin holding tightly to his hand while pretending not to be frightened of his mother's new horse or John ceasing to cry when he saw his father had mended his broken wooden sword or Tacine wrapping her arms around his neck in a hug – and were the richer for coming uncertainly and unexpected. But the orchard's beauty and his joy in it came every spring, and because Brinskep was the largest of his wife's three manors, her household had always been there six months out of a year, but when Blaunche had married him those six months had run from Whitsuntide to Martinmas, midsummer to early winter. 'Because that's how it's always been,' she had said simply when he had asked her why.

It had been only chance that brought him to stay a night at Brinskep the first spring of his marriage, on his way to Fen Harcourt for business with Sir Walter, when the orchard had been in its full bloom. He had spent half a morning walking alone there when he should have been on his way, for once able to do what he chose because he had been travelling with only two servants and no certain time he had to be anywhere. And when he had returned to Blaunche he had, for the first time in their marriage, insisted on a change in how their lives were run, that Blaunche, still happy in having married him, had agreed to with only small protest and thereafter they were at Brinskep from sometime in Lent until almost Lammastide, then moved the household on to stay through Allhallows at Wystead Manor, then shifted to Northend before winter set in, spending Christmas and the weeks afterward there until time to return to Brinskep.

The pattern was an easy and familiar one after all these years but Robert doubted he could have brought Blaunche to any such change so easily now; her pleasure in having won him was too far in the past, and she remembered too easily now, when it suited her, that the manors she had brought to their otherwise landless marriage had been hers before they were his. And he was weak, he supposed, still to think of them that way, too, when by law whatever property a wife held became her husband's when they married. That Blaunche had decided on him for her third husband and forced the marriage on him made no difference to the law: when they married, she and her properties, even those inherited by dower right from her first two husbands, had become his, no matter whether he had wanted them or Blaunche at all.

'Robert, shut the window, pray,' she said from across the room behind him. 'The wind is coming in.'

It was, and not warmly, either, but it smelled of young growing things and the rain there had been all day and the clear day there would be tomorrow and just now Robert had a craving for anything that promised life was an ongoing thing, not something that had nearly ended for him on a sword's blade in the orchard this afternoon, but he loosed his hurt hand to reach out his left one to the shutter and pull it closed. The window was of three stone-mullioned lights with a wide seat built into the wall below it and only the upper quarter of each light was glassed; their lower portion had either nothing between indoors and out or else heavy wooden shutters painted gaily on the inside with vines and flowers. One was already shut against the night; now Robert unfolded the other from where it sat flat against the stone thickness of the wall, closed it across the gap and slid its wooden bolts into the wooden catches on the other, locking them closed and to each other.

When Brinskep Manor had been built about two hundred years before, defense rather than comfort had been the concern. It had been barons then, Robert vaguely knew – barons against the king and king against the barons and barons against each other for good measure, with no one sure of not finding himself in the middle of trouble before he had time to blink twice – so Brinskep was stone-built, with only small-windowed storerooms and the kitchen at ground level. The hall was a story above them, reached from outside only by an outer stair from the yard and flanked at its west end by a squat, three-storied tower, uncrenellated because of the cost of a license to do so but defensible nonetheless. There had been no need of defense for more than a hundred years, thank God and all the saints, and even as poorly as the war in France was going in this year of God's grace 1442, the nineteenth year of the reign of King Henry VI, there was no fear of a French invasion so far inland as here in southern Warwickshire. Timber-and-plaster buildings had long since been built around the hallyard's other sides to the gateway to the outer yard, and in the hall and tower comfort came before wariness; it was a pleasant room Robert turned to, warm with lamplight, soft with Master Geoffrey reading aloud from a book of Breton lays while Blaunche, Mistress Avys and Emelye sewed and listened.

Everything in it was familiar, from his high-backed, green-cushioned chair to the tapestry painted with some scene from the Trojan War hung on one of the white plastered walls, to the scatter of the children's toys across the floor's golden rush matting, left behind when they were taken off to bed a while ago, to the women quietly busy while the household's clerk read to them, but tonight Robert was seeing all of it more sharply than he had seen it in a long while because this afternoon he had come near to being never here to see it again. This afternoon Robert had nearly been . . .

11

'Many a bold baron lay writhing in his blood, / So much was spilled the field did seem to flood . . .' read Master Geoffrey in his smooth, strong voice from across the parlor. The long settle in front of the fireplace that was Blaunche's chosen place to sit of an evening, with room around her for her sewing and sometimes for the children or, like now, for Master Geoffrey to be at its far end, reading aloud from the tale of the Earl of Toulous, by light from lamps burning on the tall wrought-iron lampstand set for their light to fall evenly over the book and Blaunche's sewing both. Tonight her work was a shirt for Robin, Robert thought, because their elder son was presently being the proverbial weed, outgrowing all his clothing at once. That at least meant John had hand-me-downs for now, but what it would be to keep Tacine in dresses when she was no longer small enough to wear the smocks that had served her brothers when they were toddling did not bear thinking on.

Thinking on it anyway, Robert smiled as he bent to pick up with his unhurt hand the less-loved of his daughter's two rag dolls, abandoned when Tacine carried the other off to bed with her; but as he straightened, his hurt hand gave a heavy throb, and dropping the doll onto his chair, he shifted the hand higher and cradled it against his chest with the other one again. It was only a pair of sprained, bruised fingers, nothing worse, he reminded himself, no matter how much they hurt. 'Didn't you ever learn,' Ned Verney had jibed at him while binding the small splint to them, 'that it's better to catch a blow on your dagger blade than with your knuckles?'

'Better on the knuckles than not at all,' Robert had jibed back. 'And best not to be in the way of it at all.'

They had both of them been making light of the hurt because if the rider's blow had not been as awry as Robert's, there would have been no making light about anything at all. As it was, the man's horse, being a palfrey instead of battle-trained, had misliked finding itself among shouting men and sword and dagger blades and women's screaming and had shied as its rider had struck down at Robert and Robert had flung up his dagger in defense, so that the sword's pommel instead of its blade had struck his dagger hand and he still had his fingers.

The trick, he reminded himself, as the throb lessened to ache, was to keep his hand raised higher than his heart so it did not gather blood, and mindful of that, he shifted Robin's wheeled horse to safety under a chair with his foot instead of bending to it. He also considered reminding Emelye she was supposed to tidy things away tonight since Katherine was helping see the children into bed, but Emelye, the younger of his wife's two maids-in-waiting, was finally quiet after a few hours of sobbing and exclaiming, as if the danger this afternoon had been hers instead of Katherine's, and was sitting on a cushion on the floor near the settle intently sorting bunches of embroidery threads by color; on the principal of letting sleeping dogs lie, Robert preferred to leave her quiet, but too restless himself to sit, he paced past his chair to the solar's far end, then back to his chair, then around the small, tall-legged table, with its evening plate of wafers and pitcher of spiced perry. He was neither hungry nor thirsty, but he would maybe after all take the valerian tonight, because if he was unable to walk away from his thoughts now, he assuredly wouldn't escape them in bed and even more assuredly did not want to lie awake with them for company. Nor with his hand's pain, come to that. He hadn't even felt the pain until everything was over, until the men were spurring away and he'd been certain Katherine was safe . . .

'Robert, will you sit, please?' Blaunche said with the slight edge that made it demand rather than request.

Robert bent and straightened too swiftly for his hand to resent it, taking up Tacine's doll and then sitting in his chair, seeing but not caring about the upward-through-her-lashes look that Emelye gave him in hopes he would sit nearer to her. Had Blaunche noticed yet the silly girl had decided to be infatuated with him now? Last year it had been Ned she fluttered at, and over Christmas it had been Benedict, and now for no good reason except lack of anyone else, Robert supposed, she had set her girlish heart toward him these past few weeks. He could only hope Sir Walter would find a husband for her soon to take her off their hands, and ignoring her sidewise looks at him, he set to straightening the doll's dress and tidying its hair.

'. . . I near die of grief. Dear Lady, grant me your love, / For love of God that sits above . . .' Master Geoffrey read on. The duties for which he was paid were in the main the daily tediousness of writing letters, keeping manorial records in order, and checking over accounts of in-come and out-go between the main audits at Easter and Michaelmas. Besides all that, the year or so he had had of legal studies was of late proving useful in the matter with the Allesleys wanting back the dower land Blaunche had been wrongfully given by her second husband, and certainly evenings had been more pleasant since he had joined the household two years back with his good voice for reading and a feel for the words. In addition, when reading was not wanted he made easy conversation. None of all that would have been enough, though, if Blaunche had failed to like him. Their last clerk had left because, he had said, he'd not take being screamed at by any woman over anything and assuredly not when the fault wasn't his. Robert, knowing the fault had indeed not been his, had paid him half a quarter's extra wages and recommended him to Ned who had hired him and since then thanked Robert for the favor rather too often.

Across the parlor Blaunche burst out her raucous laugh at some-thing in the story, and Robert's unhurt hand tightened on Tacine's doll before he could stop himself. One of the first things he had disliked about Blaunche had been her laugh, even before he had known what she intended for him. She was a Fenner, with Fenner family looks and Fenner family ways enough to have put him off her even though he was a Fenner, too. Raised in his cousin Sir Walter Fenner's household, he had been serving as a squire there in his young manhood when Blaunche first noted him. As the landless son of a landless younger son, with no likelihood of ever rising higher in life than service in someone's household, he should have been grateful when she took a fancy to him. Older than him by only six years, twice widowed and holding the wardship of her eleven-year-old son Benedict, her second husband's heir, she had quite sufficient properties to support another marriage and no one could see but what a piece of luck it was for Robert when she decided she wanted him for her next husband.

No one but Robert.

But he had had no true choice in the matter. Blaunche was a closer cousin to Sir Walter than he was, and far more in Sir Walter's favor, and Sir Walter had bluntly pointed out to him, first, what he would gain by marrying Blaunche and, next, that if he did not marry her, he would have nothing, not even his place in Sir Walter's household.

'Nor hope of place in anyone else's,' Sir Walter had added cheer-fully. 'I'll see to that.'

He would have. Sir Walter was a man who enjoyed both making threats and carrying them out, and Robert had been left with only the choice of being Blaunche's husband or a beggar.

'Robert, *please* sit down.'

He realized he was on his feet again, pacing again, still restlessly untangling the doll's hair while he did, but was saved from having to sit again by cheerful voices on the stairs warning that Ned and Benedict were returned from taking the children to Nurse at bedtime.

Ned, like Robert, was a minor member of widespread family, the Verneys in his case, but unlike Robert, he had inherited a manor from his father just to the north of Brinskep and made a quietly profitable marriage of his own choosing with a Coventry merchant's daughter. Meeting during Robert's first year of marriage, while settling a quarrel between their bailiffs over a fishing place in the stream between their manors, they had fallen easily into friendship, with much going to and fro between their manors and Ned presently here for a few days together, his wife gone to Coventry to her sister's lying-in and his company welcomed by Robert who paused to put Tacine's doll under his chair with Robin's horse, wondering as Ned followed Benedict through the narrow stairway door why Katherine was not come back, too, but only asking as he moved to the table to pour them some perry, 'You saw them into bed?'

'We saw them into bed,' Ned agreed, 'and they nearly saw me into my grave.'

'You're too indulgent with them, Ned,' Blaunche said. The woman who would send them to bed every night with too many sweets in their stomachs if she was given the chance, Robert thought. 'They need a firm hand, believe me.'

'It's not indulgence,' Ned protested, taking the bowl Robert held out to him. 'It's survival. My ungodly godson demanded three stories ere he'd let me leave or he'd not go to sleep, he said.'

'Extortion, plain and simple,' Benedict said and added, 'Thank you' as he took the perry Robert next poured for him.

'It's Robert's doing,' Blaunche said. 'He too often spoils them at bedtime.'

'What made it worse was that I've but two stories in my head,' Ned went on, 'and it would have been desperate with me except Benedict had a third.'

'John protested they already knew that one,' Benedict said, 'but Ned pointed out that Robin had asked for three stories, not three new ones.'

'You didn't!' Robert said at Ned. 'You teach him to see things that way, he'll turn into a lawyer.'

'There are worse things to be than a lawyer,' Ned answered.

'Not at bedtime,' Robert returned.

'Even if my brother is one,' Ned added thoughtfully as Emelye asked, 'Where's Katherine?'

'Gone to brew something for Robert,' said Benedict. He looked to his stepfather with belated concern. 'How's your hand hurting now? Badly?'

'It aches is all and that will pass.'

'Benedict, come sit here with us,' Blaunche said, tapping at a floor cushion with her foot. 'Geoffrey has just reached where they're killing the child to make the empress seem adulterous.'

Benedict went to fold his long legs under him and sit on the cushion beside Emelye's who smiled on him and he obligingly smiled back. Above them, Master Geoffrey took up reading again and Blaunche held up her own bowl to let Robert know he could refill it. Robert did but was thinking more of Benedict who had been old enough when Robert and Blaunche had married seven years ago to go into someone else's household for training as was the usual way, but Blaunche had claimed his stepfather could train him as readily as anyone else, indeed should train him so they could come to know each other. Despite she also claimed she gave way to her husband in everything, Robert had even then known better than to refuse her desires and after all it had worked out none so ill. He and Benedict liked each other, as it happened, and Benedict delighted in his small half brothers and half sister who in return delighted in him and that could only be to the good in future time.

But time was come – and more than come – for Benedict to have more life of his own than his mother was willing to give him, and only this morning, after some few weeks of careful wooing, had Ned managed to win Blaunche's promise that after Easter he could take Benedict into his household for the three years more until Benedict came of age to take possession of the manor he had inherited from his father. Though he and Ned had agreed to it beforehand, Robert had kept well out of it, not certain what twist Blaunche would put upon him supporting Benedict leaving her, but was pleased for the boy, who had spent much of the rest of the day telling everyone who crossed his path – which meant almost everyone heard it several times over because Brinskep was not that big a manor – of his good fortune. Robert had watched him with an inward smile, wondering if he had been that young himself at eighteen years but unable to remember; and afterwards, this evening at supper, listening to Benedict make plans with Ned, he had thought what a pity it was that it had not been Benedict instead of him who had kept that young fool Will Hayton and his two friends from carrying Katherine off this afternoon because to have rescued a damsel in distress would have made the boy's day complete.

But the thought had made pain twist deeply into him somewhere behind the breastbone because, in all bitter truth, he was glad he had been there instead of anyone else, *glad* he had been the one Katherine had clung to when it was over . . .

He jerked his mind away from that run of thought, his arm jerking, too, splashing the perry he had been pouring for himself off his bowl's rim. He set the pitcher down quickly but beside him Ned was already wiping up the spill, saying, 'Go sit. You've had more of a day than does you good.'

Robert took the excuse and his bowl of perry and went to sit in his chair again, with no need to feign weariness. Coming to sit on the cushioned stool opposite him, Ned asked with a nod at his hand, low-voiced for no one else to hear, 'Still hurting?' then answered for himself, 'A stupid question. Of course it's still hurting. How badly?'

'Not much. Only in spasms. I just hope young Hayton's head hurts as badly,' Robert said, meaning it.

'His head? All you had was your dagger and he never fell off his horse. How did you come to hit his head?'

Robert grinned. 'I didn't but I saw him run it into a tree branch as they rode off.'

'Not hard enough.'

'Not nearly hard enough. But then again, I wouldn't want to have him dead and on my hands so it's probably just as well.'

'He's that thickheaded it would likely take more than an apple branch to do him much damage.'

Robert made an assenting sound to that and took a long drink of the perry, still warm and the better for the cinnamon, ginger and touch of nutmeg Blaunche had stirred in. Among her virtues – and she did have them – was a sure way with spiced wine, ale, cider and perry.

'What happened today,' Ned said, still low-voiced, 'you know the Haytons wouldn't have dared against a Fenner even three years ago.'

'I know,' Robert said. The certainty of it had been a grim under-current to his thoughts all evening, little though he wanted to think or talk about it. The Fenners had been a power in this part of the

midland shires for almost fifty years now. Lord Fenner had supported
Henry of Lancaster's successful bid for the throne against King
Richard, and the family in almost all its various branches had flour-
ished ever since, never among the most powerful but always near
enough to them to profit and to be left alone by lesser men such as
the Haytons until now.

Henry of Lancaster had been followed to the throne by his son
King Henry V who had reopened the long war with France, won
glory at Agincourt, and made in England a peace so strong that even
after his death and the succession of his infant son to the throne, the
high lords had mostly worked together at governing well. Only of late
and for no good reason that Robert could see, with the perils of a long
minority finally over and Henry VI at last come of age to take royal
power into his own hands, the steady government the lords had kept
so carefully balanced through the years of Henry VI's minority was
somehow beginning to fracture and the Fenners' secure place beginning to fray with it. Since Lord Fenner had grown too old to be active
at court or parliament, Sir Walter was the busiest of the family at poli-
tics and if he was losing place and influence, then so were those
connected to him, even as minorly as Robert.

That was why young Hayton had dared the attempt against
Katherine. She had been barely twelve, an orphaned heiress, when Sir
Walter had given her and her wardship into Robert's hands. 'You've
done well by Lady Blaunche,' he'd said. She had lately birthed Robin,
their first son. 'But if you go on doing well like this by her you're going
to need more money in hand. This Stretton girl is mine to give just now
and I'm giving her to you. Put off selling her marriage until she's nearly
of age and you'll have the profit off her properties for years and then
the price of selling her marriage on top of it when she's old enough.'

She was old enough now, and if Will Hayton had succeeded in
carrying her off and forced marriage on her, it would have been at
Robert's expense, her properties as well as Katherine going to the
Haytons without their need to pay Robert anything without he under-
took costly legal work against them. Will Hayton's father had
probably set him on to do it because the profit balanced out against
the risk of whatever trouble the Fenners might make about it afterward and, as Ned said, three years ago that trouble would have been
considerable. Now . . .

'Sir Walter has held too long to Lord Beaumont,' Ned said.

'Beaumont is slipping out of the center of things.' Ned ever had more interest in politic matters than Robert did, complained he could talk about them forever and get no more than a nod from Robert, and it was with knowing he would take Ned by surprise that Robert said, 'The way things are shaping of late, Sir Walter would do better to shift to the Earl of Stafford and the sooner the better.'

Ned, satisfactorily startled, set his bowl down on the table beside him and leaned toward Robert with a sudden, shrewd glint in his eyes. 'You've been thinking about it after all, have you?'

'After you wouldn't shut up about it last year while I was here, how could I not?'

'Why Buckingham?'

'He has a sound place in the royal council and power in this part of the country.'

'North of here. Most of his power is in the north of the shire and over into Staffordshire. This side of the shire, I'd say it's Grey of Groby we should go with.'

'His holdings are much in north Warwickshire, too.'

'And Leicestershire,' Ned quickly pointed out. Just over the Warwickshire border eastward. 'But he's looking for a wider foothold and there's no great lord hereabouts in Warwickshire to block him. Just minor families like us with enough land to matter who ought to be looking for a lord to ally with before things go worse.'

Robert frowned. 'You really think it's going to worsen? This shift-ing apart of power?'

'What's to stop it?' Ned asked back. 'King Henry?'

'He's young yet. He's still feeling his way. We have to wait it out, is all. He'll steady to things soon.'

'He's twenty years old this year. By then his father had fought and won the Welsh war.'

'That was a different time. Nor it's not fair to judge a man by what his father did, for good or ill.' And before Ned could make answer to that, Robert added, 'Besides, young Warwick will be coming into his own soon and take up the slack his father left hereabouts.'

'I've heard stories about our young Earl of Warwick,' Ned said glumly, reaching for the perry again.

'From Ralph?' Ned's younger brother was a lawyer in the Court of Common Pleas at Westminster, and taking the chance to divert the talk, Robert asked, 'How are things going for him?'

'He still spends more than he makes and wants me to make up the difference,' Ned grumbled without sounding either worried about it or angry. He and his brother had an easy trust between them that showed itself in casual scoffs that cast Ralph as the spendthrift younger brother thrust adrift to make his way in the hard world as best he could while Ned as the elder and heir worked himself to death, according to Ned's version, or was bogged so far down in country mud he could hardly see over his sheep's backs, according to Ralph's. 'He says he has a likely marriage shaping, though,' Ned said.

'Another one?' Robert asked. These past few years Ralph had been on the verge of making a marriage rather more times than Robert had bothered to keep count of.

'One of them has to actually happen one of these times,' Ned returned cheerfully. 'This time it's a London draper's daughter.'

Robert formed a soundless whistle. 'That would be to the good, if the father's unindebted.'

'He is, or Ralph wouldn't be looking at her. I gather there's a house in Cheapside, a partner in Calais, and some land out Holborn way. The girl would have the Holborn land for dowry and some money with it.'

'Any brothers? Sisters?' Who would have share in whatever eventual inheritance there might be.

'Two sons, no sisters.'

The stairway door opened to Gil's back coming in, his voice following after because he was talking to someone below him on the stairs. Despite his claim that Blaunche's waiting-woman Mistress Avys ran him to rags with idiot errands and snored at night into the bargain, he was growing plump with wooing Mariena in the kitchen and was just now explaining the virtues of a walnut-garlic-pepper sauce for stockfish over a sauce of vinegar and pepper while not paying enough heed to the covered goblet he was carrying, and as Katherine followed him into the solar she put out a hand to steady it upright.

'Thanks, my lady,' said Gil. 'You see, it's because the walnuts and garlic work *with* the fish, while the vinegar only works *at* it . . .'

'Gil,' Katherine said, with a small nod toward the room still behind him.

Reminded he was there for more than talk, Gil broke off, turned, and bowed to the room in general though mostly to Robert. When

Robert after his marriage to Blaunche had found himself in need of his own manservant to see to him, he had taken Gil out of a place in Sir Walter's household even lowlier than his own had been. More used to serving than being served, Robert had been awkward over the change for longer than Gil had been but Gil had finally trained him to where Robert knew he would be fairly lost without Gil's cheerful overseeing of his needs and wants, even ones he did not know he had until Gil had seen to them. Now, to Robert's questioning look at the covered goblet he carried, Gil said, 'Something to help you sleep, sir.' And added before Robert could protest he did not want it. 'My lady Katherine brewed it, sir.'

Headed off from refusing the drink, Robert looked to Katherine come to stand beside Gil, smiling at him as if she knew what he had not said as she held up a fist-sized, towel-wrapped bundle and said, 'A poultice.'

There had been no reason to turn down the offer of her wardship when Sir Walter had made it and perfectly good ones for taking it, nor had the little scrap of a girl who had been delivered to them one early summer day given any trouble to make either Blaunche or him regret having the raising of her. Reasonably biddable, she had learned what she was supposed to learn and moreover been glad of the learning, unlike Emelye, taken on because her mother and Blaunche were great good friends and who learned anything only perforce and forgot most of it soon afterwards. Katherine both learned and remembered and for extra measure was patient with Blaunche's headaches, kind with the children, liked by the household, and good company at almost any time.

But when Robert had not been noticing, she had grown past being a little girl into the beginnings of womanhood, and when he had noticed, seeing her dancing in the hall one evening at Christmastide last past, with ribbons in her hair and bells tied to her sleeves, laughing up at Benedict, he must have made a sound or movement because beside him Blaunche, sitting the dancing out because she was queasy in her first month of another childing, had asked him what was the matter.

Still a little blank with surprise, he had answered, 'Katherine. She's grown.'

Blaunche had laughed at him. 'Of course she's grown. That's why I've been saying these six months past that it's time we looked out a husband for her.'

In all fairness, she had indeed been saying that but Robert had not been listening, certain it was surely too soon to be thinking of Katherine's marriage. Only that Christmas evening, seeing her laughing, dancing, for once forgetful of duties, with Benedict's admiring gaze on her, had he realized she was no longer a little girl but a young woman, a lovely young woman, and since then had spent bitter time trying to forget she was because he had no business thinking and feeling what he thought and felt when he remembered it.

But now she had drawn a stool close to his chair, was sitting beside him, the poultice in her lap, reaching for his hand, and he asked, 'Where's your Mistress Dionisia gone to?' Katherine's own waiting-woman who, like Emelye, had been in the orchard with Katherine at the attempt to seize her but, unlike Emelye for whom screaming had sufficed, had joined with Katherine in making trouble enough to keep Will Hayton from laying hands on her until Robert reached them. Since then she had followed close on Katherine wherever she went, as if another attempt inside the manor's very walls was likely, and Katherine smiled as she began deftly to unwrap the bindings holding the splints to Robert's fingers. 'She's gone to make certain Master Skipton has seen to all the doors being locked.'

'Oh-oh,' Robert said because Brinskep's long-time, much-trusted steward would take ill that doubting of his duty.

'Oh-oh, indeed,' Katherine agreed. 'She's already reminded him thrice this evening to be sure it was done.' But Katherine was more concerned with Robert's bared hand, lifting it to have close look at its bruised swelling.

Robert, preferring not to have close look, looked at the top of her head instead. Because she was unmarried, her braided hair, falling to below her waist, was uncovered, the lamplight finding chestnut sheens in its darkness, and from when she had been in his arms this afternoon he knew it smelled of camomile and was grateful now to be distracted from his thoughts as she said, 'Pray, pardon me for being quick with this, but I want to put the poultice on while it's still warm. It's mostly artemisia to lessen the swelling and bruisewort against the bruising.'

'And when, pray tell, did you learn about poultices?' Robert asked, deliberately teasing her the way he had since she was small and came to tell him of any newly learned skill.

'Mistress Avys says every woman should know herbs and how best

22

to use them.' Katherine paused, to look up at him from under her lashes as she added sweetly, 'On chance there's ever need to poison someone.'

'Mistress Avys never said anything of the kind,' Robert returned with pretended sternness.

'No,' Katherine granted, returning to her task. 'Not about the poisoning. Still, it's a thought.'

Robert tried to bend his hurt fingers and winced with the pain.

Katherine clicked her tongue at him and Ned said unsympathetically, 'What did you think it would do, Robert?'

'I'd like a little more pity here, please,' Robert complained.

Gil, waiting patiently the while, took the cover off the goblet and held it out. 'Here. This'll be better than pity. The wine's strong enough, you hardly taste the herbs or whatever she's put in.'

'And how would you know that?' asked Robert.

'I had a sip to be sure it was safe. Better safe than sorry. sir.'

'Better drunk than dry,' Ned murmured into his own drink.

Gil, who was never drunk except at holidays and Ned and everyone else knew it, ignored him with great dignity.

Robert, holding in a smile, took the goblet and drank a little. The poultice – a greenish-gray mess on a strip of waxed cloth – was laid open on Katherine's lap now, and tenderly, the way he had seen her tend to one of the children when they had a scrape or were ill, she lifted his hurt hand, saying, 'I'm wrapping your whole hand for the night and that will keep it rigid enough. The splint can go on again in the morning.'

As she set his hand carefully into the herbs, he made a small grunt of pain but when she looked up at him, concerned, he gave a slight shake of his head. 'The warmth surprised me, that's all.'

She looked into his face as if doubting him but then bent to her work again and was winding the last binding strip around the poultice as across the room Master Geoffrey neared the end of the story, 'He wedded that lady as his wife, With joy and mirth they led their life twenty year and three, / And between them children had fifteen . . .'

Blaunche broke out in her loud, raw laughter again. 'Mirth for someone!' she said. 'But I doubt the lady was laughing much after the first five or so!'

Benedict, Mistress Avys and Emelye laughed with her. Katherine, with no sign of listening, tied the binding in place while Master Geoffrey finished with, 'Here ends the tale of the Earl of Toulous,' and closed the book.

'Well done, Master Geoffrey,' Blaunche said. 'Thank you.'

She held out her hand to him and the clerk rose to his feet to take it, bow over it and kiss it with the courtly grace she particularly enjoyed and Robert had never been able to manage. Vaguely, Robert wished he could raise even a small stir of jealousy but could not. Blaunche encouraged men to notice her but it was only a game she played. Nothing more than smiling and the kissing of her hands ever came of it, and Robert wished that what he felt for Katherine was as simple, instead of simply sin.

But with the story's end the evening was ended, too, and Katherine quickly tidied bandages and splints away until tomorrow while Ned who would sleep in the solar tonight instead of riding home in the dark and Benedict and Master Geoffrey who had their own rooms across the yard made their good nights, leaving as Mistress Dionisia came in and went with Gil into the bedchamber off the parlor to bring out from under Robert and Blaunche's bed the mattresses she and Katherine and Emelye would sleep on in the parlor, while they fetched their bedding from a chest along one wall.

Robert, tired into his bones and his hand aching from being handled, only waited until they were out of the bedchamber before withdrawing with only the briefest of good nights into there himself, where Mistress Avys was now pulling out from under the great bed the truckle beds she and Gil would sleep on, to be at hand if their lord or lady needed anything in the night. With Gil to help him, he readied for bed, too tired to make much of it and hoping that somehow Blaunche, too, would be too tired for even talk tonight.

She was not. Undressed, her face, hands and feet washed and rubbed with lotion, her hair unpinned and combed out by Mistress Avys, she came finally to bed ready to say what she had held back from saying all afternoon and evening. Robert, lying with his hand as comfortable as might be on a pillow between them and halfway to sleep on the quieting tide of the medicined drink, tried to feign deeper sleep than he was in as Gil drew the curtains closed around the bed but that was an outworn ploy or else Blaunche simply did not care because, not even bothering with lying down, she leaned over him and whispered, not softly enough to keep anyone beyond the bedcurtains from hearing, 'It's going to go on happening, Robert. You know it is. Today you were hurt because of it. Who knows what will happen next time? It's only going to be worse from now on.'

'We'll keep closer watch on her after this,' Robert answered, not bothering with opening his eyes or whispering. 'It's all we can do.'

'It's *not* all we can do,' Blaunche said forcefully. 'What we can do is have her married and the sooner the better. Benedict . . .'

Robert jerked over onto his side, away from her, jarring his hand into pain that would keep him awake for a long while more, and on the pain he snapped, 'Before we deal with anyone's marriage, we're going to have to deal with the Allesleys.'

He no more wanted to talk about the Allesleys than he did about Katherine's marriage but it was the only sure diversion of which he could think and Blaunche took it, sitting rod-upright and exclaiming at him, 'Don't talk to me about the Allesleys! The Allesleys can rot!'

'Northend is theirs.' Robert started along the well-trod track again with no hope she would heed him any more than she had the other times he had said it to her, but if it kept her off Katherine's marriage and Benedict . . .

'The manor of Northend is mine and mine it stays!'

'It wasn't your husband's to give you for dower. They're not going to let the matter go. The manor is theirs . . .'

'And they want it back and recompense into the bargain, yes, I know,' Blaunche snapped, 'but they're not getting either. Not from me and not from you. I'd go to my grave first.' She abruptly fell back onto her pillow, jarring the bed and his hand again but her voice turning suddenly to reasonable. 'And don't think I don't see what you're doing, Robert. You're trying not to talk about Katherine's marriage but no matter how much we make off her lands by the year, you have to see she's not a child anymore and won't we look the fools if we lose her marriage the way we almost lost it today? Especially when all we have to do to make an end of it is marry her to Benedict. Listen to me on this . . .'

Chapter 2

With every passing day of spring the sun was a little higher, at midday the cloister walk and garth a little less shadow filled, making them today a warm, still haven from the bluster of the young wind wuthering along the roof ridges under the blue, scoured sky that was all that could be seen of the world from here. Only sometimes a gust swept down to catch and push at the three nuns' black veils and skirts where they worked among the garth's brown-soiled garden beds in the afternoon's sunlight, and only a tease of wind more astray than most found its way into the roofed north walk to catch and lift the edge of the parchment sheet on Dame Frevisse's writing desk. Just done with carefully penning 'holy fathers,' she raised the quill clear of the words and shifted the inkpot – of too heavy a pottery to be bothered by the wind – to where it would better hold the parchment down without losing her place in the book propped up before her. Or, more precisely, the portion of a book.

The latest work asked of St Frideswide nunnery's small scrivening business was a fair-made copy, to be bound in white calf's hide, of John Mirk's *Festial* that a Banbury councilman's wife was giving to herself as an Easter gift. She also wanted it done by Passiontide, and because Lent was already nigh to its second Sunday and none of St Frideswide's nuns were free of other duties but had to fit in scribing when they could, Dame Perpetua had carefully unbound the copy asked as a loan from their prioress's brother, said patiently to Dame Juliana's worry, 'Yes, I can rebind it when we're done so no one will know the difference,' and separated it into five parts, one for each of the nuns who, when they had chance, worked at their share at the writing desks set against the church wall along the cloister's north walk where the sun fell warmest. By rights, Dame Juliana should have been with the four of them presently at work there – Domina Elisabeth, Dame Perpetua, Sister Johane and Frevisse – but Dame Juliana's first love after Christ was not words but gardening and the past few forward days of spring had aroused all her gardener's urges so that Domina Elisabeth, knowing full well what the worth of Dame Juliana's scribing was likely to be if her mind was more to her gardening than her pen, had smilingly given leave at chapter meeting this morning for her to work in the cloister garth and except that Lenten silence held in the nunnery at present Dame Juliana would probably have gone singing – or at least humming – through the day. As it was, happy little exclamations kept rising over the low wall between the garth and cloister walk as she found – or her helpers Dame Emma and Sister Amicia showed her – one green thing or another thrusting back to life under last year's leaves.

St Benedict's Rule against idle talk in the cloister, though mostly let lapse anymore, was kept through Lent to help the nuns hold their minds to readying for the coming grief and glory of Easter through penance and purification. Frevisse, for one, was always glad for the silence's return but was smiling at Dame Juliana's open happiness while carefully, carefully penning, 'of the old law they fasted four times in the year against four high feasts that they had' because in her own way she was as much enjoying her work and the warm, fair day as Dame Juliana was. St Frideswide's priory had been through narrow times, troubled by an ill-managing prioress and closer to utter poverty than St Benedict's Rule required, but through these past two years of their new prioress Domina Elisabeth ruling them with a firm grasp of necessities, the nunnery had gained back its peace and something of its prosperity. Not all the hurt done by their last prioress was mended yet but the copying of books was making a needed addition to their income and last autumn Domina Elisabeth had persuaded two Banbury families to put their daughters to school at St Frideswide's, with hope there would be others. Moreover, Abbot Gilberd, her brother, had found them a wealthy Northampton merchant's daughter to be a novice, a large and very welcome dowry coming with her.

Happily, Sister Margrett had proved to be as welcome as her dowry, a bright-faced, even-humored girl who had taken readily to nunnery life and would take her final vows come Whitsuntide, bringing the nunnery's count of nuns again up to ten after Sister Cecely's flight back into the world last year. It was a pity the girl was not fair-handed with a pen yet, Frevisse thought while pausing to straighten and stretch her back, because someone else at the scrivening would be useful. With so few nuns in St Frideswide's, all had more than merely one set of duties, even Domina Elisabeth. Besides scrivening, Frevisse in the last change of offices had been made precentress, in charge of seeing that all the nuns were ready for such differences in the daily seven Offices of prayer as came with the changing holy days and turnings of the year. Along with that, she had to see to Sister Margrett being fully taught all she needed to know about the Offices before she took her final vows and, besides that, to overseeing the educating of Helen and Lucy, the little girls from Banbury. Being biddable children, they were no great trouble and Frevisse had found she minded the task less than she had thought to, but she had also become skilled at finding things that other nuns could teach them; this afternoon she had given them over to Dame Claire and Sister Thomasine for instruction in medicinal herbs until Vespers and was not missing them, instead was welcoming the chance to gain on the needed copying work.

In the while of wind-hush then, with only the small sounds of gardening and the scritch of quill tips across parchment to touch the quiet, she went on, 'Fasting it cleanses a man's flesh of evil stirring and inclination to the sin of gluttony and of lechery; for these be sins of the flesh . . .' losing track of time until a sudden loud knocking at the cloister's outer door startled heads up both at desks and in the garth. St Frideswide's was remote enough in the country for visitors to be uncommon and so small that someone – servant or nun – was almost always in hearing if someone knocked to come in; no one was needed to constantly keep the door into the guesthall yard and now, with a surfeit of nuns to hand, Domina Elisabeth said 'Dame Emma,' probably because she was presently the only one among them on her feet, taking up a basket of dead leaves cleared from a garden bed. Dame Emma, short and round and happiest when being noticed, smiled and nodded, set the basket down, made to wipe her garden-dirty hands on her skirts, thought better of it, remembered the rag Dame Juliana had left on the low wall for just that use, snatched it up, and bustled away, cleaning her hands as she went.

From her desk Domina Elisabeth said quietly, 'Continue,' and heads ducked to their work again though perhaps not so deeply as before, and certainly in the garth Dame Juliana and Sister Amicia shifted to be facing doorward, the better to see who entered. Frevisse, realizing that if she could notice that, she was giving way to unnecessary curiosity, too, bowed her head more deeply to her work, eyes firmly down, because in Lent more especially than any other time, the mind should be turned from the world to the spirit. Curiosity about whomever was at the door was surely worldly and she curbed it, fixing instead on the words in front of her – 'Then in your fast think on your death, and share your food with such that have not what you have, and then God will feed you at his table in Heaven' – even when Dame Emma came bustling back to whisper something eagerly to Domina Elisabeth who, after pause presumably to stopper inkpot and wipe pen, rose and followed her away.

Unfortunately, despite all her good intent, Frevisse could not close her ears as readily as she kept her eyes down and knew by the footfalls that it was a man and a woman – no, two women – who entered and went away with Domina Elisabeth up the stairs to her parlor with Dame Emma making a little bustle after them.

Beyond the low cloister wall, Sister Amicia whispered, 'Who do you think . . . ?' But, 'Hush,' Dame Perpetua whispered back at her and with a sigh that loudly mixed regret and resignation Sister Amicia hushed. Frevisse, resolutely holding her own curiosity in check, kept on with the copying, trying to pray the words as she wrote them to make her work and worship into one thing and was succeeding when Dame Emma came back into the cloister walk and along it to her, to lean over and whisper, 'Domina Elisabeth bids you come to her.'

Holding back from unseemly haste, Frevisse wiped her quill-point clean, stoppered her inkpot, made certain the parchment was well-weighted in place, and rose to her feet, paused then as all the nuns were used to doing of late whenever they stood up, waiting for the light-headedness of Lent's fasting to pass – as the body grew lighter, so did its burden on the soul, leaving the mind more free to reach toward heaven – then nodded to Dame Emma and followed her away along the walk toward the stairs, Dame Emma happily trotting ahead as if Frevisse, after more than twenty years in St Frideswide's, would not be able to find her own way.

The prioress's parlor was the most furnished room in the nunnery, with two chairs, a table covered by a woven Spanish carpet, embroidered cushions on the window seat, even a fireplace, because the prioress must needs deal more often than anyone else with guests important enough to need impressing or deserving of more comfort than otherwise there was to be had in St Frideswide's. Frevisse was too used to it to notice more than that while Domina Elisabeth was seated in the better of the two chairs, the man was on his feet beside the other one and the two women were standing across the room at the window as if too uncertain to sit.

That much Frevisse took in before she sank in a low curtsy to Domina Elisabeth but as she straightened, Domina Elisabeth said, 'Master Fenner thinks you may remember him,' and Frevisse looked at him, confused for a moment by the name, before she exclaimed, 'Robert!' and went toward him with an outheld hand and unfeigned delight.

His smile matching her own, he stepped forward to meet her, to take her hand and bow over it. 'I wasn't sure you'd remember me, my lady. It's been a time since we last met.'

'Six years? Seven?' Not since her uncle's funeral and then only very briefly, with only one other time together before that, when there had been two murders in the priory and Robert had not only helped but once protected her. He had been barely into his young manhood then, a very minor squire to his cousin Sir Walter Fenner, but by the look of him the years since then had been better to him than he had had hope of when she last saw him. His hair might be somewhat farther back from his forehead than it had been, but to judge by his well-made doublet of crimson wool, high leather riding boots, and fine dark-blue cloak laid on the empty chair beside him, he had prospered. But he was also wearing a quilted leathern jack over the fine doublet, as if there might have been fear of trouble on his way here, and that and something in his face brought her to ask, 'You're well?' with an edge of deeper question to it than she might have otherwise had.

'Very well,' he said almost convincingly enough, and gave her no chance for asking more but turned toward the women across the room, saying, 'And here, please you, is my ward, Katherine Stretton.'

The younger of the women – hardly more than a girl; as young as Robert had been when Frevisse first met him – curtsied gravely, her eyes respectfully lowered, making it difficult to tell anything about her except that, like him, she was well-dressed, her kendal-green gown high-waisted, simple-collared, full-skirted, and that she was unmarried, her dark hair worn braided back, the veil and wimple she must have worn while riding here laid aside with her cloak on the window seat behind her.

'And her gentlewoman Mistress Dionisia,' Robert said.

Mistress Dionisia was perhaps Frevisse's own age, plainly dressed in a gray gown with crisply coifed white linen wimple and veil, the perfect outward image of a servant, but as she deeply curtsied, the sharp assessing look from under her brows that she gave Frevisse suggested she would willingly be Katherine's protector if need be. Frevisse, with a first twinge of alarm, wondered from what Katherine needed to be protected but merely bowed her head to both women and looked to Domina Elisabeth who said easily, 'There's been a little trouble and Master Fenner has asked that Katherine and her woman be allowed to stay with us a time.'

With a second twinge, this time more definite, Frevisse repeated, outwardly matching her prioress's calm, 'Trouble?'

Domina Elisabeth looked to Robert to answer that, and with a quietness that Frevisse found she did not quite believe in, he said, 'There's been an attempt to force Katherine into an unwanted marriage by carrying her off against her will. Besides that, there's presently a dispute over my wife's dower lands. If we fail in our hope to bring it to arbitration and it comes to . . .' he paused over what word he wanted, settling again for the usefully vague, '. . . trouble, it would be better that Katherine was out of its midst, not in danger of being seized simply because she was readily to hand. For the same reason, I've brought deeds and charters concerning my wife's lands here for safekeeping.' He pointed to a small chest on the floor beside him. 'The ones that, if we lost them, would make proof of my lady's rights difficult. Your prioress has kindly given leave for Katherine to stay and promised keeping of them, too.' He bowed his head slightly to Domina Elisabeth. 'For which she has my thanks and more.'

With a smile, the prioress bent hers in return, then said to Frevisse, 'I think the documents will do best in the sacristy.' Where the priory's more costly worldly goods – the church plate, the priest's embroidered vestments, the deeds and charters of the priory's own lands – were kept. 'And Katherine will be in your charge.'

Frevisse refrained from more than opening her eyes a little wider in question that Domina Elisabeth smoothly answered, 'She can help with teaching Helen and Lucy, giving her occupation while she's here and leaving you more time for other duties.'

Such as the Banbury councilman's wife's new book, she did not say but Frevisse knew it was meant and bent her head in pleased acceptance, murmuring, 'Of course, my lady.'

'I also thought that since you and Master Fenner are acquainted, you could see his documents to the sacristy. He'll carry the chest there for us?'

'Of course, my lady,' Robert answered.

But Frevisse said, half on a question and not because she was unwilling but careful of how Sister Amicia, presently sacristan and therefore with the church and sacristy in her charge, might feel about her place being usurped even so briefly, 'It's rightly Sister Amicia's to do?'

'Master Fenner asked to see you and you needed to be told about Katherine and may as well deal with this, too,' Domina Elisabeth said. 'It's enough that one of you be interrupted at your work.'

Cleared of fault no matter how Sister Amicia took it, Frevisse smiled at Robert. 'Then I'll be pleased to.'

'I'll make my farewells then, please you,' Robert said to both her and Domina Elisabeth, 'and leave directly I've set the chest away.'

'You're not staying the night?' Frevisse asked, surprised.

Domina Elisabeth answered for him. 'He wants it noticed as little as possible that he was here at all. For Katherine's greater safety.'

Robert made a slight bow in agreement with that and crossed to Katherine, held out his hands to her, and said as she took hold of them, 'No need to fear. You'll be home again soon.'

Looking for the moment very young, her eyes large and fixed on his face, Katherine clung to his hands, careful, Frevisse saw, of his right one where some of the fingers were bound and splinted even as she pleaded, 'You'll come for me as soon as may be?'

'I'll come myself or else send someone for you with token that it's safe. Just as I promised.'

She managed a smile. 'Remember you promised to be careful of yourself, too.'

'As careful as may be,' he said.

Little girl turning back into young woman, Katherine clicked her tongue at him with pretend impatience. 'I'd like a better promise than that, sir.'

Robert laughed at her. 'It's the best promise you're going to have.' He drew her toward him and kissed her on the forehead. 'Just mind you're as careful of yourself as you want me to be of me.'

'Will I have much choice otherwise, being in here?'

'I trust not,' he said, let her go and stepped back, ready to take his leave, but she reached out, caught him by the wrist, and said, a little desperately, 'You'll be in my prayers.'

For a moment he only looked at her, then answered, very softly, 'And you in mine.'

'I know.' She smiled at him, letting him go. 'Now bid Dionisia good-bye, too, or she'll be difficult after you're gone.'

'Katherine,' her woman said quellingly but did not resist the quick, smacking kiss that Robert, smiling, gave her on the cheek, and while Katherine had stayed pale to his kiss, Mistress Dionisia blushed, fighting a smile as she said, pushing him away, 'You've neither of you any sense.'

'Mayhap not,' Robert agreed, 'but now you've no grounds to say you were neglected.'

'Which I'd not have said anyway. Be off with you and don't worry over Katherine, we'll all see to her well enough here.'

'I know.' Robert turned and made a deep bow to Domina Elisabeth. 'Again, my thanks, my lady.'

'And equally our thanks to you for seeing fit to trust us with both your treasures,' Domina Elisabeth returned graciously.

While Frevisse made a parting curtsy to Domina Elisabeth, Robert threw his cloak over one shoulder and took up the chest, then followed her out of the parlor and down the stairs, but at their foot, before passing out into the cloister walk again, she paused and turned back to him to ask with a nod toward his splinted hand, 'Was it in saving Katherine you were hurt?'

As if unwilling to admit it, Robert hesitated, then said, 'Yes.'

'There was a fight?'

'A brief one. No blood was spilt.'

'How dangerous is this thing you've asked us to do?'

Robert blinked, seemingly taken by surprise, before answering straightforwardly enough, 'I don't know. Not dangerous at all so long as no one knows she's here.'

'Or your papers.'

'Or my papers,' Robert agreed.

Nor was there any way, even if it was only her choice to make, that Frevisse would have refused refuge to the girl or anyone else who asked it, despite what danger there might be; she simply wanted to know and nodded and went on into the cloister walk. The sacristy lay on the cloister's far side and the shortest way to it was leftward and around, past the writing desks where Dame Perpetua and Sister Johane were still at work. To leave them undisturbed by going the other, longer way around was reasonable and Frevisse did but with another purpose in mind: at the corner of the cloister's square she said to Robert, 'Wait here a moment, please,' and before he could ask why, hurried away along the side passage to the infirmary.

There Dame Claire, Sister Thomasine, Helen and Lucy were together at the shelves where the boxes and pots of medicines and baskets and hanging bunches of herbs for making more were all kept, Dame Claire holding one of the bunches for the girls to look at closely, saying in a voice surprisingly deep for so small a woman, 'This is betony. Powder of it mixed with honey is . . .'

The rule of silence could never be held to utterly. Here, as in Domina Elisabeth's parlor, necessity intruded, but when Dame Claire broke off and everyone looked to Frevisse as she came in, Frevisse made sign with her hand to ask that Sister Thomasine come with her. Dame Claire nodded agreement and Sister Thomasine came away without a word, taking off her apron and laying it aside on her way out of the room. She had been still a novice, young and desperate with piety and fear, when Robert – equally young – had first seen her and fallen into love with her. Sister Thomasine had never noticed his love but Frevisse had; had also seen the moment when Robert knew his beloved was completely given to God and watched him let go of any hope of her. Now, though Sister Thomasine was walking toward him with bent head and eyes down, Frevisse saw him recognize her in the same moment that he saw her, with sudden remembrance and pleasure lightening his face back toward boyhood, and in a whisper, to disturb the cloister's quiet as little as might be, she said, 'Sister Thomasine, do you remember Robert Fenner?'

Sister Thomasine raised her head and to Frevisse's relief her thin face was lighted with both remembrance and pleasure, as if she were encountering a familiar friend, gladly met after long parting as she said, 'Of course I remember him. He's been in my prayers ever since he was here.'

Fleetingly Frevisse wondered if Sister Thomasine prayed for everyone who had ever crossed her path, then had the wry thought that probably she did, while Robert said with surprised pleasure, 'You've prayed for me? Oh, Thomasine, my thanks for that!'

Sister Thomasine looked momentarily surprised, either at his thanks or at being called simply by her name for probably the first time in all the years since she had taken her final vows, but all she said was, simply, 'You're very welcome.'

In a quick whisper Frevisse explained why he was here and asked, since it would be unseemly for her to be alone with him, would Sister Thomasine come with them into the sacristy? Sister Thomasine nodded that she would and they went on around the cloister walk, past the refectory, the kitchen passage, the door to the warming room, the stairs that led up to the nuns' dorter, finally to the narrow door into the sacristy beside the church.

Frevisse opened it for Robert to go in with the chest and followed him, with Sister Thomasine coming last and the door left open behind them for more light because the room's single window high in the east wall was both too small for any but the smallest of children to squeeze through and closed with thick green glass that kept the sacristy in perpetual twilight even on the brightest days. But there was light enough for Frevisse to point to a place in the far corner beyond the great storage chests ranged along the walls and Robert set his own small chest there, almost out of sight, stepped back from it, and nodded with satisfaction. 'That will serve very well.'

'You'll come for it yourself?' Frevisse asked.

'I hope to. Else I'll send someone with a token that Katherine knows and no one else.'

'We'll need either you or the token and Katherine's word to release it.'

'That's what I want,' Robert assured her but his gaze strayed to Sister Thomasine standing just inside the doorway, her hands tucked into her opposite sleeves, her eyes lowered. His gaze lingered a moment, then he looked back to Frevisse and said, 'I'll go now. With good riding I might make Banbury by dark or not long after.'

'You're not alone?' she asked.

'I've a man with me. He's seen to the horses while I've been in here.'

They moved to leave the sacristy and Sister Thomasine faded out the doorway ahead of them into the cloister walk again as Frevisse asked, 'Do you mean to go directly home?'

Robert shook his head. 'No. I mean to swing eastward a ways and come back from a different direction than we left by, to confuse things if anyone is interested. I'll be home the day after tomorrow rather than tomorrow, making it more unclear how far we actually went.'

That told Frevisse something more about how much it meant to him to keep Katherine and his papers safe but they were in the cloister walk again, going back the way they had come, Sister Thomasine following and silence between them until at the passage back to the infirmary Sister Thomasine said softly, 'By your leave, I'll leave you here.'

Robert turned quickly around to her. For a moment he looked about to reach out to take hold of her hands as he had with Katherine but her hands were still tucked up their opposite sleeves and he held back, only saying, 'It was good to see you again. To see you're doing well.'

Sister Thomasine raised her eyes to him. 'And you, too.' And then, out of her usual way of things, she asked, 'Are you married? Do you have children?'

'I'm married,' he said. 'We have three children. Two boys and a little girl. Robin and John and Tacine.'

Frevisse's hands, tucked out of sight in her own sleeves, tightened on her forearms, because just as Robin was the little name for Robert, Tacine was for Thomasine.

Gravely regarding him, Sister Thomasine said, 'I'll add them to my prayers.'

Equally grave, Robert answered, 'Thank you.'

There was a pause then while it became clear there was nothing more to be said between them, before he simply bowed to her and she bent her head in return, turned, and walked away toward the infirmary, Robert watching her leave with something of the boy he had been showing in his face, the years and troubles smoothed away to feelings as simple as they had been then despite all he must have learned since of how unsimple love was, how complicated by too many things ever to be simple except maybe in the first moment it existed.

Turning away from so much laid out so openly, Frevisse went on toward the outer door, Robert following her, both silent until with her hand on the latch, she turned back to him and said, smiling, 'I'm sorry it was trouble that brought you here but it's been good to see you again.'

All look of the boy was gone from him; he was a man with a man's troubles riding with him as he answered, smiling, too, 'It's been equally good to see you.' And softly, after a moment's hesitation, 'And Sister Thomasine. Thank you.'

Frevisse bent her head to him in both acceptance of his thanks and in farewell and with a murmured prayer for his safe journeying pulled open the heavy door, let him out, and closed it behind him.

Chapter 3

†

Well into this third week of Lent the lightness of hunger was become familiar as well as welcome but nonetheless Frevisse sat back on her heels, scrub brush in hand, with a deep sigh and thankfulness to be nearly done with washing the choir floor's paving. How somewhere no one ever walked but nuns come in from the equally paved, often-swept cloister could be so constantly in need of cleaning she did not understand and in Lent hunger made the work only the harder. But – *Advenerunt nobis dies poenitentiae, ad redimenda peccata, ad salvandas animas.* To us have come the days of penance, for redeeming sins, for saving souls. And that made the burden a blessing.

But she was still glad to be done with it for today and nodded pleasantly to Sister Margrett, just finished, too, and sitting back from her work at the far end of the choir. They had started in the middle between the choir stalls where the nuns gathered six times a day for the Offices of prayer that were their main duty among the tasks that made up their lives, beginning with Matins and Laud together at midnight, then Prime at dawn, with Sext, Terce and None through the day and Vespers near its end. Only Compline was usually done simply in the warming room at the end of the nuns' daily hour of recreation, just ere bed. And none of that explained how the choir floor came to so often need washing, Frevisse thought impatiently and inwardly laughed at herself at the same time, recognizing the short temper that came to her with fasting and must needs all too often be countered with prayer.

Sister Margrett made question with her hands, asking if they were done here, and Frevisse nodded that they were and together, Frevisse not so briskly as she had done when she was younger, they stood up, took up the pads they had been kneeling on and the buckets and left the church, going around the cloister walk to the kitchen and the scullery beyond it, keeping clear of the servants busily preparing supper under Dame Perpetua's direction. Unfortunately there was no way to keep equally clear of the warm, thick smell of the fish mortrewe with its almond milk and ginger, and Frevisse's stomach clawed at her with unhappy protest of its hunger but supper would not come until after Vespers and wishing she could hold her breath she hurried with Sister Margrett through putting the kneeling pads on the shelf where whoever would need them next would expect to find them, poured the dirty water down the drain, rinsed the buckets and brushes and put them away under the stone sink, and was just going back into the kitchen as the cloister bell began to ring to the Office.

The servants were not required to go to services nor, being busy at things that could not be left, often simply could not, but Dame Perpetua broke off in midword telling one of the women she needed to cut up another onion, took off and laid aside her apron, and joined Frevisse and Sister Margrett going back toward the church. From wherever else they had been throughout the cloister the other nuns were coming, too, in haste and silence save for the hush of soft-soled shoes on stone and the rustle of the rain as another of the day's many showers passed over. In the church the choir's candles, lighted by Sister Amicia as sacristan, made an island of bright welcome among the gray shadows and in a whispering of skirts each nun went to her place, the choir stall she had been given when she first came into St Frideswide's and which would be hers until she died unless she was elected prioress and must needs move to the more elaborate seat that went with her office.

Frevisse, glad that honor was never likely to burden her, sank into her own familiar place, made sure of her breviary and Psalter in front of her, then slid forward to kneel in prayer until everyone was in place and the Office began, continuing the unending weave of prayers and psalms begun years into centuries ago and never ceasing, prayed and sung by so many women and men in so many places, their lives given to the prayers and petitions and their lives lost to all memory but God's, that sometimes it seemed to Frevisse that here and now this hands-count of nuns no more made the prayers than someone made a river: they simply stepped into the endless flow, to be carried by it the way a river carried whatever came into its way.

Across the choir the nuns chanted, *Deo gratias* – God be thanked – and answer was made by the other nuns, *Fidelium animae per misericordiam Dei requiescant in pace*. The souls of the faithful through the mercy of God rest in peace. To be answered from across the choir, 'Amen,' and like a long sigh of someone coming to rest, the Office ended.

The stillness then lasted until Domina Elisabeth stirred, shut her prayer book, and rose to her feet, setting off a bustle of others following her. There would be supper now, the first food of the day since a little bread and cider in early morning, and it was discouraging, Frevisse always thought, how quickly she returned from the wonders of prayer to the tyranny of the body's needs – hers wanted to be fed and fed *now* – and only by severest will did she close her breviary gently, rise slowly, move quietly out of the stalls.

Others of the women were less restrained, making unseemly haste about their going, with even something of a slight scuffle between Sister Amicia and Sister Johane in their haste into place in the small procession of nuns meant to follow Domina Elisabeth out of the church, and their prioress turned to glare them to quiet. Not until everyone was standing still did she move on, slanting across the nave toward the door to the cloister, acknowledging with a nod the deep curtsies the girl Katherine, her Mistress Dionisia and little Lucy and Helen between them made as she passed.

In the while since Robert had brought them here, Katherine and her woman had come to fit quietly into nunnery life. As hoped, Katherine had been a help with Lucy and Helen, and Frevisse had left them to her more of each day until finally shame had moved her yesterday to ask Katherine's pardon, but Katherine had laughed and said she did not mind. 'It's better to have something to do rather than nothing, and I do better with children than with a great many other things.'

Mistress Dionisia seemed content here, too, keeping herself to herself for the most part but somehow always being helpful to someone. Two days ago in the recreation hour between supper and Compline, the only time of day there could be free talk among the nuns, Dame Perpetua had been rejoicing over the sheets Mistress Dionisia had mended for her. 'As fine a darning as you'll ever hope to see on three of them, and the one that needed to be turned sides to middle she whip-stitched end to end so smoothly you hardly know it's been done.'

For good measure, both of them came to all the day's Offices except the midnight ones and Compline and brought Lucy and Helen with them and kept them quiet, which was more than any of the servants who had had the task had ever managed to do.

Once outside the church Domina Elisabeth stepped aside and stopped, to bless each of her nuns as they passed by her. They were free then to make their best haste to the refectory and a certain degree of scurry overcame some of them but Frevisse held back, forcefully repeating to herself the Lenten prayer, *Utamur ergo parcius Verbis, cibis et potibus, somno, jocis, et arctius Perstemus in custodia* – Let us be the more sparing of words, food and drink, sleep, jests, and more narrowly stand on guard – while keeping moderate pace with Sister Thomasine and Dame Claire.

Nor did hunger count first with everyone else; ahead of them Sister Johane abruptly turned aside from her near-trot with Sister Amicia to Domina Elisabeth's gray-and-black-striped cat on the cloister wall. Like most cats, this one had a well-developed sense of its own dignity and a thorough mind of its own. Come with Domina Elisabeth to the priory and provided with its own bed near the parlor's hearth, it too often preferred one or another of the nuns' beds in the dorter, usually Dame Claire's because she had no use for cats, while Sister Johane courted its attentions and in return was usually ignored. But this afternoon, now that the brief rain and its clouds had passed, Mistress Cat was taking advantage of the westering sun's watery sunshine to have a warm bath on the wall, was seemingly in a mellow mood and rose to be stroked, strolling and twisting under Sister Johane's hand to its best advantage while she made happy sounds and told it what a dear it was.

How long that would have kept Sister Johane from her supper went unlearned as a firm rap at the outer door paused everyone where they were with the surprise of it, even Sister Amicia about to be first into the refectory, but before any could move toward the door, Ela of the guesthall servants, having followed her knock with letting herself in, came hastening into sight and both Domina Elisabeth and Dame Juliana as hosteler and in charge of the priory's guests and guesthalls changed course to meet her because her coming had to mean something or someone out of the ordinary had happened.

Curiosity balanced against hunger held the others where they were and even stayed Sister Johane's hand so that Mistress Cat with a

41

disgusted twitch of its tail at the fickleness of humans flowed off the wall and into the garth, just as everyone realized Ela was not come in alone but was followed by two women, moving slowly enough that she had reached Domina Elisabeth and begun saying something before they came from the shadowed passageway into the cloister's better light. Frevisse had time to note they were both well-dressed for travel before Katherine, not far off from them with Mistress Dionisia and Lucy, and Helen, made wordless exclaim and started toward them, instantly raising Frevisse's curiosity well past her hunger. But in the same moment Domina Elisabeth turned from Ela to gesture her nuns on toward the refectory, and perforce, with only slightly dragging pace and watching over their shoulders, they went, leaving their prioress, Katherine, and the two newcomers in head-near talk too far away for anything to be heard.

Once into the refectory, curiosity gave way to hunger again, and as she began on the gourd-onion pottage waiting for them, Frevisse was sorry for Sister Thomasine whose turn it was this week to read aloud while the others ate, her own meal put off until afterwards; but she would be more sorry next week when it would be her own turn to be reader and almost as sorry the week after that when it would be Dame Emma's, because Dame Emma read with the grace and pace of a spavined horse. But for now Sister Thomasine's low, even voice kept them company – 'For the contemplative life has joy in God's love, and savor in the life that lasts for always, in this present time, if it be right led. And that feeling of joy' – through the fish mortrewe that was their main dish and the apples cooked in cider with nutmeg that was the meal's end. By then Dame Juliana had come to her place at the long table but since silence held during the meal no one could ask her anything, even whether Domina Elisabeth was going to join them. Curiosity was kept waiting until they had finished and grace was said, but once they were out of the refectory and into the cloister walk, recreation's hour was begun and talk could flow freely and it did. With evening shadows and cold quickly coming on together, no one lingered on their way to the warming room but that did not slow the questions tumbled at Dame Juliana who answered them in the order she chose to deem important, beginning with, 'I bade Alsun in the kitchen take supper to Domina Elisabeth and the others in the parlor. That's all seen to. And spiced cider, too.'

'My accounts,' murmured Dame Perpetua, momentarily diverted

because now she would have to record the guests' food and drink with the kitchen expenses when otherwise they would have been a guesthall matter.

'But who *are* they?' Dame Emma cried out in distress.

'If I caught the name a-right, she's Lady Blaunche Fenner. Katherine knows them, anyway. It's her waiting-woman with her.'

Frevisse and Dame Claire were gone ahead into the warming room. Most rooms in the cloister were warmed only by braziers or, most often, not warmed at all, making for cold goings to bed through the winter, let be rising at midnight for Matins and in the mornings. Only the kitchen, the prioress's parlor, and here had fireplaces, and now was the last chance there would be today for warmth, and because whatever Dame Juliana might tell would be told and talked over again all through the coming hour nothing would be missed for long by reaching the fire first.

Frevisse's sigh and Dame Claire's matched as they held their hands out to the low flames' heat but behind them Dame Juliana was saying as she and the others came into the room, 'come to take Katherine away,' and Frevisse, diverted from her comfort, looked around sharply to ask, 'Away? Katherine?'

'Oh, yes.' Dame Juliana was sure of it. 'Something about dower lands and dealings and Katherine's marriage. It was all jumbled but that's why Lady Blaunche is here.' The others were crowding to the hearth now as Dame Juliana added, 'It was her husband brought Katherine, I gather.'

'I suppose so,' Frevisse agreed. Robert had never said his wife's name. She started to ask more but was interrupted by a sharp single knock at the door that no one had time to answer before Mistress Dionisia was quickly come in, saying as she came, 'Dame Claire! Pray you, come!' urgently enough that Dame Claire left the fire without question, casting a look around for Sister Thomasine as she went and, not finding her, ordered, 'Sister Margrett, come, please,' startling the novice up from a stool she had drawn near the hearth to follow her out.

In their haste none of them shut the door, Mistress Dionisia's voice disappearing into the darkness with, 'She's in the parlor . . .'

Following after them to close the door, Sister Johane said, 'Well, what was . . .' as Dame Emma exclaimed, 'But what's this about Katherine going away?' to Dame Juliana.

Unfortunately there was nothing else Dame Juliana could tell beyond what she had already said but that did not keep the others from drawing their stools into a cluster beside the hearth and setting to talk it over some several times more. Only Frevisse kept aside, intent on enjoying the fire and this small while of nothing to do. But she found she could not keep away from the thought that if Katherine left then Lucy and Helen would be back on her hands and found besides, with a slight surprise, that she would miss Katherine. Little had passed between her and the girl and most of it had been about Helen and Lucy but Frevisse had begun to like her and to suspect that under the quiet good manners, there was more than Katherine let show and was interested in what it might be. At ease and warm, she let her thoughts drift to wondering what had happened that Robert had felt it well to send for Katherine and had Lady Blaunche come with the promised token or was it enough she had come herself?

In the way of drifting thoughts, she somehow wended from there to wondering what could be done with Lucy and Helen when the weather would be warmer . . . and how much longer the copying would take . . . and on to nothing in particular, maybe even into a small drowse, pleasant beside the fire and despite the talk around her until of a sudden Domina Elisabeth swept in, bringing a draught of cold air despite how hurriedly she shut the door against the cloister's darkness. She sometimes joined her nuns at recreation but they had not expected her tonight and stood up in flustered haste, Frevisse shoving sleep away, all of them offering her places beside the hearth.

Rubbing her hands and holding them out to the fire, she refused Dame Juliana's offer of a stool with, 'No, thank you,' and a smile. 'I'm not staying.' Adding, 'It's raining again.'

Not bothering with pretense of interest in anything else, Dame Emma asked, 'What was Dame Claire needed for?'

'To see to Lady Blaunche,' Domina Elisabeth answered readily enough. 'The lady is in her fourth month with child and was having not pains but some discomforts out of the ordinary and was a little frighted at it.'

There were soft exclaims among the nuns and Dame Perpetua said gravely, 'We'll pray for her.'

'That would be to the good, though all seems well now. Dame Claire says it was only that the riding tired her. She's given her something to ease and quiet her and says there's no danger to the child.'

There were quick and knowledgeable nods among the nuns. Though it was no part of their own lives, they all had been at other women's birthings before they came into the nunnery and knew something and sometimes too much of the uncertainties of childing.

Solemnly, Dame Emma said, 'Every dram of delight hath a pound of pain.'

Too used to Dame Emma's fondness for ill-placed proverbs to pay this one any heed, Domina Elisabeth went on, 'Dame Claire will spend the night with her in the guesthall with Lady Blaunche's woman to help her if need be. Tomorrow, all being well, she purposes to return home, taking Katherine with her.'

'Whatever was wrong has been settled?' Frevisse asked.

'I gather so. Though it seems the chest is to stay since it's not been asked for.'

Several mouths were open to ask more but Sister Thomasine, who had likely been not at supper all this while but eaten and then gone to pray in the church as was her wont, slipped in, bringing another cold draught and reminder from Domina Elisabeth that, 'It's time for Compline, my ladies,' the end of the day's chance for talk.

Chapter 4

The next day began simply enough. Awakened by the cloister bell in the darkness before dawn, Frevisse rose and dressed by feel more than sight in the dim light from the lamp burning at the head of the dorter stairs, with all around her the rustle of the other nuns doing the same, and shortly, silently, they gathered in pairs in the passage between their sleeping cells, to go down to the cloister walk and along it to the church. The rain dripping softly off the eaves was hardly louder than the pad of their own soft leather shoes as they hurried to their choir stalls as quickly as if they would find warmth there. They did not, of course, except for what the candles gave once they were lighted and that was barely enough to warm fingers held to the small flames now and again for comfort and to make the turning of pages easier. Domina Elisabeth joined them, coming with equal haste from her own rooms, and the quiet gave way to their voices taking up Prime's prayers and psalms of greeting to the day, tempered now with the necessities of Lent and turning to admonition – *Quaerite Dominum, dum inveniri potest: invocte eum, dum prope est.* Search for the Lord, while he can be found: appeal to him, while he is near – with Dame Claire's sure voice missed on her side of choir but all else as usual, familiar as the east window beyond the altar graying with dawn as they came at last to *Dominus nos benedicat, et ab omni malo defendat, et ad vitam perducat aeternam* – The Lord bless us, and defend from all evil, and guide to eternal life . . . and Prime's end, the final word drifting into a silence with only the distant hiss of rain on the roof, before Domina Elisabeth drew a deep, satisfied breath, quietly closed her prayer book, and led the nuns in rising to their feet and out of the church, into the cloister walk again and around to the refectory for what passed for breakfast in Lent.

Today that meant bread and ale and a small boiled fish that had long since lost any sense of what it might once have been before being salted down in a barrel months ago and lately boiled, then made somewhat – but not much – more agreeable with ginger and cinnamon. But it was enough to hush if not greatly comfort bellies when they returned to the church immediately afterwards for the Mass. Dame Claire joined them on the way, and Frevisse was pleased to see in the nave not only Katherine, Mistress Dionisia, Lucy and Helen but the two women who must be Lady Blaunche and her woman. With the satisfied thought that yesterday's trouble must have indeed been as slight as Domina Elisabeth had hoped, Frevisse turned her mind to the Mass, and when it was done and Father Henry gone to the sacristy to put off his vestments, the nuns left the church again, this time to the warming room for the daily chapter meeting where the nunnery's business was talked through, decisions made, faults confessed and penances given. In past times there would have been a fire waiting for them, lighted by a servant during Mass, but among the things they did without these days of less than certain prosperity was a morning fire, so there was nothing to take off the damp chill steadily creeping through the layers of wool gown and undergown and linen chemise as they waited for Domina Elisabeth to join them. At Mass's end she had gone aside to the women in the nave, nor had Dame Claire come to the warming room either and Frevisse was wondering what that might mean when Domina Elisabeth opened the door, said with no greeting to anyone else, 'Dame Frevisse, come, please,' and turned away again without explanation. Frevisse shared startled looks with the other nuns even as she obeyed, following her prioress into the cloister walk.

'The door, please, dame,' Domina Elisabeth said, and Frevisse closed it. The rain had stopped for now, leaving only an irregular dripping off the eaves as she followed her prioress again, a few paces farther along the walk, away from the door, before Domina Elisabeth turned and said. 'Lady Blaunche is leaving this morning with Katherine as soon as may be. She took comfort from Dame Claire's care of her yesterday and has asked that Dame Claire be allowed to go with her, to see her safely home. I've granted it.'

Because no nun should leave the priory unaccompanied by another nun, Frevisse knew what was coming then but had no way to avert it.

'I want you to go with her.'

'It's Lent,' Frevisse protested.

'It's Lent outside the nunnery, too,' Domina Elisabeth returned, unbothered.

That was true enough, but it would be far harder outside the nunnery to keep it in all the ways it should be kept – in body, mind and spirit all at once – but Frevisse knew Domina Elisabeth well enough not to protest that, tried instead, 'What of the copying work if I'm not here?'

'God will provide.'

Frevisse had the unbidden thought that what Domina Elisabeth hoped God would provide was a gratefully large gift – preferably in coin – from Lady Blaunche or her husband but she bit back on the words, bent her head in obedience, and said instead, trying to leave feeling out of her voice, 'Sister Thomasine would do best as precentress while I'm gone, I think.'

Domina Elisabeth accepted both that and Frevisse's obedience easily and went on to practicalities. 'Dame Claire has gone to gather what she thinks she may need in way of medicines. Let you fetch what you'll both need for travelling. A change of clothing. Cloaks. You know.'

Frevisse bent her head again, acknowledging that she did.

Domina Elisabeth hesitated, then added, 'You might wear your cousin's gift.'

Her cousin's gift of a few years back was a fur-lined gown, properly Benedictine black and of wool but altogether too fine for the vow of poverty every nun took, however well or ill she kept it afterwards, and assuredly too fine to wear among the other nuns – or anywhere else, if Frevisse had choice in the matter. By Domina Elisabeth's leave it was kept folded away with herbs in the storeroom, for use if ever Frevisse's cousin was to be met with – or to impress a possible patron – but Frevisse said quickly, 'It would look ill for me to wear such and Dame Claire not. Better that we go just as we are.'

'I suppose,' Domina Elisabeth agreed with a regretful sigh. On the priory's behalf, Frevisse hoped; but the small thought arose, as it sometimes did, that Domina Elisabeth, despite she kept her nun's vows well, had not only a useful understanding of the world's ways but sometimes a longing for them, too. Such as for a rich gown to impress another lady, even if on the priory's behalf, not her own. But if she did, she rarely gave way to them and was saying now, crisply, as she moved toward the warming room door, 'See to the other things, then. Father Henry and I will come give our blessings before you go.'

Gathering what she and Dame Claire needed and packing it into bags for travel took very little time but she had barely done before a servant was come to say Lady Blaunche was set to leave. Frevisse sent the woman to tell Domina Elisabeth and went herself to the infirmary for Dame Claire, finding her at the worktable there, strapping closed the box she carried medicines in when she had to go elsewhere.

Not bothering with the silence they would have to let go of anyway once they were outside of St Frideswide's, Frevisse said, 'They're ready to leave.'

Dame Claire gave the strap a final pull, secured the buckle, and said, 'So am I. You're in this with me, then?'

Frevisse granted that with a rueful nod.

'Ah, well.' Dame Claire took the box from the table and came toward the door. 'What can't be cured must be eaten with a long-handled spoon, as Dame Emma might say.'

With a slightly further sinking of her spirits, Frevisse realized by Dame Claire's cheerfulness that she had no regrets at all about this going out. With her, love of God came first, love of medicine next, and love of prayers only somewhere, though probably closely, after that. For Frevisse it was otherwise; for her, her love of God was so closely bound about by praying that she had no way to unbind one from the other. To have to leave behind the Offices, knowing how difficult it was to keep to them even a little while dealing in the world . . .

'We're ready, then?' Dame Claire asked, picking up the box.

Frevisse held up her arms, a saddlebag and a cloak over each. 'Change of clothing, change of shoes, night things, our breviaries and Psalters.'

Dame Claire set the box down. 'Best I put the cloak on here. Has the rain stopped?'

'For a little. It looks likely to start again, though.'

Going back through the cloister walk, they met Domina Elisabeth coming from chapter meeting to see them off and in the guesthall courtyard found Lady Blaunche's four men waiting with the horses and Father Henry. While one of the men strapped Dame Claire's bag behind her saddle and another took the medicine box to pack into one of the hampers on the packhorse, Father Henry and Domina Elisabeth gave their blessings and made farewell, with Father Henry at Domina Elisabeth's prompting formally releasing them both from the saying of the Offices at length while they were gone. Such pardon was commonly given and, 'Do as you can, best as you can,' Father Henry said. 'God knows what's in your heart.'

Frevisse, doubting God would approve of what was in her heart at the moment, bowed her head more low, trying for humility and acceptance where she was hard put to want either.

'You're freed, too, from heavy fasting,' Domina Elisabeth said. 'There'll be greater demands on you bodily outside the cloister. Fast, but only so far as does you no harm.'

The man had taken Frevisse's bag and was strapping it behind her saddle now, leaving her free to put on her own cloak as Lady Blaunche came out of the guesthall, Katherine with her, Mistress Dionisia and Lady Blaunche's woman following after. Frevisse did not know whether Katherine had spent the night there instead of in her cloister room or had simply breakfasted with Lady Blaunche. What she did know, by her first look at Katherine's face, was that the girl was showing no feelings at all, one way or another, either to gladness or sadness, at leaving. She merely looked . . . nothing.

It came to Frevisse that most of the time she had been in St Frideswide's, except maybe when she had been playing with Lucy and Helen, there had always been a careful stillness to Katherine, as if she were waiting for whatever might come next. As if, maybe, she was afraid of what might come next.

But Lady Blaunche was making a cheerful bustle down the guesthall stairs, coming to thank Domina Elisabeth for all she had done for Katherine and for letting Dame Claire go with her, adding, 'And?' with a meaningful look at Frevisse before Domina Elisabeth could have a word in.

'Dame Frevisse,' Domina Elisabeth answered. 'Our precentress.'

'Dame Frevisse,' Lady Blaunche repeated with a gracious nod and smile in Frevisse's direction. 'Yes, you're one of the ones Katherine mentioned.'

'My lady,' Frevisse murmured but Lady Blaunche was already turning away with a sweeping look around at everything and everyone. Like most Fenners, she was of moderate height and a solid build. Years and childbearing were working their ways to broaden her but she was not yet run to fat and likely never would, Frevisse guessed, watching as she set to organizing Katherine and Mistress Dionisia to their horses with the busy assurance of someone who knows nothing will turn out right if they do not see to it. Girths were fussed over, baggage made certain, questions about the horses asked before finally Lady Blaunche allowed the men to set to helping her and the other women into their saddles. The man seemingly given charge of the nuns for now led Dame Claire's horse toward the mounting block when she asked him because, unused as she was to riding, she wanted all the help she could have, but Frevisse, left beside an unimpressive bay gelding, gathered up its reins for herself, shook back her skirts to clear her foot for the stirrup, took hold of the saddlebow, and swung herself up into the saddle, glad there was no fashionable nonsense over side-sitting in box seats, even by Lady Blaunche. Finished with settling her skirts and cloak, she found everyone else was ready, too, however uncertain about it Dame Claire might look, with Lady Blaunche sorting them into the order she wanted: two of the men to ride ahead, the women in pairs behind them, Lady Blaunche with Dame Claire, Frevisse beside Katherine, the two waiting women together and the other two men behind.

Domina Elisabeth and Father Henry had faded back toward the cloister door, out of the general way of things but now the priest came forward, to raise a hand and make general blessing at them for their journey. They all crossed themselves in answer and then the lead men swung away toward the gate, leading the way into the outer yard. Priory folk were there about their morning business among the byres, barns, sheds and stables that served the worldly side of the nunnery's life and some paused to watch the riders go by because even though come-and-go was part of the nunnery's life, it was rarely nuns who came and went, and as they neared the outer gate, a tall boy somewhere in the awkwardness between childhood and youth came to stride at Frevisse's side, asking up at her, 'When will you be coming back?'

'Good morning to you, too, Dickon.'

'Good morning, my lady,' he returned belatedly and unabashedly. The steward's son, he had grown up at St Frideswide's with no awe of nuns. 'Going to be gone for long?'

'As God wills,' she said, smiling at him.

'Safe journeying,' he said and as he dropped aside she turned in her saddle to raise her hand in farewell. He waved back cheerily, the last familiar face before they rode through the priory's outer gateway into the world and it was only as they swung rightward into the narrow

51

road between the greening hedgerows did Frevisse realize she had no thought of where they were going except away. Ahead and behind, the other women were already in talk with one another and she turned to Katherine to ask, 'Where are we bound for?'

Katherine looked at her, momentarily surprised, before lightly laughing, saying with sympathy, 'It's come of a sudden, hasn't it? To Brinskep, Master Fenner's Warwickshire manor.'

'More than a day's ride?' Frevisse said, remembering something of what Robert had said.

'It could be a long day's ride if you start earlier than this and ride at a hard pace.'

'And for us?'

'Likely midday tomorrow, the roads allowing.'

Rain spattered down in answer to that and Frevisse reached back to pull her hood up. Katherine reached over to help her set it over her wimple and veil, then Frevisse helped her with hers. The close-felted wool would serve against all but a heavy rain and happily the low-swept clouds looked likely to be too busy on the wind to bother with much more than showers.

Ahead, likewise busy with hoods, Lady Blaunche was saying to Dame Claire, 'It was yesterday the rain was bad. There was rain all the morning. When I awoke and heard it, I nearly didn't want to bother with getting out of bed. You could tell it was the kind that would go on for hours. This looks like it will pass, though.' She turned in her saddle to say back at Frevisse and Katherine, 'We'll likely have sun by this afternoon. You'll see.'

Katherine agreed they likely would and Frevisse nodded, too, and Lady Blaunche returned her attention to Dame Claire. Frevisse called up her manners and asked Katherine, 'Are you glad to be going home?'

'Yes,' Katherine said, paused, then added, 'Of course.' And after another moment, 'In some ways.' And very quietly, 'But I was far happier in St Frideswide's than I'd expected to be.'

'I'm glad,' Frevisse said, for awkward lack of a better answer.

Katherine smiled almost apologetically, as if the awkwardness were her fault instead of no one's. 'I've never spent days in a nunnery before. I didn't know it was like that. The busyness mingled with the quiet. And the prayers. The Offices. They're so . . . beautiful.' She looked back and Frevisse looked with her. The road was cresting a small rise and through a field gate's gap in the hedge there was a last glimpse of the church roof and the top of its squat tower. 'I'm sorry to leave. I've been . . .' Again she hesitated before saying, '. . . happy with being safe here.'

They were beyond the hedge-gap now, St Frideswide's lost to sight, and Frevisse, giving in to the curiosity, asked, 'What changed to bring on this sudden leaving? From the way Master Fenner talked of it, I thought you'd be longer with us.'

'So did I. But there's been ongoing trouble over Lady Blaunche's dower land from her second husband and it seems that all of a sudden the Allesleys and Master Fenner have finally both agreed on arbitration, to settle outside the courts if possible.' She paused but so clearly with something more to say that Frevisse held silent until slowly Katherine went on, staring forward at her horse's ears. 'From what Lady Blaunche says, the Allesleys have said they're willing to consider my marrying their heir as part of the recompense Master Fenner would otherwise have to pay for them for having been wrongly kept from their land this while.'

If Katherine was as wealthy an heiress as seemed likely, she had probably understood all of her life that her marriage would be something arranged for her, to one person or another's profit, and Frevisse passed by the question of her marriage to, '*Have* the lands been wrongly kept?'

Katherine looked up from her horse's ears toward Lady Blaunche's back. 'Master Fenner says so, but Lady Blaunche' – Katherine dropped her voice even lower than it had been – 'holds to her own way of seeing things.'

Held to it come what may and in despite of everybody, Frevisse silently suspected and had the regretful thought that she was probably not going to like the trouble into which she was riding; but since there seemed no help for it, she might as well know more and asked, 'Have you met this Allesley heir they're thinking of for your husband?'

'No.'

A flat and simple statement that invited no other questions that way. Frevisse tried instead, 'Is it much land in question?'

That Katherine answered readily enough. 'The smaller of the Northamptonshire manors.'

'Master Fenner has others, then?'

'One other in Northamptonshire and Brinskep where we're going in Warwickshire. The one the Allesleys claim is the least of the three.' Katherine hesitated, then said on a rush, 'And Master Fenner says it would be worth being rid of it for him not to be bothered over it anymore.' Katherine turned her head to look at her, still remembering to keep her voice low as she went on, as if glad to say it out, 'The mother of Lady Blaunche's second husband was married first to an Allesley. She had the manor of Northend for her dower from him. When she was widowed, she married again and had her only child, Sir Ralph, and inherited everything from his mother. But when she died, the dower land should have gone back to the Allesleys and instead Sir Ralph kept it and gave it to Lady Blaunche as her dower when they married and she's kept it ever since, declaring it's hers and that the Allesleys can go hang before they have it from her.'

'She's not pleased that her husband is trying to settle with them, then?'

Katherine gave Lady Blaunche's back a worried glance. 'Not pleased in the least.'

'But she brought the token from Master Fenner and you're certain he's sent for you?'

As soon as she had asked it, Frevisse wished she had not because there was nothing to be gained by alarming the girl. But come to that, why had it even crossed her thoughts that there might be cause for alarm?

But Katherine said without worry, 'Oh, yes.'

'Look!' Mistress Avys exclaimed behind them. 'Blue sky!'

There was a patch of it indeed and when that diversion was done, neither Frevisse nor Katherine took up their talk where it had been but rode silent save when Lady Blaunche or either of the waiting-women passed comments to them that must needs be answered, until somewhat late in the morning the road passed through Banbury's south gate, became a street and opened out among the houses and shops into the marketplace with its finely wrought Eleanor cross and, more to the present necessity, a choice of inns for their dinner. Lady Blaunche had been happy enough with the Green Lion on her way to St Frideswide's to return there now and the meal they were served at one of the long tables in its main room justified her choice though Frevisse and Dame Claire perforce made do with ale and bread and a simple pease pottage meant for servants. But it was a new brewing of ale, and the bread, though rye, was satisfyingly crusty outside and soft

– for rye bread – within. They had to refuse butter on it and as the tormenting smell of the other women's mutton stew reached them Dame Claire said aside to Frevisse, 'This is not going to be easy'; but no one had stinted on the herbs in the pease pottage and it was savory enough that all in all they did none so badly.

Trouble only came at the meal's end, when Lady Blaunche was paying the host and he asked where they were bound for and she answered, 'North into Warwickshire.'

To that he frowned worriedly and asked, 'By the direct way, my lady?'

She frowned back at him. 'Of course by the direct way. Why?'

'The northward bridge into Warwickshire is out. Yesterday's rains did for it, seems like.'

'It's out?' Lady Blaunche's voice rose. 'I crossed it yesterday. It can't be out!'

'It is, my lady. Two different carters have been in here today, not half angry about having to turn back and take another road.'

'But I have to go that way,' Lady Blaunche said. 'That's the road I want to take!'

'I can't help you there, my lady.' The man was regretful but too used to travellers and their upsets at what he could not change to be much bothered by this present one.

'What about fording anywhere that way?' one of the men asked.

'Shouldn't have much hope of any ford,' the host said. 'Not if the water's been bad enough to take that bridge out. Your best hope is east over the Cherwell bridge here. It's—'

'I don't want to go east!' Lady Blaunche protested.

'Or else try westward to the first bridge upriver. There's no trouble that way that I've heard.'

He withdrew across the room then, leaving Lady Blaunche speechlessly near to distraught and no one knowing what to say, until she sat herself abruptly down onto a bench and said at no one in particular, 'I don't want to go that way.'

'My lady,' Mistress Avys tried soothingly, 'it's not that great a matter to be upsetting yourself for it.'

'I *have* to go that way,' Lady Blaunche repeated.

'But you can't,' one of the men dared. 'There's not point in even trying, what with the bridge out. Best we can do is go straight for the first bridge upriver and be done with it.'

Lady Blaunche shot angrily to her feet. 'But that puts us on a whole different road to home!'

'It makes no odds, my lady,' Mistress Avys said, beginning to be distressed with her. 'We'll be a little later home is all. Isn't that so, Jack?'

'By tomorrow eventide, sure. Only a little more riding that would have been,' the man Jack agreed.

Mistress Avys made to pat Lady Blaunche's arm. 'See? There's naught—'

Lady Blaunche flung her hand aside, exclaiming at her, 'That isn't the point! That . . .'

'What *is* the point, my lady?' Katherine asked in an oddly careful voice.

Lady Blaunche spun around to face her but stopped short of answering and after the barest pause said instead of whatever she had been going to, 'The point is where are we going to stay tonight? I don't know anywhere on the way you're all wanting me to go. What will we do if there's nowhere?'

'There'll be somewhere,' Jack assured her. 'There's always somewhere.'

Between one moment and the next Lady Blaunche had turned to piteous, her voice rising with desperation. 'But what if there isn't? I can't just sleep in a ditch! I can't . . .'

Jack started to protest that and Mistress Avys to flutter toward her with soothing sounds but Dame Claire came in her way, going to take Lady Blaunche by the arm and turning her back toward the bench, saying firmly, 'You know no one is going to let you sleep in a ditch, my lady.'

'My baby—'

'Will do well so long as you do well. Upsetting yourself over what can't be helped is not the way to do well. Now sit.'

'We have to be going—'

'We will. Sit you down, I pray.'

Perforce, guided by Dame Claire's strong hand, Lady Blaunche sat as Dame Claire raised her voice to order, 'Host, warmed cider well spiced with cinnamon for my lady, please. Dame Frevisse, would you bring my box, please?'

Frevisse went willingly, one of the men with her, knowing which hamper it was in, and in the innyard while he undid the bag's straps, she asked him, 'Does Lady Blaunche often fret herself this way?'

Sounding long resigned to it, the man said, 'Aye, she does and not just when she's bearing, either.'

Frevisse had been afraid of that. If all it was with her was the unbalance of humours that so often came on a childing woman as her body resorted itself to the growing child, making her feelings as changeful as her body, then mayhap Dame Claire could balance them again, but if Lady Blaunche commonly flung about this way . . .

The man pulled out Dame Claire's box of medicines and made to carry it himself but Frevisse held out her hands to take it from him, aware as he gave it to her that Katherine was coming from the inn, Mistress Dionisia following her in rather flustered haste, as if Katherine's going out was sudden, and in truth the girl moved sharply aside from the doorway and Frevisse coming back toward it, only stopped from going farther by Mistress Dionisia catching her by the sleeve and turning her around to bring them face-to-face.

What Katherine said then, Frevisse did not catch except that she seemed angry. Or maybe frightened. Of what? Of rain-swollen rivers and washed-away bridges? That was all there had been to distress her unless Lady Blaunche being upset had upset her, too. But she must be used to Lady Blaunche's ways by now. Everyone else around the lady seemed to be.

Dame Claire took the box from her with thanks as the host brought a cup of the same spiced cider Katherine and Mistress Avys had had with their dinner and set it beside her.

'Baby's drink,' Lady Blaunche said with distaste.

'And you're drinking it for your baby,' Dame Claire said crisply, choosing two little packets from among the other packets and small stoppered jars packed in the box.

'What are those?' Mistress Avys demanded.

'Don't be so suspicious, Avys,' Lady Blaunche said impatiently. She handed the innkeeper a coin for the cider and asked as if maybe he could be persuaded to change things if only he'd change his mind, 'Master host, you're certain there's nowhere near that's a sure crossing northward?'

'I'm sure as can be, my lady.'

On that, he bowed and withdrew again and Lady Blaunche said grimly to the wall across the room, 'This wasn't supposed to happen.'

'Here, my lady.' Having crumbled and stirred some dark, dried leaves into it, Dame Claire held out the cider to her. 'Drink while it's still warm.'

Lady Blaunche took it, sipped carefully, made an appreciative sound, and drank deeply, Dame Claire, Frevisse and Mistress Avys watching in silence. All the men were gone out now and Katherine and Mistress Dionisia not come back in, and when Lady Blaunche had finished and set the emptied cup aside, she stood up and said, calm and determined, though it was too soon for the herbs to have begun to work on her, 'Well, if change roads we must, then change roads we will and we'd best be about it. Let's be on our way, shall we?'

Chapter 5

That afternoon's riding had an unease the morning's had not, even though before they were far out of Banbury Lady Blaunche had given over being outwardly upset and was keeping up an almost constant talk to Dame Claire riding next to her again. It made Frevisse grateful for Katherine far more silent beside herself, but somehow Katherine's silence was not a comfortable silence, no more than Lady Blaunche's talk was easy talk, mostly about her ailments and her children with occasionally other things thrown in as they came randomly to mind and none of it of any interest to Frevisse. But just as Katherine's quiet and few brief, stiff words came, after the first while of riding, to seem like a guard wrapped around thoughts she was keeping to herself, so Lady Blaunche's almost ceaseless rattling began to have the feel of things said to hide thoughts.

What things? Frevisse wondered.

Or maybe it was simply her own and everyone's unease at the weather that instead of settling was shifting from rain to not to rain again but never one or the other for very long; and the riding was less easy than it had been, the roads more muddied from more rain here, forcing them too often to ride aside, when hedges or walls allowed, onto the grassy verges or else to cut through pastures or fields not yet spring-plowed. All of that slowed their going so that it was nigh to mid-afternoon before they came around and down a steep curve of the road toward a village and into sight, at its near end, of a bridge with the water running high under it and a clutter of village men and a few women at both ends, some of the men knee-deep in water among the bridge timbers along the bank, everyone else standing above, calling suggestions down at them.

In immediate distress, Lady Blaunche exclaimed, 'Jack!' and he answered as quickly, 'I'll find out, my lady,' and rode forward while the rest of them drew rein. Dame Claire leaned to say something quietly – and probably quieting – to Lady Blaunche who gave her only a curt nod in reply without looking away from Jack while he talked briefly with some of the men on the bank below; calling down impatiently at him when he reined his horse around to come back, 'Well?'

'They say we can cross, no fear, my lady,' Jack called back.

From the rear Mistress Avys cried out, 'Are they sure or are they just saying it?'

'If they weren't sure, they wouldn't say it,' Lady Blaunche said, heeling her horse forward.

'But how can they be sure?' Mistress Avys insisted.

'Because they are,' Lady Blaunche returned impatiently.

Still holding her horse where it was, Mistress Avys protested, 'They're not the ones crossing it!'

'Nor will we be if you go on sniveling,' Lady Blaunche snapped. 'It's safe enough if they say it is. Come on.'

Directly ordered, Mistress Avys came, making small, unhappy sounds until, just short of the bridge, Lady Blaunche drew rein, looked back at her and said, 'If you're all that afraid, come ride with me but be quick about it.'

Frevisse did not see why riding with Lady Blaunche would make the crossing any safer but she kept the thought to herself while they re-sorted themselves, Mistress Avys riding forward to join Lady Blaunche, Katherine swinging her horse around to Mistress Dionisia's side, Dame Claire drawing back to ride beside Frevisse. The men waited with the patience of men who have no choice in a matter, Jack saying when it was done, 'We'll cross two at a time, please you, my lady?'

Lady Blaunche agreed with a nod and Jack and the other forerider set their horses forward, rode onto the bridge followed by Mistress Avys's prayers aloud to St Christopher, and in only moments were across without mishap, Jack calling back, 'All's well. No trouble.'

Mistress Avys's prayers redoubled in might as she and Lady Blaunche rode forward in their turn, and Frevisse took this first chance to say anything alone to Dame Claire to ask, low-voiced and quickly, 'How is it truly with Lady Blaunche? Is she endangering herself or the baby with this riding?'

'She's not that far along with child that riding is any way likely to do her harm,' Dame Claire returned, as low and as quickly and neither of them looking away from the women now almost over the bridge. 'By all I've been able to tell, she's a well woman.' Dame Claire lowered her voice even further. 'The only ills she has are the ones she frets herself into, and because she's one of those people who thinks the world will fall to pieces if they don't manage everything and everyone within their reach, she frets herself into a great many ills.'

From the far side of the bridge Lady Blaunche said, 'Open your eyes, Avys. It's done.' And raised her voice to add peremptory order, 'The rest of you, come on.'

They did, Frevisse and Dame Claire next, with Frevisse knowing as soon as she felt the bridge under her horse, the wood ringing hollow to its hoofs, that there was no danger. The bridge's small trembling to the force of water rushing under it was no more than it should have been. She had crossed worse in her time and left all the prayers to Mistress Avys who went on at St Christopher without pause until everyone was over, then finished fervently with, 'Praise be to St Christopher and all the saints,' as she made the sign of the cross on herself.

Lady Blaunche clicked her tongue at her impatiently and said, 'Jack,' with a nod at him and the other forerider to lead off.

As they did, the rain began to spatter down again. There had been none heavy enough yet to soak their cloaks through nor was this, and with the road soon climbing to higher ground they had better going than they had had since Banbury, and Frevisse, settled into the riding now, was surprised when Lady Blaunche said of a sudden, with still several hours of riding light left and no sign the weather would worsen, 'I'm minded to stop the night at one of my cousin Sir Walter's manors not far ahead from here.'

Her foreriders seemed as surprised, both of them looking back at her, Jack saying uncertainly, 'My lady?'

'The bailiff knows me,' Lady Blaunche said. 'There'll be no trouble over our spending the night.'

'But . . .'

Lady Blaunche snapped him short. 'I'm tired.'

With a shrug the man faced forward again, while on her own part Frevisse found she did not mind the thought of stopping sooner than they might have. The pace had been easy, suited to a childing woman and nuns far along in Lenten fasting but she had been too long away

61

Margaret Frazer

from any riding at all and knew that in a day or two she would be feeling today's miles, with tomorrow's still to be added to them. But her next thought, rising unbidden and unsought was that Lady Blaunche had protested at having to come this way out of fear there might be nowhere to stay the night and now she had a cousin's manor she was sure of. How was that?

Frevisse shoved the wondering firmly away because whether the protest had been a slip of Lady Blaunche's memory or not, it hardly mattered and there was nothing to be done about it, anymore than there was anything to be done about the heavy-hanging wilt of her veil beside her face, the day's damp having long since defeated its every pretense of starch. That that was beginning to annoy her told Frevisse she was more tired than she had been realizing and she did not try to deceive herself over how grateful she was when they turned through a gateway into a small manor yard where the bailiff was already coming out of the hall door to meet them, probably warned that strangers were nigh by the skein of small boys who had left off playing in a flooded wayside ditch a ways down the road to run for the manor with cheerful yells. They had probably also told him that most of the newcomers were women, meaning they were likely simply travellers coming, not trouble, and the man greeted them smiling even before Lady Blaunche rode forward past Jack and the other forerider to announce herself and add, 'Do you remember me, Master Humphrey, and can we have lodging for the night?'

The man's smile widened. 'Bless me and yours, of course I remember you and you know you're welcome to anything we have, from a roof' – he glanced up at the gray-hanging sky, the threat of rain still there – 'to beds to a good, hot supper.'

'All of those will be welcome,' Lady Blaunche said. 'Thank you.'

It was altogether a small place, a grange more than a manor, with no particular accommodation kept for the lord if ever he came to visit. Instead there was merely the hall with the kitchen off one end and a bedchamber off the other and nothing else except the byres and barns around the yard. Even the village was a good quarter-mile farther along the road and Frevisse briefly wondered where the bailiff's family would sleep that night as his wife cheerfully cleared children and their things and her own and her husband's out of the bedchamber that was apparently also parlor during the day while giving servants orders for stripping the beds and bringing fresh sheets to make them up again, while directing one of her women to be off to the kitchen to see what could be added to the evening's pottage and ordering someone else to be off to the village to see who might have baked bread today.

'Three loaves. That would be good. Four would be better,' she called after the woman hurrying away.

Blankets, too, Frevisse thought but did not say, because the family's blankets would go back onto the beds readied for Lady Blaunche and the rest of them, leaving the bailiff's family – she had so far failed to sort out how many children there actually were among the bustle of skirts – to take the servants' bedding probably and the servants to make do as best they could. But there were always the byres and dry straw for the night, she supposed, and assuredly the woman seemed only cheerful about the whole business, shepherding children and stray servants ahead of her out of the bedchamber and into the hall where Lady Blaunche was sitting on a bench and the rest of them were standing, with Jack to hand in case he was needed and the other men gone off with Master Humphrey to see to the horses.

Shooing servants and children on their way, Mistress Humphrey, with a basket of sewing on one arm and a year-old child on the other, paused to give Lady Blaunche a quick curtsy and assurance that all would be ready shortly. Lady Blaunche thanked her with a smile and a few coins. 'Toward our supper,' she said, and with a pleased blush Mistress Humphrey thanked her and hurried on, saying over her shoulder that she would have ale brought for them, there was a new brewing.

Before it came, the two servants readying the chamber finished and came out, one of the women coming to tell Lady Blaunche she could go in, if it pleased her. Lady Blaunche thanked her, gave each of the women a penny for their trouble and received their thanks and pleased assurances that if there was anything she wanted she need only ask for it.

'I'm sure, and you have my thanks, but all I'm longing for just now is lying down,' Lady Blaunche said kindly and sent them on their way.

The bedchamber was larger than Frevisse had feared it would be, with a sufficiency of stools for sitting if one were unparticular about comfort but no fireplace for warmth or to take off the chill; for that someone would have to go back to the hearth in the center of the hall when the fire was built up for the evening, she supposed, and unfortunately there was only one standing bed with a truckle bed under it, and unless mattresses were to be brought from elsewhere, it seemed they would sleep three to a bed tonight. While wondering if anyone snored, she took off her cloak along with the other women and was looking for somewhere to hang it to dry when Lady Blaunche settled the problem by saying as she gave her own over to Mistress Avys, 'We'll have them taken to the kitchen. They'll still be damp come the morning otherwise. Jack, everything seems well enough here. Go fetch our bags. The men should have them off the horses by now.'

Jack bowed to the dismissal and went but scarcely two breaths later Lady Blaunche exclaimed, 'Oh! I forgot to tell him . . .' and was out the door after him before she had finished.

Frevisse, occupied with shaking out her skirts and wondering if anyone would mind if she shut the single window's shutter against the chill draught, did not see Katherine go a few moments later, only heard Mistress Dionisia say, 'Katherine, dear, where . . .' and looked up to find Katherine gone and her woman staring worriedly at the empty doorway.

Katherine was of an age to see to herself – not fall into the fire or run out the back door to play – but one clear look at Mistress Dionisia's face told Frevisse that tiredness was overtaking the woman rapidly now that they were done with the day's riding and that nonetheless she was about to go after Katherine, her worry more than her weariness, and without thinking Frevisse said, 'Let me go for her, Mistress,' and was out the chamber door before Mistress Dionisia could more than protest, 'But . . .' But neither did the woman come after her, and after all Katherine had not gone far. The place was too small for the bother of a screens passage between the hall and its outer door and Frevisse saw her there at the hall's far end, just inside the door to the yard but going nowhere, simply standing still, her head to one side as if she were listening. And she was, Frevisse realized as she neared her and heard Jack close outside, saying, as if not for the first time, 'No, my lady. I can't. Master Fenner was clear on it.'

The hall was dirt-floored but with rushes over the packed earth and no way to come on Katherine silently; as Frevisse neared her, the girl looked briefly around and raised a hand, asking her to quiet as Lady Blaunche said, a little shrill with anger, 'I know what Master Fenner said but I'm bidding you differently.'

'Makes no odds, my lady. I can't. None of us can. Master Fenner said you weren't to be left. Not for any reason.' Jack was apologetic but stubbornly certain. 'Makes no odds if things have changed. Master Fenner said . . .'

Surprised at Katherine eavesdropping nor even minding she was caught at it, Frevisse turned away, back toward the bedchamber and the other women, then just short of there thought better of what she was doing and turned back to Katherine, meaning to bid her come away.

She was too late. She had no more than turned when Lady Blaunche came in at the hall door, face to face with Katherine so abruptly that Katherine took a step backward and Lady Blaunche froze where she was, both of them staring at each other, rigid, before Katherine said, a little too loudly, her voice high with strain, 'Where did you want Jack to go?'

Lady Blaunche looked sharply past her to Frevisse, too far away to have overheard anything she must have thought, and said to Katherine with a haughty lift of her head, 'If you're rude enough to overhear other people's talk, you should at least have manners enough not to ask about what you missed,' and swept past her in what would have been a swirl of skirts if they had not been heavy with damp.

As it was, she came so swiftly Frevisse had only time to step aside and let her pass, with Katherine close enough behind her there was no chance to stop the girl and ask her what was toward even if Frevisse had wanted to and mostly she did not. What she mostly wanted was chance to catch up on the day's missed Offices as best she might and hopefully serve Vespers' prayers better, but as she left the hall, servants were coming from the yard with wood for building up the hearth fire and to set up the tables for supper, while the crowded bedchamber offered no better hope of quiet and Frevisse knew nowhere else away there might be here.

Nor did it seem Dame Claire had any hope of escape; Lady Blaunche was complaining she felt a headache beginning and had a hand laid high on her belly as if expecting trouble there shortly, too. That set Dame Claire to asking her questions and Mistress Avys to fussing over her, leaving Mistress Dionisia and Katherine to see to unpacking what was needed from the bags two of the men just then brought in, with Frevisse to meet Mistress Humphrey and a servant bringing a pitcher of ale and tray of cups and assure them all was well, nothing greatly wrong with Lady Blaunche, only the weariness of the journey.

'Yes, indeed. Poor lady,' Mistress Humphrey said with an understanding nod. 'Will she dine in hall, think you?'

'I will,' Lady Blaunche said from the bed, 'and hope you and your good husband will keep me company at table.'

Mistress Humphrey beamed with pleasure, curtsied, said, 'We'll gladly, my lady, thank you,' and added to Frevisse and Dame Claire with another curtsy, 'There's thought taken for your fasting, too, my ladies. I've set cook to making a lovely gourd pie, please you.'

They thanked her and she hurried out, sweeping a half-grown child peeping in at the door along with her as she went.

After that it was a matter of seeing to Lady Blaunche's care while trying to sort things out to their comforts, too, and everything made less easy by Lady Blaunche refusing to take anything Dame Claire offered her that might have quieted or made her drowsy.

'That would hardly be kind to our host. I won't come to table unable to make talk with him,' she said.

'If you kept your bed and had supper brought in . . .' Mistress Avys started.

Lady Blaunche waved the possibility aside. 'Neither my husband nor my cousin Sir Walter would pardon such ill manners.'

And in truth when supper was called, she rose to it readily enough, leading the way from bedchamber into hall as if naught had ever been amiss with her. Master and Mistress Humphrey had done well by her, with shiningly white linen on what was the 'high' table, though the hall had no dais at all to make it higher than the only other one there was, and the pewterware at Lady Blaunche's place shined to its best glow. The rest of them would make do with bread trenchers and wooden cups but the cups were clean and well-polished and the bread thickly cut. There was merely a momentary confusion after Lady Blaunche had gestured that she meant Master Humphrey to sit on her right side, Mistress Humphrey on her left with Katherine beyond her, when Katherine said no, she would wait on Lady Blaunche at table, please her; and added, before Lady Blaunche could more than begin to frown objection, 'If you would grace me with the favor, my lady,' making a deep curtsy and glancing sideways as she straightened from it at the manservant hovering nearby, clearly assigned to see to Lady Blaunche and, equally clearly, unnerved by the task, uneasily shifting from foot to foot, giving point to Katherine's very low murmur, 'Your gown, my lady.'

Mistress Avys, more direct, with a hard stare at the hapless man, muttered, 'Let Mistress Katherine have her way, my lady.'

To Frevisse it looked that Lady Blaunche gave way then more because longer delay would be ungracious than because she wanted to but give way she did, with a curt nod at Katherine but a brief smile and kind word at the man who only looked much relieved at being spared his ordeal and more than happy to be left to seeing to only his master and mistress.

They all sat then, with Frevisse on the bailiff's other side and Dame Claire beyond his wife, and Mistress Avys and Mistress Dionisia at the head of the 'lower' table with some of the manor's other folk and Lady Blaunche's four men beyond them. The first remove was brought promptly and warm from the kitchen, and Frevisse guessed that meals here did not usually run to more than one remove but Mistress Humphrey had managed this one into two by accompanying fish cooked with a thick pepper sauce with a salad of very young greens, probably the first her garden had given this year, to make the first and created a second by following the gourd pie with apples cooked in wine and cinnamon, so that all in all the meal was both well done and filling and Frevisse more than satisfied to be left alone to enjoy it, which she was because Master Humphrey spent the meal giving almost all his heed to Lady Blaunche.

So did his wife and so did Katherine who hovered at Lady Blaunche's shoulder even when it put her in the way of the manservant's serving the rest of them, to the point where Frevisse found herself watching the girl, wondering if it was only chance she seemed most particularly there whenever Lady Blaunche turned to talk with Master Humphrey. But if she was, why?

Nor did the meal's end bring an end to Katherine's close attending. Instead, in the little while Lady Blaunche stood in talk with Master and Mistress Humphrey before pleading weariness and withdrawing to her chamber, Katherine was never more than a few paces behind her, still attending though Mistress Avys hovered not far off, more than ready to take her place, and Mistress Dionisia's occasional look toward her was puzzled.

Lady Blaunche ignored her as if she was not there at all, until talk with Master and Mistress Humphrey was done and thanks again

given and good nights said. Then Lady Blaunche led Katherine and
the other four of them into the bedchamber with a fine sweep of
skirts, Frevisse happening to come last, turning from shutting the
door between them and the world in time to see Lady Blaunche across
the room turn on Katherine, all graciousness gone as she snapped,
'Enough! Back off and leave me alone!'

Katherine flinched from the suddenness, bobbed the slightest of
curtsies, and swung sharply away from her without an answering
word.

Servants had been in since supper to pull out the truckle bed and
make up both it and the other with the fresh sheets and aired blankets
Mistress Humphrey had earlier ordered, leaving the room smelling
faintly of lavender. The window had been shuttered, too, and two
lamps lighted, and with all that and the promise of a comfortable
night after a very good supper, things should have been pleasant
enough but having started with Katherine, Lady Blaunche went on
giving sharp orders she did not need to, impatient when there was no
need for impatience, and at the last bursting into tears and flinging
herself into the bed, telling everyone to leave her alone.

The two waiting-women exchanged looks with each other, all but
saying aloud that this was just how it so often was with childing
women, while Dame Claire, standing tight-lipped by the bed with a
cup of warmed ale mixed with soothing herbs, had the air of someone making a slow count before saying anything, and Frevisse, before
she could think not to, looked across the room to Katherine.

Since Lady Blaunche's ungraciousness had begun, the girl had kept
aside nor made a move now to come near but stood where she was,
coldly staring at Lady Blaunche's sobbing. As if angry at her, Frevisse
thought. And afraid. Because there was fear as surely as anger in her
look.

Fear of what? Anger at what?

Neither made sense.

But then neither did Lady Blaunche's flaring out at her for nothing
more than keeping close attendance through the evening.

Too close attendance?

Frevisse carefully took her mind away from wherever next her
thoughts might have gone. Whatever trouble Katherine was making
between herself and Lady Blaunche, there was no need to let it
become a trouble for her, too, and firmly not thinking about anything

except going to bed, she stripped down to her undergown, slipped into the far side of the truckle bed that indeed she was to share with the two waiting-women, pulled up her share of the blankets, shut her eyes, and set to saying Compline's prayers in hope that sleep would soon come, leaving the others to sort things out as they would.

Chapter 6

The shutters had been set wide open from the narrow, tall windows down both sides of Brinskep's great hall to let in the cool wash of the overcast day's lean light and the warming day's spring-scented air – not being from the pigsty side of the manor today, Robert thought wryly. The windows were too high in the walls for anything to be seen from them but pale sky with thin clouds instead of thickly gray and raining ones. Without the rain, even with the roads still muddied, travel should have gone well enough today and even while he agreed aloud with Master Durant that the weather looked likely to clear, he was thinking that they should have been here by now, Katherine and the others. But aloud, to keep up his share of the talk, he said, 'If the weather holds dry for a few days, we might be plowing by next week's end,' because after all Master Durant was one of the six arbiters who were to help sort out matters with the Allesleys and it was better they liked each other than not, and from the little he had seen so far of Master Durant and his fellow Master Hotoft in the hour or so they had been here, he liked them both well enough. It was simply that he was not as ready as he could wish for all that was happening. The matter of arbitration had moved forward more swiftly than he would ever have deemed possible in the scant weeks since he had no more than raised the possibility with the attorney's clerk who had come with Sir Lewis Allesley's latest demands. Sir Lewis had answered back by swift messenger that he was more than willing to it, and after that, among the possible ways arbitration might be done and the difference in place and power between himself and Sir Lewis, they had settled on each bringing three arbiters to the dealing, rather than on trying to find a neutral lord who might after all have interests one way or the other; and because Sir Lewis Allesley, as the Earl of Stafford's man, would draw his arbiters from the earl's council, Ned had advised Robert he should ask Lord Grey of Groby's help in providing his own.

'It would obligate me to him,' Robert had protested.

'You're going to have to be obligated to someone to balance the Allesleys or else you'll have no chance in this at all. Grey is the coming power this end of Warwickshire. You'll likely have to align with him soon or late. Why not now and have some good out of it right off?' Then, knowing perfectly well the answer, Ned had added, 'Unless you'd rather ask Sir Walter's help?'

Because any Fenner help would reach no further than flat refusal to consider parting with any land, Robert had turned away from that possibility without second thought, had sent word to Lord Grey of his need, been promptly assured of Lord Grey's willingness to help, and now here were Master Durant and Master Hotoft, with Master Fielding due to arrive tomorrow when the Allesleys and their arbiters were likewise expected, with the talks among them to begin the day after that.

And all Robert found he was truly mindful of was that Blaunche should have been here with Katherine by midday and it was now late afternoon and neither they nor word of them had come.

Beside him, Ned had been keeping Master Hotoft in talk but they had moved on from weather to other things and Master Hotoft now turned to Master Durant to ask, 'Tom, do you remember the name of that family in my lord's Coventry case last year?'

'The Coventry case? Last year?' Master Durant pursed his lips in thought. 'Wasn't it Godyng?'

'Was it? That doesn't sound right.'

As Robert understood it, both men were attorneys, with Master Durant on Lord Grey's council for good measure and Master Hotoft frequently in Lord Grey's service. Gowned soberly in three-quarter-length black houppelandes and dark hosen, with velvet caps that differed only in the garnet-set jewel Master Durant wore on his, they were a matched pair of men confident of their skills, at ease already with where they were, Master Hotoft turning to ask across the hall toward the clerks who had come with him and Master Durant, 'John, do you remember my lord's case in Coventry last year?'

Clumped in talk of their own with Geoffrey Hannys, the men all looked toward him and one offered, 'Boteller, wasn't it?'

'That was the grazing case on the Leicestershire border two years ago.'

'Was it?' The clerks drifted across the hall to join their masters, the talk turning complicated over whether Master Durant meant the Coventry case at all or another one, while several servants circled with pitchers, offering more wine where it was needed. Robert, refusing with a small shake of his head, drew backward from among the clustered men to answer a question Master Skipton brought him from the kitchen about tonight's supper and made no effort to rejoin the talk when the steward went off again but simply stayed close to hand as if paying heed.

Ned, turning aside to hold his goblet out to be filled, took the chance to say low into Robert's ear, for no one else to hear in the general talk around them, 'They'll be here. It's naught more than that the rains have made the roads slower going than we thought they'd be.'

Robert nodded agreement he wished he felt. Even when the matter of arbitration was fully in hand and going forward, Blaunche had gone on opposing any dealing at all with the Allesleys as fiercely as she had from the first, only adding bitterness to her anger. Then suddenly, giving it all up, she had agreed there was no help for satisfying the Allesleys' desire to see Katherine. 'If it has to be, it has to,' she had said, still bitter but finally near to accepting that the arbitration was going to happen. More near than Robert was to accepting that Katherine's marriage to Sir Lewis' heir was likely the price the Allesleys would demand for settlement.

Even so, with already too much to hand and everything happening too quickly, he had been simply grateful when Blaunche – to make amends for having made him so much trouble, she'd said – had offered to see to fetching her back, and blind and dull-witted he must have been, he thought bitterly now, to have trusted her change of heart without a second thought. Not until the day after she had gone, when Benedict was suddenly gone, too, had his first doubt stirred. There was no reason Benedict should not come and go at his choice and he had taken two yeomen with him, as was right, and left word that no one need expect him back until they saw him. It was so ordinary a thing that no one had seen reason to say anything to Robert about it and, busy at accounts that day, he had known nothing until suppertime.

His first thought then had been that if Benedict was not back before Blaunche was, she would be fierce when she found out. Then on that thought's heels there had come a worse one: that Blaunche already knew where Benedict was gone because she had sent him.

Robert, despite that he knew too well how stubborn Blaunche could be toward having her own will, had seen too late this time that if she could not have Katherine for Benedict one way, she might well mean to have her for him by another. And what way would be more certain than to hand Katherine over to him herself, leaving Robert nothing but his anger once the marriage was forced and done?

As he had realized all that, his first urge had been to take horse and set out to overtake Benedict, but almost as quickly he had seen there was nothing he could do except wait it out. Neither he nor anyone he sent could reach St Frideswide's before Blaunche had Katherine out of there and after that there was no way of knowing which way they might go because if Blaunche's purpose was not to bring Katherine home but to give her over to Benedict she might go any way but the direct one. The men he had sent with her had had their orders to keep with her, but that only meant they would go the way she told them to, riding Katherine into Benedict's hands.

So helplessness and hidden anger had curdled in Robert's guts these two days past while he had gone on with everything needed to make the arbitration work, able to tell no one, not even Ned, only knowing that if he was right and Blaunche had done this thing . . .

With his back to the wooden screens that hid the hall's door toward the yard and his attention trying to be on the talk going on around him, he did not see Gil had come in until from just behind his shoulder Gil said low-voiced, 'They're back, sir. Lady Blaunche and the rest. Eudo's just called out he's seen them.'

Eudo had been set to keep the watch on the gatehouse roof for these few days when there would be so much come and go, and holding in his mingled rush of relief and fear, Robert said with outward ease to the two attorneys, 'By your leave, my lady wife is returned,' bowed to them, received their bows in return and assurances they would do well while he was gone, and left them, saying to Gil as they headed together for the door, 'Everything looks well? No sign of trouble?'

'Not that Eudo said. That it was Lady Blaunche coming and it looks to be two nuns with her is all he yelled down.'

Robert's stride shortened with surprise. 'Two nuns? And Katherine, too, yes?'

'Lady Blaunche and two nuns, that's all Eudo yelled. I didn't wait for more.'

Robert could have cursed both him and Eudo but he would know for himself in bare moments and bit back the words. The screens passage shielded the hall from draughts when the outer door to the yard was opened in ill weather but today the door stood wide to the afternoon's soft air and Robert came out of the passage's shadows onto the top of the stone stairs down to the cobbled yard without need to break stride. From there he had clear view over the yard and crowding of people there. Some were his own men, some were Ned's, others were Masters Durant's and Hotoft's and would have nothing much to do these days but be there. He remembered too well that idle hanging about from his own days as Sir Walter's squire, and because he had never had great inclination to drinking, games of chance, or wenching, the tediousness between the times he had been needed for something had sometimes been nigh to unbearable. Remembering all of that, he had already given the maidservants word they were to keep clear of the yard this while and warned his men they could game with the newcomers but anyone who either got into a fight because of it or drunk enough to make trouble of any kind would be in need of a new master come quarter day.

As it was, Eudo must have been dozing at his watch because as Robert paused at the top of the stairs, Jack and Matthew rode through the gateway arch, followed by Blaunche, with Katherine beside her and no sign there had been any trouble.

Fear drained from Robert, leaving him half-sick and with nothing between him and the anger that had been building these two days under the fear. More quickly than was wise on the stairs' stone steepness he went down to the yard, was waiting at their foot for Jack and Matthew to draw rein, bowing to him from their saddles as he demanded, 'All went well?'

'There was a bridge washed away north of Banbury,' Jack said. 'It was going around to another set us back. Otherwise, no trouble.'

'Well done. My thanks,' Robert said, dismissing them, leaving them to bow to his back and turn their horses aside, out of his way to

Blaunche through the momentary crowding and sorting out of men and horses as other household men hurried forward to take hold of the women's bridles and help them dismount. Courtesy would have taken him to his wife first anyway, in the usual way of things, but this time it was his anger that needed to see her, even if he could not give way to it here or yet. Nor did sight of her white face lined with tiredness touch him in the least. He knew too well how willfully she pushed herself against her strength; if she was overtired, it was by her own choice and he was in no humour to pity her for it.

Maybe she read that in his look before ever he spoke because she gave him no more greeting than he gave her, only leaned over into his hands to let him lift her from the saddle and down. It was something she had begun with their marriage, a little feigned helplessness she saw as womanly, but today Robert was in no humour for it either and clamped hold of her waist and lifted her down with more force than grace, setting her on her feet so ungently that she tightened hold of his arms to keep her balance and said at him, 'I'm not a grain bag, thank you.'

Brittle with his anger, Robert snapped back, 'No. A grain bag doesn't have sons. Where's Benedict?'

He had not loosed her, felt her stiffen between his hands and saw thoughts shift rapidly behind her eyes before she returned curtly after too long a pause, 'He's here for all I know,' and pulled roughly free from him.

Robert caught her by the arm, determined to have more out of her, but a short, brisk nun ducked around the man beginning to lead Blaunche's horse away and took hold of Blaunche's other arm with, 'Master Fenner? I'm Dame Claire from St Frideswide's. Your lady wife needs her bed now. By your leave,' but already drawing Blaunche away from him toward the stairs, Mistress Avys hurrying after them from among the horses.

Balked of his anger, Robert turned sharply away, almost into Katherine brushing past him after Blaunche. Without thinking he caught her by the arm almost as roughly as he had Blaunche and turned her toward him, saying, 'Katherine.'

Only that; and she said nothing at all; but her other hand came up to cling to his and in her eyes as she looked up at him was such desperate relief and closeness to tears that he understood, hard as a blow, certain as words, that she had been very afraid, and he wanted

75

to take her in his arms and hold her close and tell her she was safe, that he'd never let her be afraid again.

He crushed the urge as it rose because in bitter truth there was next to nothing he could do to protect her and instead loosed her and demanded as she stepped away from him, 'What happened?'

'Nothing.' And then, 'Is Benedict here?'

'He left the day after Lady Blaunche did,' Robert said, and added deliberately, 'with no word of where he was going or when he'd be back.' Watching her face, he saw that Benedict's sudden going meant the same thing to her that it had to him, which meant that some way Blaunche must have betrayed her plan or at least given enough suspicion of it that Katherine had been riding in fear. For how long? All the hours from St Frideswide's?

The thought made him want to shake Blaunche and strike Benedict, but Katherine was drawing another step away, making him a quick, slight curtsy before turning to follow Blaunche as behind him an unexpected voice said, 'Master Fenner,' and he swung around to find Dame Frevisse there. Past the brief wondering at what she had understood of what she might have overheard, he was only happy to see her and said gladly, 'Welcome, my lady. I hadn't thought we'd meet again so soon.'

Chapter 7

Because the business he had in hand was more his duty at the moment than she was, Frevisse took no offense when Robert, barely after greeting her, gave her over to Mistress Dionisia. The waiting-woman took her on with the same evenhandedness she was giving to overseeing their baggage being unstrapped from behind saddles.

'You go ahead with those,' she told one of the two men doing as she bid. 'They go to Lady Blaunche's chamber. That one there,' she told the other man now carrying Frevisse's and Dame Claire's, 'you follow me with it.' She looked suddenly to Frevisse. 'Where will Dame Claire want her medicines, do you think?'

'With her,' Frevisse said. She was finding, now that they were done with riding, that she was as tired as she had feared she would be and more than willing to leave thinking to anyone else so long as there was shortly somewhere she could sit quietly a time or, better, lie down until tomorrow. Not that she really thought she would have the chance, but as she followed Mistress Dionisia up the stairs and into the hall and past the clusters of men in busy talk there, she gratefully refuged in her nunhood, keeping her head bowed, her hands tucked into her sleeves, removing herself from need to see or be seen until at the hall's far end Mistress Dionisia led her through a doorway into a large room where no one was, with a fireplace with carved stone mantle at its far end, a mullioned window looking out toward trees, a scattering of chairs and a large table, and on the near wall to the right of the door a large painted hanging bright with armored, smiling men attacking an unlikely small tower from which equally smiling ladies in blue- and carnation- and primrose-colored gowns were pelting them with flowers. Crossing toward a door standing open to a tight spiral of stone stairs, Frevisse and the baggage-burdened man following faithfully, Mistress Dionisia said without any particular look at the room, 'This is the solar where they'll do their talking once they set to business. Above is the parlor and my lord and lady's bedchamber. I'm not certain where you and Dame Claire are to stay, so by your leave we'll just go up . . .'

She was stopped by Katherine sweeping down the stairs and into the room. The girl had put off the veil she had worn for travelling, her hair was untidily pulling free from its braid, and she had not yet changed from her riding gown with its mud drying around the hem just as Frevisse's was. She was flushed and a little flustered and while making quick curtsy to Frevisse said to Mistress Dionisia, 'Lady Blaunche says they're to share Nurse's chamber. I'll take her there and see her settled. You go see what you can do to help Mistress Avys.'

'She's being troublesome, is she?' Mistress Dionisia said, not meaning Mistress Avys, Frevisse thought.

'She is,' Katherine agreed tersely.

Mistress Dionisia gave a crisp nod. 'You keep clear, then. I'll see to her.'

'Dame Claire wants her medicines.'

Mistress Dionisia nodded again, went to unstrap Dame Claire's bag the man was carrying, and took out the needed box. 'You go on then and don't hurry to come back,' she said to Katherine. 'You go with them,' she added at the man and went away up the stairs alone.

'This way, if you will, my lady,' Katherine said and turned toward the painted tapestry, saying to Frevisse following her, 'It seems best to put you and Dame Claire in with the children's nurse and maid. But not with the children,' she added.

Frevisse was relieved to hear that. Thus far she had worked out that they must be in the tower whose top she had glimpsed at the hall's end from the road as they came toward Brinskep. Now, close to the door back into the hall, Katherine lifted the corner of the hanging to reveal another door, set deep into the six-foot thickness of the tower's wall and while the manservant came forward to hold the hanging aside she knocked firmly, then opened it and went through before anyone would have had time to answer, Frevisse following her, too travel-tired to care so long as there was shortly some place she could stop moving for a while.

The room they came into was plain and not overlarge but with freshly white-plastered walls and a large, unglazed window, its shutters open to the day's mild light and air, looking out across the manor yard toward the hall stairs. It was furnished for several people's daily living with two beds against one wall, a small wooden chest beside each, a table in the room's middle with a pair of joint stools at it, and rush matting on the well-scrubbed wooden floor. There were also two other doors across the room, toward which Katherine pointed and said, 'One of them leads to the necessity and the other to the children's room and the stairs to the yard. On this side of the yard the rooms are made in pairs, a shared door between the two rooms below and shared stairs from the yard to the rooms above.'

She was talking while pointing the manservant to set the bags on the table, nodding her thanks to him when he had and saying while he bowed to her and left, 'The children's nurse and their maid share this room. The children have the next. The rooms beyond there – they aren't reached from here but only from the yard – are Benedict's and Master Geoffrey's. Benedict is Lady Blaunche's son, and Master Geoffrey the household clerk and anything else he's needed for. He's with Lady Blaunche now . . .'

She trailed off that line of talk, her eyes busy about the room. 'I'll give order to have a towel and basin brought for your and Dame Claire's own use, and Nurse and the maid take turns sleeping the night in the children's room so there's a bed for you and Dame Claire to share. I don't even know why there are two beds in here . . .' She broke off again, saying with sudden worry, 'Or would you rather I had a mattress brought and one of you sleep on the floor?'

'I don't mind the floor,' Frevisse said. 'That might be best.' After last night with Mistress Avys's and Mistress Dionisia's snoring, she was longing for the solitude of her bed at St Frideswide's; anywhere to lie down would, at this moment, be acceptable, she was so tired.

Katherine gave a crisp nod much like Mistress Dionisia's. 'I'll see to that, too, and—'

'Katherine,' Frevisse said quietly, stopping her in midsentence and would have added there was no need to worry, she and Dame Claire would do well enough, but before she could, Katherine caught a quick breath and said on a short laugh and a smile, 'I'm galloping my tongue to market, aren't I? I'm sorry.'

'No need for sorry. Everything has been of a sudden these three days. Will the arbiters and the Allesleys and their people all be staying here, too?'

'I don't know.' Katherine sounded surprised at herself. 'No one has said.'

'There's hardly been time.'

'There hasn't, has there?' Katherine sat suddenly down on a joint stool. 'Oh, my, I'm tired. And so must you be.'

Frevisse was about to take the chance to say that, yes, she was and would not mind being left on her own for a while if Katherine had other things she should be away to see to, when a sudden rise of voices from the yard brought Katherine to her feet and both Frevisse and her to the window side by side in time to see three horsemen draw rein at the foot of the hall steps. Not strangers, Frevisse guessed. For one thing, there had been no warning shout from the gateward, and for another, aside from shifting out of their way and shouted greetings, no one seemed much stirred to see them.

Two of the riders, by their plain doublets and plain horses, were attendant on the third, a young man in dark riding doublet and tall leather boots, his horse a long-legged, wellbred bay. Horse and boots were well-muddied, as if from hard, fast riding, and so were the other men and horses; but while they looked merely tired, the young man was plainly something much more like angry if his tense seat in his saddle and the abrupt jerk of his head sideways as he answered a question from someone in the yard was anything to judge by.

'Who . . .' Frevisse began to ask.

'Benedict,' Katherine said curtly. 'Lady Blaunche's son by her second husband.'

Katherine said the words so near to spitting that Frevisse looked at her, startled. Hands clutched together and between her breasts, the girl was standing tautly, her eyes rigid on the man as he jerked his horse to a stop at the foot of the hall stairs. Frevisse looked back to him in time to see him fling himself from his saddle and his reins at one of the men standing there. Young, fair-haired, a little long of leg perhaps, like a colt still growing, he was not, except for the anger, uncomely. Nor was he much older than Katherine. With a sideways look toward her, Frevisse said carefully, 'I wonder what he's angry at.'

Staring at him as he went up the hall stairs, Katherine said sharply back, 'He's angry at having failed to cut off my coming home. At having failed to seize me and make me marry him.'

Openly startled, Frevisse turned toward her. 'What?'

Katherine faced her in return, now as openly angry as Benedict.

'Do you really think Lady Blaunche had forgotten her cousin had a manor along that road we were forced to take yesterday because of the gone bridge?'

'She might have . . .' Frevisse began, ignoring her own doubt about it.

'There was never Fenner yet forgot where any Fenner land is. What she was protesting was having to go a different way than she had purposed. She—' Katherine stopped her words short, said instead with a quick curtsy and only a little strangled on the effort to shove her anger down, 'Pray, pardon me. I must needs tell Nurse that you're here and Lady Blaunche will want to know how the children are. By your leave.'

She was backing away even as she said it, turned without waiting for Frevisse's answer and left, going by way of the door toward the nursery.

Frevisse let her, not having right to bid her stop and in doubt that Katherine would have anyway, angry as she was; but unless Katherine chose to go down the stairs and across the yard, she would have to come back through here and Frevisse spent the while until she did by unpacking her bag and Dame Claire's, shaking out their spare habits and laying them flat across the foot of one of the beds for the travel's wrinkles to fall out as best they might. The clean wimples and veils, tightly rolled, had not much rumpled, would do, she thought and laid them beside the habits. Then, with nothing else she could do, she sat herself down on one of the joint stools.

Prayer should have been a possibility then but instead her thoughts were an unhappy mingling of uncertainty over what to do with herself now she was here, an uncomfortable wondering about how much pleasure she could manage to show when inevitably confronted by Nurse eager to show off Robert's – three, had he said? – children to her, and – though she tried not to – an even more uncomfortable wondering over what Katherine had said. Because if the girl was right and Lady Blaunche had been plotting with her son to thwart Robert both over Katherine's marriage and this arbitration that was underway – and if Robert found out-matters here were going to be more difficult than ever she had thought.

She heard a door snick quietly shut across the landing and stood up, ready when Katherine came back into the room, thankfully alone and composed, pausing to say with a smile, 'I told Nurse that you're

81

tired from travel and wouldn't want to see the children today. I'll see to sending someone with warm water and a towel now.'

She was going for the tower door before she finished speaking but Frevisse said, 'Mistress Katherine, a moment please.'

Already past her, Katherine stopped short, visibly drew a deep, steadying breath, and turned, not bothering to feign any smile now, to face her again.

Not smiling either, Frevisse asked, 'How do you know a forced marriage is what Lady Blaunche and her son intended against you?'

Katherine's eyes darkened with anger as she answered, her voice edged, 'Because of yesterday. Beginning with how more angry than upset she was when we first found out the bridge was gone. And then she lied.'

'About being afraid of nowhere to stay, you mean.'

'She never forgot that manor was there. And then I overheard her trying to send Jack somewhere.'

'You followed her deliberately to overhear her, didn't you?'

'If she'd wanted Jack for something usual, she'd have sent one of us after him, not gone herself. By then I was beginning to be afraid. I didn't know of what. Just afraid. And then I heard her trying to order him to go somewhere.'

'You think to Benedict. To tell him where we were,' Frevisse said.

'I think so, yes. But Jack wouldn't go. He's more Master Fenner's man than Lady Blaunche's, and Master Fenner had given orders the men weren't to leave us for any reason. So Jack wouldn't.' In the relief of saying it all aloud to someone, Katherine was talking rapidly now. 'Then she was willing to dine with the bailiff and his wife in the hall. That wasn't like her, either. Tired as I know she had to be and little as she likes to spend time on "lesser" folk, she should have been more than willing to have her supper in bed.'

'She was maybe merely being well-mannered.'

'No, she wasn't,' Katherine said flatly. 'She was seeking a chance to talk alone with the man, to set him to send someone, or go himself, to Benedict.'

'And you kept her from it.'

'Yes.' Katherine shivered. 'I had to.'

'Would it be so bad to marry Benedict?' Frevisse asked gently. 'At least he's someone you know.' Or was that the trouble?

Katherine drew a deep breath, gazing past Frevisse as if into her own thoughts before she said carefully, 'I know him and there's nothing amiss with him. But . . .' She looked at Frevisse, pleading for her to understand. 'We don't suit. We simply . . . don't.'

'It may be the same with the Allesley marriage if it goes through.'

'I know. But Master Fenner needs that marriage. Lady Blaunche hates that he's willing to have anything to do with the Allesleys, has fought him at every step, but it has to be done, and if my marriage is what . . .' Her voice broke. She had to stop to steady it, and went on, 'My marrying Benedict would serve no purpose but Lady Blaunche's greed.'

Frevisse hesitated but, having gone so far into what was no business of hers, went further. 'Will you tell Master Fenner?'

Katherine paused in her turn, before saying carefully, 'From how angry he was at Lady Blaunche in the yard just now, I'd guess he knows already.'

Frevisse had not noticed Robert was angry in the yard just now but that was maybe because she had been too busy being grateful to be done with riding to heed much else. 'How would he know?' she asked.

'He could guess easily enough. He knows Lady Blaunche's mind as well as anyone does. It was partly their quarreling over the Allesley marriage and Benedict that set him to take me to St Frideswide's in the first place. Then if Benedict disappeared from here while Lady Blaunche was gone for me – and surely Benedict did and without any word to anyone because he doesn't lie well . . .' Katherine's voice rose, fear and anger twisted together in it. 'That's all Master Fenner would need to guess the rest and by then there was nothing he could do about it!'

'He should have foreseen the treachery,' Frevisse said.

'He trusts,' Katherine said, as if made angry by it. 'He believes in the good until the bad is forced on him.'

'Couldn't he have sent men after Benedict?'

'To where? He couldn't know Lady Blaunche purposed to come back from the nunnery the same way she'd gone. I wouldn't have, if I'd been planning it. And how long was Benedict gone before Robert knew about it? If Benedict had too great a lead . . .'

Katherine broke off, hands pressed over her mouth, eyes shut, until she had steadied. Then she dropped her hands and said, subdued, her eyes toward the floor, 'Your pardon, my lady. This isn't anything I should be troubling you with.'

'I asked.'

'And have kindly listened. But it's done. They failed and we're safely here.' Katherine swept down in a low curtsy and came out of it moving toward the tower door, saying over her shoulder as she went, 'I pray you pardon me, I've other things I should see to,' and was gone.

Chapter 8

Not much ere sunset, while Ned was gathering Masters Durant and Hotoft and their men to ride with him to his manor for the night, word came that the Allesleys were indeed arrived at the Bishop of Coventry's grange where they were to stay the nights, hardly farther off than Ned's manor though in a somewhat different direction and bespoke for them by the Duke of Buckingham, both he and the bishop being often together on the royal council, making double point by this favor to Sir Lewis that he had strong backers to be reckoned with.

Already in the saddle, Ned grinned down at Robert. 'That they're come means, likely, that his grace of Buckingham's arbiters and Master Fielding are at my place waiting for me. Barring trouble or vile weather, we'll be back first thing in the morning, Allesleys and all.'

'I dare say we'll be here,' Robert said back, managing to sound easy about it, slapped Ned's horse on the shoulder, and stepped back, making farewells to Master Durant and Hotoft and waiting where he was while they and Ned rode away, their men after them and the yard abruptly back to its usual quiet once they were gone, no one there except household folk about their work. As if everything were simply as it always was, Robert thought as he returned up the stairs and into the hall, relieved at being done with pretense for a while but knowing the thought that everything was as always was pretense, too, and now there was the evening to be gone through with Blaunche and Benedict.

And Katherine.

He tried to close off thought of her as soon as it arose. He needed her as near to not in his thoughts as he could possibly keep her, and he would to God he did not have to see her again, ever, until this was over with and she was married to the Allesley whelp. And, for the best, he would not ever see her then, either, because what he had felt – in mind and body both – at seeing her this afternoon, safe and back with him, had been too near to overwhelming. He was supposed to feel that way for no one but his wife, and for Blaunche he felt . . .

What did he feel for Blaunche?

Anger, he decided. For now, anger would do. Better anger at her and at Benedict for what they had planned than memory of his sickened relief at seeing Katherine safe, here, not wed to Benedict.

God help him, in the moment he had seen her and known she was safe, he would have seen Blaunche and Benedict and anyone else who came to hand into hell before he would have had her at risk again.

And that was sin.

The sin of pride, to begin with – putting his own desires ahead of whatever cost there might be to anyone else because of them – but the sin of covetousness, too, because he would, if he could have, kept Katherine for himself alone, away from anyone else who wanted her. Sin upon sin and the sin of lust added to them, no matter how much it shamed him, no matter how much he wanted to deny it. Worse yet, he could make no confession of any of it to the priest because confession meant he wanted not only forgiveness and penance but to cease the sin and, God help him, he did not want to stop loving Katherine.

Which left him to the sin of wrath, in a kind of blind hope that if he gave way to it fully enough, it would obscure all else he was feeling.

In the hall the servants were setting up the trestle tables in readiness for supper, the familiar evening business that would be mirrored at the meal's end by taking down and setting away the tables. Keeping out of his people's way rather than they out of his, Robert passed among them, paused to answer the butler's question of whether Lady Blaunche would be coming down to supper by saying he did not know, and went through into the solar. For a wonder, there was no one there and he was alone, as he so rarely was during any day or night, and he nearly turned aside, to linger in the quiet; but that would leave him with his thoughts and he was better without them.

But his steps lagged nonetheless, resisting the stairs up to the parlor and Blaunche. Momentarily he considered going to see the children instead but they were likely already at their own meal and Nurse would not care for his interfering with that, he knew and, left with only the shove of his conscience, he went up the stairs.

He had forgotten the nuns. The surprise of that was as sharp as the surprise of seeing them in the parlor, Dame Frevisse in talk with Mistress Dionisia and Katherine at the window, the other one – Dame Claire, she'd said – and Master Geoffrey keeping Blaunche company on the settle. Mistress Avys was a little aside from them, intent on her embroidery, and Benedict was well apart, sitting in Robert's chair, leaning forward in earnest talk to Emelye on a cushion on the floor in front of him, her blonde little head tipped back to look up at him. In his craven relief that confrontation with Blaunche would have to be put off because the nuns were there, Robert said with the best seeming of good humor he could manage, 'All here then, I see.'

He sounded false even to himself, but as it was he feigned better than Benedict who looked toward him with a start and made to rise, then when Robert gestured him to stay, looked nervously toward his mother, uncertain what to do until she nodded tersely at him to keep where he was. Confused into surliness, Benedict subsided, scowling, and Robert would have settled for greeting Dame Frevisse and meeting the other nun but Blaunche said to him, 'You couldn't have come sooner?'

His in-held anger stirred to rise into the open at that but he kept it down, saying evenly, 'Ned has only just left with the arbiters. No, I couldn't have come sooner.' And then, to have it over with, 'There's word that the Allesleys are at the grange.'

'So you'll be going there tomorrow, I suppose.'

'They're coming here,' Robert answered stiffly. 'It was agreed on after you left.'

Blaunche stabbed her needle into the piece of linen she was embroidering and snapped, 'So you're giving them the roof over our heads, too. Next it will be the clothes off our backs.'

On either side of her Master Geoffrey and the nun were suddenly very still, understanding as surely as Robert did that she was set to quarrel. And once Blaunche was set to quarrel there was little chance of stopping her . . .

From across the room Dame Frevisse said mildly, as if noticing nothing amiss, 'Well, I certainly hope the weather holds well if there's to be all that to-and-froing these next few days.'

Robert turned toward her, momentarily blank of any answer to such a bland nothing comment because he had never found Dame Frevisse either bland or given to nothings. It was Katherine who said, bright-voiced, 'Oh, I think it's going to be dry. We've had our rain for a while, surely.'

'Red sky at morning, shepherds take warning,' Mistress Dionisia put in. 'But this morning was all gray, wasn't it? Overcast. No red at all.'

'But clear skies at night, shepherds' delight,' Dame Frevisse said with a nod at the sky above the orchard.

Then, for a mercy, because Robert did not know how long they would be able to go on heading off Blaunche's quarreling, there was a knock at the stairway door and Nurse came in with the children. She was holding John by the hand to help his short legs up the steep stairs and carrying Tacine on her hip but Robin at five was more than proud to be on his own and squeezed past her skirts to be almost first into the room. He must have been warned there would be strangers because sight of the nuns did not pause him as he made a quick, bright-eyed survey of everyone there, grinned at his father, then trotted first to his mother, to make her the very fine bow he had been practicing while she was gone. Blaunche, her sewing already put aside, clapped her hands in delight and drew him to her with admiring exclaims.

'Father taught me,' Robin said, wriggling up onto the seat beside her, between her and Master Geoffrey to whom he gave a quick smile, then leaned forward to grin at the nun on her other side.

'And very well he taught you,' Blaunche said, her arm around him, squeezing him to her, then letting him go as she added, 'This is Dame Claire. You should bow to her, too.'

Robin willingly slipped off the seat and made his bow again. Dame Claire, with dignity to match his own, bowed her head to him.

'And there's Dame Frevisse,' Blaunche said. 'You should bow to her, too.'

Happy to show off his skill, Robin headed obediently away and John, held back by Nurse's hand until then, shot forward to scramble up beside his mother and wrap his arms around her neck. Laughing, trying to keep her wimple and veil on with one hand, Blaunche managed with the other to swing him around and set him firmly on her lap. She was months away from being too great with child to have a lap and that was good because while Robin at five years old had begun to lengthen to long arms and legs, John at three and a half was still in the soft, round puppy stage and ever ready for the cuddle

Blaunche was ever ready to give him. Happy to have her back, he set to telling her busily about everything that had happened to him, and Robert turned to Tacine. Still on Nurse's hip, one foot swinging in idle beat against Nurse's skirts and a knuckle in her mouth because she was not allowed to suck her thumb, she was regarding the proceedings solemnly until Robert held out his arms to her. Then she regarded him with equal solemnity before, all in an instant, mischief lighted her face and she flung herself out of Nurse's hold and toward him. Both Robert and Nurse were ready for that and with practiced skill Nurse loosed her and Robert caught her, swung her up to make her burst into delighted laughter, and brought her down to settle her on his own hip. In their familiar game, he poked a quick finger into her ribs and she answered by puffing at his chin. He ducked from that as from a blow and she laughed again, burrowed her head into the curve of his shoulder, and then wriggled mightily to be set down. She rarely deigned to talk yet, probably because she could make her wishes known without it, and when Robert obliged her now by setting her down, she took him firmly by the hand and led him away to where their parlor toys were kept.

In a while, Blaunche sent John to join Tacine and his father and called Robin back to her from his earnest talk to Katherine and Dame Frevisse about something that had them both nodding agreement to him. Tacine took the chance to desert Robert for Katherine, leaving him to John's demands and then with a fine sense of how much time there was until supper took her mother away, left Katherine to go to Blaunche, pressing against her skirts until she was noticed and lifted up onto her mother's lap and held there while Blaunche went on questioning Robin about everything he had done while she was gone.

It bothered Robert that Blaunche so obviously preferred her sons to her daughter, but if it bothered Tacine, it did not stop her from taking a share of her mother's attention when she wanted it and being happy with her father's and anyone else's – usually Benedict's – the rest of the time. Benedict returned the pleasure by, most evenings, joining in readily to play with his halflings, but tonight he stayed where he was, turned as much away from Robert as might be and seeming to heed no one but Emelye who in return was gladly heeding only him.

With the distraction of the children and help from Dame Frevisse, Mistress Dionisia, and sometimes Katherine, talk kept away from places it should not go until, to Robert's relief, they were called to supper. The children would stay playing in the parlor, letting them be somewhere other than their nursery for a while longer, be there when their parents came back from supper to bid them good night, and then be herded away to their beds. It was the usual way of things but as Nurse was drawing Tacine and Robin away from Blaunche and Robert was disentangling himself from John's clutch around his neck, Katherine said, 'I'm more tired than hungry, I think. I'll stay with the children rather than come down to supper, please.'

'If you like,' Blaunche said without a look at her, and all Robert could be was cravenly relieved not to have to deal with being near her through supper. He made it even better by seeing to it that Dame Frevisse was seated beside him at the high table, and though there was no help for Blaunche being seated on his other side, he left her to make what talk she would with Dame Claire and Benedict beyond her while he gave his attention to Dame Frevisse.

They kept to merely general things – how the roads had been, the weather, the children – while the first remove was served to them, until the servants had drawn off. He had shifted some of the fish tart, thick with fruit and dark with spices, from the platter between them to her trencher of thick-cut bread and was serving himself when Dame Frevisse asked, 'This arbitration I keep hearing of. I know something of the why of it but how does it happen these Allesleys are coming here rather than you to them or somewhere in between?'

A servant came to refill their goblets, pausing their talk, but when he was gone Robert answered, 'Here was near to midway for all the arbiters. It was for their convenience more than anything.' With a sideways look toward Blaunche and a bitterness he should have kept buried, he added, 'Though elsewhere could well have been better.' And then, to be away from it, he said, 'Has anyone told you we have a chapel here, rather than needing to go into the village to the church? It's across the yard, near to the gateway. I'll have Master Geoffrey show it to you tomorrow. You're more than welcome to use it while you're here.'

'Thank you. That would be good,' she said with a smile whose warmth changed her sometimes too-austere face to a different, younger woman's.

How old was she? Robert wondered for the first time. Wimples and veils and the loose-fitted habits concealed, as they were supposed to, a nun's womanhood and made difficult any close guess at her age in the years between very young and old. As he thought that, he had a sudden vision of Katherine as nun, garbed so and shut away into a nunnery for all her days, lost to him just as his first love had been, and his heart seemed to contract as if he had taken a blow there. Afraid he was showing the pain, he grabbed his goblet and feigned a long drink of the ale until he was sure of himself. What Dame Frevisse saw or guessed he did not know, only that she took their talk away into general matters again – more questions about the children, what a fine manor Brinskep looked to be, how large a household did he have – that he doubted she cared about but were at least safe.

Servants brought the second remove – a fish pottage and baked apple tart from last year's dried apples – all there would be for tonight, it being Lent for one thing but also because there would be an overly fine dinner tomorrow midday when the arbitrators and the Allesleys would be here, so that overworking the cook and kitchen servants tonight would have been ill sense. But that also meant that, with supper finished, there was nothing for it but to go back up to the parlor and see the evening through. The children took up only a while of it, but when Nurse was gathering them up to go, both Dame Claire and Dame Frevisse claimed readiness for sleep, too, and left with them, Dame Claire advising Blaunche that bed for her as well would be a good thing. Mistress Dionisia put in that Katherine looked tired, too, and Benedict and Master Geoffrey accepted all that for sign to make their good nights and betake themselves away to their own rooms across the yard. Soon enough – or too soon – with the parlor left to Katherine, Emelye and Mistress Dionisia's bed-going, Robert had nowhere else to be but in his own bedchamber. With Blaunche.

Alone together for the little while it would take Gil and Mistress Avys to fetch the wafers and light ale that would be kept to hand should Blaunche or Robert hunger or thirst in the night, there was no reason not to say something to her at last about what she had intended between Benedict and Katherine, but Robert found that he did not want to, that he was tired and past his anger. There had been too much time for it to fade, too much time for him to realize that neither his anger nor his fear were any use now. Whatever Blaunche had purposed, Katherine was safe for the present. And besides that – and almost despite himself – he could not help seeing how tired Blaunche was as she sat on the bed edge, combing out her hair.

Loosed for the night from pins and wimple and veil, swung forward over one of her shoulders, its soft, straight fairness fell nearly to her waist. In the low lamplight the gray that was beginning to weave through it was merely fairer than the rest, silver-shining, and years, too, were shadowed from her face; she might have been no older than he was, the age she had been when they married, and wearing her loose bedgown and because she always carried her babies small, hardly showing she was childing until well along, there was no sign she was bearing except, because Robert knew her, her face's thinness.

Instead of flourishing outward as other women did when bearing, Blaunche seemed instead to fade inward, as if she nourished her babies to life by feeding them on her own. No one else seemed troubled by that change in her – the women merely made certain she ate strengthening foods – but Robert had always been frightened by it, wondering what it was like to give over your self so thoroughly to another's need, even this one that brought another life into being. And tonight he was more troubled to see, watching her from across their bedchamber, that she was combing her hair with such a slow weariness that the comb might almost have been too heavy for her to lift. If things had been different between them, he would have gone to her, taken the comb and combed her hair himself, but as things were, he was not even sure she would accept his help and stayed standing where he was, not wanting the moment when they would have to lie tensely in their bed together, silently unfriendly.

That undesire was maybe what Blaunche saw on his face that moment when she looked up at him, because her own face, that had been softened, harshened and, tossing the comb down on the chest beside the bed, she demanded, 'So. Are you going to draw back from this Allesley matter while there's time or not?'

That was to be the way of it, then: attack him on the Allesleys before he could attack her on Benedict, Robert thought wearily. He should have been ready for it but he was not, taken up with too much else, and his own weariness came down on him so heavily that instead of answer he let his head fall back, looking up at the painted ceiling beams among the lamplight's shadows instead of at her, with no answer to hand nor any desire for one, only for quiet.

But, 'You're going through with this, aren't you?' Blaunche demanded at his silence. 'Robert, look at me!'

He looked. She had shoved her hair back over her shoulders, out of her way, was staring at him with the harsh glint of anger in her eyes, and because there was no use in trying to go sideways from it, Robert said with answering harshness, 'Yes, I'm going through with it.'

'Then I'm taking the children and going. I won't be here for this.'

'You're staying here and so are the children,' Robert said, so flatly certain of it that for a moment Blaunche was brought to a full halt, something he rarely managed to accomplish.

But only briefly. She rallied, flushed with anger, and said, 'I'm at least sending Benedict away. He shouldn't be here for—'

'Benedict stays. I won't have him on the loose while this goes on.' To make who knew what kind of mother-inspired trouble.

'He's not going to be here while you give away his lands!'

Robert was sick to death of going that way and said angrily back at her, 'They're not his lands. They're not even your lands.'

'They've been my lands for nearly twenty years!'

'And shouldn't have been for even one!'

Blaunche ignored that as deftly as she always ignored it, saying instead, 'You're giving away a third of our lands. You're going to leave us hardly above yeomen. There's going to be next to nothing to leave our children. How can you want to do that? Can't you see what you're doing?'

Robert saw clearly enough but saw other things, too, and said back at her with weary anger, 'What I see is that if the Allesleys aren't given back what's rightfully theirs, they're going to use force to have it.'

'Let them. We'll meet and match them any way they want to go. Northend is mine!'

'It's not yours!' Robert flared back at her, for the first time between them giving up all hold on patience. 'It's *mine*. Because when you married me everything that was yours became mine, to do with as I will.'

'And well that was for you,' Blaunche blazed in return, 'because you had nothing, *nothing*, until I . . .'

Too late she heard herself, caught back the rest with an inward gasp, and left them staring at one another, the unsaid thing hanging in the air between them, the thing there had always been between them but never said aloud until now. And Robert, finally, with his belly clenched around hollowness, said into the silence, 'Yes. I had nothing until you married me. But once you did, then by the law I hold everything. And equally by the law Northend belongs to the Allesleys, and has ever since your first husband's mother died twenty-seven years ago. And by law they're going to have it back. And the best we can hope for is that what they ask in compensation for the wrong we've done them doesn't cost us more than we've ever made from it.'

'If we don't give it back—'

'If we don't give it back, the Allesleys are going to use force to have it, and when they do, the ones who'll have the worst of it are our manor folk caught in the middle, and not just at Northend. There'll be people hurt who had no part in either the wrong we've done or the profits we've had, and I won't have that if I can stop it happening.'

'But there's going to be so little left! Benedict will have Wystead from his father and all the saints know that's little enough but with Northend gone, there'll be only Brinskep to go to Robin, with some sort of provision to be made for John out of that, let be how we'll ever provide a dower for Tacine. And this child.' She laid a hand over her belly, her voice gone suddenly tender, the anger turned to worry and soft persuasion as she added, 'All that would change if Benedict marries Katherine. Northend or no, there'd be money enough then and he's fond of her . . .'

'I doubt the thought of marrying Katherine would ever have entered his head except for you,' Robert said coldly.

'Better Benedict than some Allesley brat!' Blaunche flared. 'Can't you see—'

Robert had suddenly had enough and demanded, 'Come to that, madam, where was your son yesterday and today?'

The change of attack caught Blaunche unready. She paused, visibly regrouped, and said, trying for defiance, 'He's man-grown. I don't know everything he does or where he goes.'

'But you knew this time, didn't you?' Robert flung at her.

Blaunche glared at him, both fierce and cornered, not ready to lie but equally unready to admit the truth. Instead, she swung aside from either, turned on the instant back to soft pleading, holding her hands out to Robert with, 'Think what it means if you marry her off to an Allesley. We'll likely never see her again.'

It was Robert's turn to be caught unready. 'I know,' he said and shouldn't have, because the words caught in his throat.

Blaunche stood up from the bed edge, back to fierce. 'But maybe I shouldn't mind that, should I? Maybe that you never see her again is exactly what I should be wanting!'

Robert stared at her, knowing his mouth was open but not knowing what to say – denial was too cheap, admittance too dear – and instead of either, he said desperately, 'Blaunche, what do you want of me?' And realized as he said it that she had only been flinging words at him, did not believe what she had come near to accusing him of, because at his desperate question her face crumpled toward tears and she cried back at him, 'I want you to love me!'

'I do!' They were both keeping their voices low, aware of the thin wall between them and the parlor and that Gil and Mistress Avys would be back at any moment, but his cry matched hers for desperation. 'God be my witness, Blaunche, I love you!' And the terrible thing was that he did. How could he not? She had given him everything – a better life than he had ever had hope of, his children. The trouble was that he loved her but not the way she wanted to be loved – not with passion, not simply for herself. That he could not give her. But he gave her what he could and said again, 'I do love you.'

And Blaunche with the suddenness that came too often on her when she was childing burst into tears, was suddenly, simply a tired, frightened woman in need of comforting and held her arms out to him, saying, 'I know you do. Forgive me, Robert. Please. I love you, too. I love you so much. Please.'

Because it would bring at least temporary peace, he crossed the room to her, into her outheld arms and put his own around her, saying to the top of her head as she pressed against him, 'I know, Blaunche, I know.'

'It's the baby,' she whispered against his shoulder, past her sobs. 'You know how it is with me when I'm childing. But I love you. I truly, truly do.'

'I know.' He was holding and rocking her much as he would have held and rocked Tacine in a fit of weeping grief, repeating like a lullaby, 'I know.'

Gil rapped his foot against the doorframe to let them know he was here and pushed the door open with his hip, needing both hands for the pitcher and goblets he carried. Behind him, Mistress Avys was bringing the covered dish of wafers and dried fruit, and beyond her Robert had glimpse of Katherine, Emelye and Mistress Dionisia making up their beds across the parlor, before Blaunche gave a great, trembling sob and went weak against him, forcing him to lose heed of all else in the need to lift her off her feet, one arm around her shoulders, the other under her knees, cradling her against him, while Mistress Avys put down her plate and hurried toward them; but Blaunche, her arms tightly around Robert's neck, said wearily but firmly, 'No need, Avys. There's nothing wrong. I'm tired is all.'

'Tired and with no sense,' Mistress Avys grumbled. 'Gil, help me here and be quick at it.'

Together they folded the heavy woven bedcover to the bedfoot and turned back the blankets and sheet while Robert held Blaunche, quiet in his arms, then clinging to him when he set her on her feet, letting go of him only long enough for Mistress Avys to take her bedgown off, then briefly squeezing his hand again before she lay down and moved away across the bed, making room for him beside her as always; and as always he slipped free of his own bedgown and in beside her.

Sometimes that was the end of it and sometimes she wanted more. Tonight, when Gil and Mistress Avys had drawn the covers over them and closed the curtains around the bed, leaving them alone together in the bed-shadows, she shifted to be close against him again, nestling into the curve of his arm with a small child's whimper, her head resting on his chest. Robert waited and was thankful when he understood she would want no more than holding from him tonight; waited and was more thankful when she was safely gone to sleep, leaving him to the loneliness of his bed and thoughts, his own sleep taking far longer to come.

Chapter 9

In the pleasure of escaping from too long a time among too many people not saying too many things all through the evening, Frevisse momentarily cared only for being away as she left the parlor, following Dame Claire down the stairs into the solar. But the certainty that 'away' was something neither of them could really be so long as they were here came hard on the heels of her relief and darkened it. Whatever was wrong between Robert and his wife, it was more than the trouble of the moment and present angers. Added to that, Katherine's place here was difficult to judge. She had been almost a daughter, Frevisse guessed, but now she was become something to be used to someone's best profit, the question seeming to be whether the profit would be Robert's or Lady Blaunche's. Nor was young Benedict to be envied either, caught between his mother's wishes and his stepfather's and whatever his own might be. He had kept too thoroughly apart from everyone except young Emelye for Frevisse to judge much about him. Did he want Katherine for herself or because he was told he ought to have her? Was it truly to Benedict himself that Katherine objected, or to being forced into a marriage, any marriage, the way Lady Blaunche had meant to force her? If the complication of the Allesleys had not happened, where would her affections naturally have gone except to the boy – young man, Frevisse amended, but they all seemed so young, even Robert; sure sign she was growing old, she supposed – whom she had grown up with and knew best of anyone she might be likely to marry?

Unless knowing someone best of anyone was grounds for *not* wanting to be married to them. Frevisse could readily suppose it was, but then . . .

Turning around short of the tapestry over the door to their chamber, Dame Claire said, 'Lady Blaunche told me there's a chapel here that we're welcome to use. Should we, do you think?'

'For Compline?' Frevisse's heart rose. She had put by thought of the chapel as something for later but to go there would be very welcome just now. 'Do we know where it is?'

'We'll ask. Someone else is coming.' Dame Claire took a step back toward the stairs as Benedict, followed by Master Geoffrey, entered from them, both men pausing for a slightly startled moment at being confronted by two nuns, before Benedict bowed and said, 'Do you need something, my ladies?'

It was the first time Frevisse had heard him speak more than a sullen word or two in answer to questions from his mother, and was surprised to see that on his own he was simply a well-mannered, pleasant-faced young man; but Dame Claire had been beside him at supper and was maybe not so surprised, answering him easily, 'We're wondering if someone could tell us where the chapel is. We'd like to make our evening prayers there.'

Benedict started to point. 'It's across . . .'

But Master Geoffrey said with a smile and a bow, 'I'll gladly take them to it, if they please.'

Not of a mind to see if they could lose their way if left to themselves, they accepted his offer willingly and Benedict bowed and went on to wherever he had been going while Master Geoffrey said in answer to Dame Claire's thanks, 'It's my pleasure.'

Because Dame Claire had been in his company through the evening, diverting Lady Blaunche, Frevisse easily left them to walk together while she fell half a pace to the side and behind them, following into the hall and taking the chance to have clearer look at the clerk who was likely Dame Claire's best ally in dealing with Lady Blaunche, judging by how deftly he had managed her too-obvious ill humour both before and after supper, even bringing her to smiling a few times. He was near to Robert's age, his face smooth and open, his manner warm and easy, his plain black clerk's gown neither too rich nor too poor to his place in a squire's household and as neatly képt as his manners. He had no tonsure to go with it, though, and among the casual talk he made while leading them through the hall among the household servants beginning to bed down there for the night, he mentioned he was only in minor orders and doubted he would ever take greater.

'The urge simply isn't in me,' he said as if both puzzled and regretful over that, going now into the screens passage, turning toward the outer door. 'I simply have to hope that what I'm doing is sufficiently to God's will.'

Beginning to feel her tiredness to the full, Frevisse wanted to tell him she did not care whether he was in greater, minor, or any orders at all; all she wanted was to be at her prayers; but that was mean-spirited and, knowing it, she chided herself that Master Geoffrey was making talk for courtesy's sake, used to it as part of his duties here, not understanding that to her and Dame Claire silence was not only perfectly acceptable but even welcome.

Dame Claire, doing better than she at courtesy, murmured in answer to him, 'All anyone can hope is that we're doing God's will.'

Outside, the clear, early evening sky was still full of light from the sunset's afterglow, shaded from shining green above the roof of the buildings enclosing the courtyard's west side to a deepening blue pricked out with the first silver glint of a star overhead. The evening's damp chill as much as the hour had probably driven most people indoors; there were thin yellow bands of candle-, lamp-, and rushlights around shutters' edges at some of the closed windows overlooking the yard but in the yard itself there were only two men talking at the gate and one of them was on his way out, the other closing the gate after him. For the night, Frevisse thought.

Pointing as he started down the stone steps to the yard, Master Geoffrey said, 'The chapel is there, between the gatehouse and my own chamber. I'll see you to it, then find a lantern and come back to light your way to your chamber, if you will.'

Dame Claire gave him thanks and Frevisse added her own, because by the time they had finished their prayers, full darkness would have filled the yard except for the islands of light around the lantern burning for the night beside the gateway and the other at the head of the hall steps, now behind them and confusing their feet with shadows as they followed Master Geoffrey down; a light of their own in an unfamiliar place would be welcome.

But just where the hall lantern's light was altogether lost to the thickening dusk Master Geoffrey stopped and turned to Dame Claire, his easy manner dropped as he asked with concern in his voice, 'Now that there's no chance we'll be heard, can you tell me how well or ill it truly is with Lady Blaunche? Is it what she says? That she's only over-tired and will be well enough by and by? Is that all there is to it or is she hiding worse and we should be afraid for her?'

Dame Claire paused, probably considering how much he could be told, then seemingly decided to take him for the ally he had been so far and said, 'It's true she's overtired, more than she should be from merely childbearing, but I gather from what I've been told that it's always that way with her.'

'Yes,' Master Geoffrey agreed. 'Always.'

'I gather, too, she too much tends to make it the worse by pushing herself beyond her strength.'

'She goes at everything with her full heart,' Master Geoffrey said. 'It's both her boon and bane. Nor is Master Fenner, in all truth, as kind to her over it as he might be, I must needs say.'

He need say no such thing, it wasn't his place to, Frevisse thought but kept the thought to herself while Dame Claire asked, 'You don't think he can be appealed to for much help with her?'

Master Geoffrey hesitated, then said, 'No.'

Dame Claire bent her head, considered that, looked up and went on, 'This Allesley business isn't helping, either. She's wrought herself too high over it when what she needs is quiet, both for her own sake and the child's.'

'That's Master Fenner's doing again,' Master Geoffrey said, 'and I don't know what's to be done to keep her from taking it all too deeply to heart the way she is.'

'For her own sake and the child's, she has to stop it,' Dame Claire said. 'I'm giving her as strong doses of valerian as I dare and a borage cordial to soothe and cheer her some but she agitates herself out of their quieting sooner than I like. You know her better than I do. Is there anything that would serve to divert her even a little from fretting herself so continually?'

'I read to her,' Master Geoffrey said. 'That helps sometimes. Or I keep her in talk about anything except what worries her. I've done that often and often. She enjoys my talk. Say the word and I'll keep her as much company as I can, divert her as much as may be. Once this Allesley matter is done and over with and past undoing, she'll maybe let it go and be herself again and quieter, I can only pray.'

'We all pray so,' Dame Claire said. 'Yes, any distraction you can give would be to the good. I'll set her woman to it with you, and Dame Frevisse and I will do what we can that way, too.'

Frevisse had no pleasure at hearing herself pledged to helping with Lady Blaunche, but Lent was a time for penance and helping see to Lady Blaunche would serve as well as other things toward humility of spirit, she supposed as they crossed the darkening yard to the chapel. Master Geoffrey left them at the door, promising to return with a lantern, and Frevisse followed Dame Claire into the chapel's hush, leaving the heavy wooden door ajar behind them.

The silence of sanctified places always seemed different, deeper, to her than the silence of other places and here was no different. A quieting of spirit came on her as she made obeisance, then went forward to kneel at the altar. By the little ruby glow of the altar light, it was plain this was a cherished place. Gold thread gleamed in the embroidery of the altar frontal and although she understood that the household made do with the village priest rather than one of their own, the pleasant smell of well-polished wood told that someone saw to more than merely the daily replenishing of the altar light's oil. With a deepening ease of spirit, she set to Compline's prayers, both she and Dame Claire knowing them well enough to have no need of their breviaries that they could not have read anyway by the slight light there was, intertwining antiphon and response and psalms through to the quieting petition *Divinum auxilium maneat semper nobiscum.* Divine aid remain always with us.

They were still kneeling, each in her own silent prayer, when lantern light from the doorway behind them made sudden sharp shadows around them, telling that Master Geoffrey was returned as promised. Not ready yet to leave either the chapel's quiet or her prayers, Frevisse nonetheless crossed herself and rose with Dame Claire, going to join the clerk who murmured something about hoping he had not come too soon but otherwise respecting the quiet they brought out of the chapel with them, leading them across the yard to a doorway where he gave them the lantern, saying only, 'My own door is back along on the right from here. I can find my way well enough but you've stairs to manage. Up them and to your left is where you want to go. May you rest well,' he added.

They thanked him again and he bowed and drew away into the darkness as Dame Claire, lantern in hand, opened the door where he had left them and went in, past shut doors that led to ground-level chambers on the right and left, and up narrow wooden stairs, turned a little sidewise to let light fall past her for Frevisse to see her way, too, to the top and the door on the left that opened indeed to the chamber Frevisse recognized from this afternoon.

In one of the beds someone was already snoring softly in deep sleep but the other one was still empty. No third mattress had been brought but Frevisse did not care. With the lantern set on the floor where its light would not disturb the sleeper, she and Dame Claire took off their stockings and shoes, put them beside a stool at the head of their bed, took off their gowns, wimples and veils, and laid them carefully folded on the stool. Any washing would have to wait until morning, and when Dame Claire had slipped into bed and to its wallside, Frevisse blew out the light and joined her, as grateful to be at last lying down as she had been to go to prayers and asleep almost before she had pulled up her share of the blanket.

She awoke in what she supposed was the middle of the night, used to it from always rising then in St Frideswide's to go to Matins and Lauds. From Dame Claire's breathing, she could tell she was awake, too, but there was no question of them going out to the chapel in the middle of the night here, nor should they be discourteous to the other sleeper by rising and praying aloud where they were, and silently, supposing Dame Claire was doing the same, she set to saying the Offices to herself as best she could and afterwards slid easily into sleep again, to awaken when Dame Claire did, again by habit, somewhat before dawn, in time for Prime. Without need to say anything or see what they were doing, they dressed in the room's darkness and, having no way to light the lantern, groped their way down the stairs to the yard where the graying of the sky toward dawn gave them light enough to make their way back to the chapel.

When they had finished and left the chapel, full light was not come yet but the yard was busy with people off to their early work, and chilled but satisfied, they returned to their room, to find it was Nurse who had been asleep in the other bed and was awake now, dressed and not in the least bothered by two strangers sharing her room, saying crisply while putting on her coif and tying it under her chin, 'It's only every other night I sleep in my bed anyway. The other nights, turn and turn about, I sleep with the children, and Anabilla – she's the nursery maid – is in here. It's her snuffling in her sleep you'll have to bear with tonight. Now which of you is which? No one bothered with telling me yesterday. Dame Claire and Dame Frevisse, yes?'

Dame Claire sorted out for her who they were and asked, 'And your name? We aren't to call you only Nurse, are we?'

'It's what I'm mostly called,' she said cheerfully. 'But if you've a mind to more, I answer to Mistress Welland, too.' Not over-tall but brisk and sure of words and movement, she finished pinning her starched, sharply pressed, shiningly white veil to her wimple and cocked her head while fixing both nuns with her merry black eyes as she added, 'Or, if we turn friendly enough, I'm Florence. So mind your manners and we'll see.'

Something of the constriction that had bound Frevisse through the two days since leaving St Frideswide's eased, for no better reason than that here at least was one person without open confusions in her life.

But there were increasing, cheerful child noises from beyond the stairward door and Mistress Welland said, slipping an apron over her head and tying it behind her while moving toward the door, 'I'd best be off to see to them so Anabilla can fetch their breakfasts. By the by.' She turned back in the doorway. 'I mean to tell the children that if they're very good this morning, one or the other of the nuns might tell them a story this afternoon.'

Then she was gone, before either Frevisse or Dame Claire could give answer to that, leaving them sharing a rueful look; and before they had gone beyond that to choosing what to do next, Mistress Avys knocked and entered from the solar, bringing them a breakfast of bare bread and weak ale.

'Master Fenner said that's as it should be, because of your Lenten fasting,' she said worriedly, 'but my lady says that if you want more, you've only to ask and you'll have it.'

Frevisse's stomach made a soft sound that told her more would have been welcome but she agreed, along with Dame Claire, that this was exactly what they should have and thanked her for it before Dame Claire asked, 'How is it with Lady Blaunche this morning?'

Mistress Avys pursed her lips and heaved a sigh. 'Not so well as we could wish, I fear. She slept well enough, once she came to it, but she's keeping to her bed this morning and said I wasn't to say anything until you'd eaten, but since you ask, she wants to see you as soon as might be, please you.'

Bread untouched in one hand and cup of ale in the other, Dame Claire asked, 'What's amiss?'

'Now you eat,' Mistress Avys said, nodding at the bread. 'You need your strength and she'll bide till you come. I can't say there's any one thing greatly wrong with her, just too many things altogether, if you take my meaning.' She dropped her voice as if giving a secret. 'The Allesleys come today.'

Dame Claire questioned her between bites of the bread and sips of the ale, and Frevisse listened while eating her own, not learning much except what Mistress Avys had already told but gaining a suspicion that there were other things that could have been said but Mistress Avys would not. About what? Frevisse wondered, then quickly shut the wondering away because she had no business wondering about what was no concern of hers.

Done with her breakfast, Dame Claire brushed at her habit to be rid of crumbs that were not there and hasted away with Mistress Avys without even asking if Frevisse would go with her. They knew each other well enough for her to know Frevisse would prefer not to, but when they were gone, Frevisse found herself left full in the awkwardness of being a guest where she did not wish to be and with nothing to do. Dame Claire at least had occupation but nothing was needed from her but to be here. She was no use to Lady Blaunche in her illness and, being uninclined to idle talk, had no interest in keeping company with the other women in the parlor; but neither was there anywhere else for her to be, and by the sounds beyond the one shutter set open to the growing daylight, the yard was even more busy with folk than it had been and surely everywhere else was, too, leaving her nowhere to be out of the way but here, with time on her hands and nothing to do with it.

Except pray, she suddenly thought; and the day, dismal ahead of her a moment before, lightened. Prayer – the slipping aside from the world's passing concerns into the greater quest of nearness to the eternal – was one of the pleasures that had deepened through her years of nunhood but oddly enough time for prayer alone, outside the hours set for the Offices, was one of the most difficult things to come by in the nunnery.

Nunnery life was a formed and carefully kept thing; a nun shaped herself to it, not it to the nun, and while that at its best provided a surprising freedom of spirit, it also provided for almost every moment of a day and so after all there was maybe something to be gained by being here at Brinskep, Frevisse thought as she slid from the edge of the bed where she had been sitting to her knees on the floor, drew a deep, quieting breath and set, as the blessed Richard of Hampole directed, the love of her heart upward and her thought as greatly as she might on what she prayed.

Eyes closed, head bent over clasped hands, she wound herself far into the intricate simplicity of prayer, losing thought of time and everything about her and when eventually she returned to where and when she was, she did not know how long Katherine had been standing at the window looking out into the yard; and when, still a little light-headed from her praying, she drew a deep, steadying breath, Katherine swung around from the window to say in quick apology, 'My lady, I'm sorry. I tried to keep as quiet as possible.'

Using the bed for help against her knees' stiffness – she never felt the pain of them while she was praying, only when she was done – Frevisse rose to her feet, saying while she did, 'I never heard you come or knew you were here, Mistress Katherine. You didn't disturb me.'

The girl tried to smile. Today instead of the plain gown she mostly wore, she was dressed in a full-skirted overgown of light wool dyed bright spring green, held in at its high waist, just below her breasts, by a wide belt of silver and enameled roses, its neckline collared with darker green velvet and plunging in a deep vee between her breasts to show her rose-colored undergown of fine linen. Rose velvet lined the overgown's wide, open-hanging sleeves, too, that were turned back the better to show off both the velvet and the undergown's close-fitted sleeves brought down to a careful point over her white, slender hands, and for good measure the rich darkness of her hair, loosed from its usual braid to fall down her back to well below her waist, was held back from her smooth forehead by a circlet of more silver and enameled flowers.

All in all, both she and her wealth were well-displayed, to be admired and desired, and the only flaw was that her face was as bleak as a winter's day, her eyes flat with pain, so that without thinking Frevisse said, 'Is it as bad as that, Katherine?'

Tears that seemed to take her by surprise brimmed in Katherine's eyes and her voice caught as she said, 'You're the first person this morning who hasn't told me how beautiful I look. Thank you.'

'They say it because it's what they think you want to hear. Besides that, it's true.'

'It doesn't matter whether it's true.' Katherine's voice tried to rise toward breaking; she forced it down. 'What matters is that they've all stopped seeing me. Everyone. I'm only something to be dressed and disposed of to everyone else's best advantage. They don't see *me* at all in this anymore.'

That was hurting her to the heart, and with an answering pang Frevisse remembered her mother saying once, long ago, about her marriage, 'Everyone knew how I was supposed to marry. They had it all planned, down to the last pence they would make from it, but I listened to no one but myself and married your father.' And went off with him into a life they had both loved as much as they loved each other and because of it had been exiled from everyone else who had ever been dear to them.

Frevisse had never needed to ask if it had been worth the cost. Even if she had not known before, the remembered joy in her mother's face even then, when she had lain widowed and dying, had been all the answer there need be.

Which was no use to Katherine who had no such other choice, it seemed – no lover to whom she could turn, her only choices acceptance of what was intended for her or flat refusal of it, with whatever troubles and outrage that would bring down on her.

Katherine tried another smile, saying contritely, 'I'll be all right. It's only that I'm frightened a little. I'm sorry I broke into your prayers.'

'You didn't,' Frevisse repeated, and because she had no help to offer, added, 'Am I wanted somewhere?'

'No. I only came here to hide awhile. Until my courage came back. I couldn't think of anywhere else to go.'

Where was Mistress Dionisia? Frevisse wondered. She surely knew Katherine best, was best suited to comforting her. Lacking her and not knowing Katherine well enough to guess what comfort to offer, Frevisse settled for asking, 'Has it come back? Your courage?'

Katherine's smile was bleak. 'Enough.'

Knowing she should leave it at that but not able to, Frevisse said, 'You think it will happen, then? Master Fenner will make an agreement with the Allesleys and your marriage will be part of it?'

'Sir Lewis wants compensation for the years he's been deprived of his land. Master Fenner has no other way to pay it except with me.'

'Is he maybe fond enough of you not to force you to it if you refuse?'

'I won't refuse. He has to have this peace with Sir Lewis. The cost and loss if he doesn't will happen to too many people who don't deserve to suffer for wrongs they didn't do. If I'm what has to be paid to keep that from happening, then I will be.'

'And Lady Blaunche?' Frevisse asked. 'She'll come to accept it, you think?' and was startled by how swiftly Katherine's resignation turned to blazing bitterness as she snapped, rawly angry, 'She'll have to, once it's done, but she'll make Master Fenner's life hell for it from now until she can't anymore.'

'She's not well . . .' Frevisse began.

'She's as well as she wants to be,' Katherine said, then quickly returned to contrite with, 'I'm sorry. I shouldn't have said that. I . . .' She shook her head, changed what she had been going to say to repeating, 'I shouldn't have said that.'

'Dame Claire has draughts that will maybe serve to soothe her.'

Katherine refused that with another shake of her head. 'When she's wrought herself this high, there's little chance of soothing her.'

'Is she often like this?'

'Often enough.' Bitterness surfaced again. 'It's what she does best. Ah!' Angrily, but at herself this time, Katherine covered her mouth with both hands, then clutched them to each other and dropped them to her waist. 'I'm sorry. I shouldn't have said that, either. It was unkind.'

But true, Frevisse said to herself, and was saved from struggling with how much more she should ask about what was none of her business by the gateward's ringing cry, 'They're coming!'

Katherine gasped, 'Blessed Virgin, no,' and spun toward the window with fear so plain in her that Frevisse crossed the chamber to her side, and Katherine, one hand pressed to her belt over her heart, reached with the other to take hold of Frevisse's near one, whispering, 'I'm not ready.'

Ready or unready made no difference and Frevisse held back from any of the useless things she might have said, leaving them to wait in a silence taut with Katherine's fear while below them in the courtyard manor men went and came, some of a purpose, some seemingly not, before Katherine said, 'There's Master Fenner,' come out of the hall door to the head of the steps.

He was more finely dressed than Frevisse had ever seen him, in a calf-length azure houppelande over dark hosen, the gown cut full and belted into his waist, the wide sleeves hanging long but gathered to his wrists, the collar high around his throat, with a slender chain glinting gold in the morning sunlight over his shoulders and across his chest. From above the yard he called out orders to men below him and they responded with bows and a swift sorting out that cleared most of them to the edges of the yard or away altogether, leaving a half-dozen men grouped near the foot of the stairs, all dressed in the brown surcoats that told they were household officers, high in their lord's service. They would likely have no direct part in what was to come but nothing was ever lost by playing up dignity in a matter like this, Frevisse supposed.

There was hardly time for the grouped men and onlookers to begin to fidget before there was a shouted order from the gateward and men were swinging the gates wide, back against the gatehouse walls, but rather than toward the gate, Frevisse – and Katherine, too, she noted – looked toward Robert in time to see him, still alone at the stairhead, straighten his back and lift his head, one hand coming to rest on the hilt of the sword on his left hip. There was small likelihood any weapon would be drawn today but neither would Sir Lewis nor Robert choose to face each other without his and so lessen his place against the other. It was a man thing that Frevisse had seen often enough not even to shake her head over anymore and in the next instant altogether forgot about it as riders cantered into the yard, too many and too quick to count, a burst of maybe a score of men and horses and the clatter of shod hoofs on stone and the chink and ring of harness before most of them drew rein in the midst of the yard, leaving three others to ride forward at footpace to the stairs as Robert came down to meet them.

'The man in gray is Ned Verney,' Katherine said. 'He's Master Fenner's friend who helped set this all toward.'

'Then the older man' – with a long, well-fleshed face, dressed in scarlet houppelande slit up the side for riding, with tall leather riding boots and brimless, high-crowned hat – 'will be Sir Lewis,' Frevisse said.

'I'd guess so,' Katherine agreed, tight-voiced, because that meant the third man was most likely his son and heir, Drew Allesley, angled from them so they could not see his face, only tell that he was fair-haired, his short-cut green houppelande showing a well-shaped leg above his low riding boot, before he, his father, and Ned Verney were swinging down from their saddles and going forward to meet Robert, with everything after that lost in a scurry of servants come to take the horses and the six arbiters dismounting in their turn, coming forward, more servants going for their horses and those of the other men now dismounting, too, while at the stairs Robert had turned to lead everyone up and into the hall where, if all went as planned, they would shortly sit down to dinner.

When Robert and the Allesleys were gone inside, out of sight, Katherine let go of Frevisse's hand, turning from the window and saying with credible steadiness, 'There. That much is done at least. Now for . . .' Her control faltered. '. . . the next . . .' Turned farther away, she pressed her hands over her mouth as if to hold in the anger and pain her unfinished words had betrayed.

To her back, gently, Frevisse said, 'There's no wrong in being angry at what's being done to you, or in being afraid. You've reason to be.'

'But it isn't my place to be, is it?' Katherine swung to face her, bitter. 'I'm not supposed to be angry or anything else except obedient. That's all that's wanted from me. To be obedient and a profit to whoever can sell me or buy me or carry me off by force!'

Frevisse, with no answer to change the grief and truth of that, held silent and Katherine, with unabated bitterness, demanded, 'Aren't you going to at least tell me how obedience is my duty and I should be glad of doing my duty?'

At least to that Frevisse had answer, saying dryly, 'I haven't found doing my duty and being glad of it the same thing often enough to tell you so. And obedience aside, I surely don't see why it should be your duty to be glad over being grabbed at by greedy men, especially when it's for the sake of righting a wrong that isn't even yours.'

Katherine gazed at her fixedly, balanced between tears and anger before willing herself away from both toward a smile that, once begun, was more real than any she had yet had this morning. She even managed, on a half laugh, to say, 'And once I'm married, if he's not to my liking, I can always begin to hope for an early widowhood.'

It was a bitter thought, better than despair but not by much, and before Frevisse had to answer it there was a hurried knock at the tower door and Mistress Dionisia came in without waiting to be bid, her somewhat frantic look changing to open relief as she saw Katherine and then to hen-clucking annoyance as she hurried forward saying, 'There, child, you gave us a turn. Gil came looking for you . . .' She began to twitch and straighten at Katherine's skirts. '. . . thinking you'd be in the parlor or with Lady Blaunche and you weren't and I've had to come find you. You're wanted in the hall, as well you knew you'd be.'

Katherine backed away from her a step. 'I have to go in now?'

Mistress Dionisia followed her, busily smoothing her sleeves. 'Of course now. Don't be a silly.'

Katherine backed another step. 'I'm not ready.'

Mistress Dionisia stopped, drew herself straightly up, and said firmly, 'Mistress Katherine, you were told this would be the way of it. Don't play Lady Blaunche with me.'

Katherine flushed. 'That isn't a fair thing to say!'

'Nor is it fair what you're doing, making trouble where trouble isn't going to do you any good.' But she softened even as she said it, reached out to smooth Katherine's hair back from one cheek, and said more gently, 'Sweetheart, I know, but it can't be helped and Gil says he's a comely young man. You'll take a liking to him, certain as daylight, and he can't help but like you as soon as he sets eyes on you, you're that lovely. Now come. They're waiting.'

For all her gentleness, she was unshiftingly certain that there was no gainsaying necessity, but Frevisse thought it was more Katherine's own courage than Mistress Dionisia's urging that brought her, after standing frozen-still a moment, to bow her head and move toward the tower door in an at least outward seeming of submission.

Chapter 10

'You, too, my lady, please you,' Mistress Dionisia said to Frevisse. 'What?' Frevisse asked, alarmed.

'Lady Blaunche refuses to have any part in this, she says, and won't come down to dine but she wants Dame Claire and you should be there.' Mistress Dionisia was as firm with her about it as she had been with Katherine. 'Otherwise there'll be no women at table but Mistress Katherine and that wouldn't be right. All those men and only her.'

No, it wouldn't be right, but that did not make Frevisse like it any the better. But, as with Katherine, liking or not liking had nothing to do with duty and, like Katherine, she bowed her head and went, to wait in the solar, joined by Dame Claire, while Robert's man, Gil, went to tell Robert they were ready; and when he returned, there was nothing for it but to make small procession with Dame Claire and behind Katherine, Mistress Dionisia following after them. into the hall where everyone was already standing to their places at the high table and along the two tables down both sides of the hall. Robert came forward to take Katherine by the hand and lead her forward, her eyes lowered, as was proper for a maiden among so many men, to her place on his left at the middle of the high table, with Frevisse able to see no more, her own eyes toward the floor as was equally proper for her, a nun, as Gil led her and Dame Claire aside, down from the dais and along the nearest table to their places just below three men she guessed were half of the arbiters because, once she was seated, she could see three other men who matched them for sober dress and solemn faces at the facing table. Everyone else looked to be men of Robert's household or else come with the Allesleys and the arbiters, and indeed she and Dame Claire were the only women seated there. Master Verney could at least have brought his wife, she thought. But maybe his wife did not get on with Lady Blaunche. That was a likelihood Frevisse had no trouble believing. Or maybe, to be slightly more charitable, it had been guessed Lady Blaunche would prove difficult and Mistress Verney's being here would serve no purpose.

It hardly mattered, Frevisse supposed. Whichever way it had been, things were as they were, and once the meal had started, it was none so bad as it might have been for her at least. The man on her left and the one on Dame Claire's right spoke with them each briefly, enough to satisfy manners, and then turned to talk with the men on their other sides, leaving her and Dame Claire to their meal and each other's company. Keeping in mind their Lenten fasting, she and Dame Claire took only small portions of all the dishes set out with the first remove, and though they ate slowly, they finished before anyone else could and were left, not feeling free to talk here among so many men, with nothing to do except exchange a glance at each other past the edges of their veils and then, on Frevisse's part, with everyone else busy at their food and talk, to look to the high table to see how things went there.

Mistress Dionisia had withdrawn, she saw, to the corner near the solar door, quietly out of the way, keeping discreet ward on her young mistress. From nunnery talk, Frevisse knew she had been Katherine's nurse in the girl's babyhood and her waiting-woman ever since. She had come into the Fenner household with her and therefore it was likely that when Katherine married she would go with her again and so must be almost as desperately interested as Katherine in what these Allesleys were like; but from the utter quietness of her standing there, with hands folded at her waist and eyes downcast, she might have been feeling nothing, thinking nothing, noticing nothing beyond the floor at her feet, and despite that was probably seeing as well as Frevisse could that between Katherine and Drew Allesley, seated on her other side from Robert, all seemed to be going amiably just now.

Certainly to the eye there was no more amiss with the young man from the front than there had been from the back. He and Katherine made a couple good to look on as they sat there, his fair head and her dark one close together in what looked like lively talk, broken off only sometimes while he served her from whatever dish was set between them or he made brief talk to Master Verney on his left and Katherine turned, equally briefly, to Robert on her right.

The second remove was brought, occupying Frevisse a while, but when she had done, she turned her heed to Robert and Sir Lewis who looked to be, surprisingly enough, almost as easily in talk together as the others. If nothing else, that meant they were both able to put manners before angers, and in such dealing as they were to have after this, that could only be to the good, Frevisse thought. Only Benedict, seated on Sir Lewis's other side, was making a poor show, unable to summon up good manners enough to hide how displeased he was to be there, leaving him on what looked like the constant edge of being openly rude. He made sorry contrary to young Allesley but Frevisse was less sorry for him than for Robert, forced into pretending he did not see his stepson's ill manner while probably hoping it would go no worse, and mercifully it did not as they passed on to the third remove, but Frevisse, for one, was relieved when the meal was done, thanks given, and everyone was drawing back from the tables.

Her own hope, said quickly to Dame Claire under the scrape of benches being shoved back and voices shifting to louder around them, was that they could go to the chapel to say at least something of the day's Offices, and Dame Claire gave a quick nod of agreement but they had only begun to wend their way around benches and men toward the outer door when Gil slid around a clot of arbiters and to them so purposefully that Frevisse's heart sank even before he bowed and said, 'They're going to start their talking now and Mistress Katherine and Master Drew are going out to walk in the garden awhile, or maybe the orchard, and Master Fenner asks if you two would keep them company.'

'Keep them company?' Dame Claire repeated uncertainly.

Gil stepped closer, saying too low for anyone else to hear, 'He wants someone besides Mistress Dionisia there.'

Frevisse traded looks with Dame Claire that told each other the request was too reasonable to refuse but that they both wished they could, before Dame Claire said to Gil as mildly as if nothing else could have been more pleasurable to them, 'Of course we will.'

Gil cleared a way for them the rest of the way down the hall, to join Katherine and Drew in the screens passage to the outer door, with Mistress Dionisia and an Allesley servant there, too. Katherine gave Frevisse's name and Dame Claire's to Drew and his to them and he made them a low bow and polite greeting and said to Katherine, gesturing toward the door, 'By your leave?'

She smiled on him and led their way out into the bright spring day, with a pause at the head of the steps while she gathered her skirts a little higher in front and Mistress Dionisia picked them up in back to keep them off the stairs. Then Drew held out his hand and she rested her free one on it for him to lead her down, with another pause at the stairfoot while Mistress Dionisia set down her back-skirts and Katherine reached around to gather them up. She was dressed to show both that she was able to afford such a wealth of cloth and lady enough to have no other need for her hands than managing her skirts and she made a quick and graceful movement of clearing them from the ground behind with one hand while still holding them up in front with her other, all without showing more than the tip of her shoe when she'd finished and smiled at Drew to show she was ready to go on.

Many of the lesser folk with no part in the afternoon's talks had already spilled out of the hall but they cleared way as Drew and Katherine crossed the yard toward the gate, followed by Dame Claire and Frevisse – glad her own skirts were far less full and made to clear the ground, even if only by a scant inch – followed by Mistress Dionisia, followed in turn by Gil and Drew's servant. Outside the gateway, they turned leftward and went by a graveled path between the manor's wall and a granary, turned a corner of the manor's wall and were at a penticed gate set in a waist-high withy fence, with beyond it the garden laid out narrowly between wall and orchard in a pattern of graveled paths and square beds where only a few early plants showed young green, with a hedge and arbor closing it in at its far end and a turf bench along the low earthen bank that separated it from the orchard.

As Drew held the gate open for her, Katherine murmured that it was not so pleasant a place this early in the spring as later in the year.

'No matter what time of year we were here,' he answered, 'you'd be the fairest flower in it.'

Katherine turned her gaze aside, looking down, accepting his fair words in the best of maidenly manners, and remembering the fiercely frightened girl of hardly two hours ago, Frevisse wondered if this change in her was purely by will or if, after all, she found Drew Allesley to her liking. If it was the latter way with her, all this might not turn out so ill after all. At least for Katherine.

Meanwhile Gil hurried forward to hold the gate open for Frevisse,

Dame Claire, and Mistress Dionisia to pass through, leaving Drew and Katherine free to stroll off together by the nearest path, Katherine saying something about the grapevine over the arbor. There being no need to more than keep them in sight, Frevisse hesitated over what to do now. Gil and the Allesley man were in no doubt on their own behalf; they propped themselves against the pentice posts as if ready to hold them up for the afternoon, and Mistress Dionisia, saying to no one in particular, 'There now, I've been on my feet long enough and want to be off them, by your leave,' sat herself down on a wooden bench beside the gateway, adding to Frevisse and Dame Claire, 'Come sit, too, if you like. There's room enough.'

'We'd rather walk a little,' Dame Claire said with a smile, moving away toward a path that Katherine and Drew were not on. 'Dame Frevisse?'

Unaware she had any particular urge to walk until Dame Claire said she did, Frevisse joined her, the two of them falling without thought into the familiar, matching, measured steps they so often used when circling St Frideswide's cloister walk together, hands tucked into their opposite sleeves and eyes to the ground a few yards ahead of them. The silence between them was familiar, too, and Frevisse would have been content with it and with the thinly warm spring sunshine and no more sounds than the small crunch of gravel underfoot, the bird sounds in the hedge at the garden's end, the low murmur of Katherine and Drew's voices across the garden and Mistress Dionisia and the two men beside the gate; but she sensed Dame Claire tense beside her, and when they had walked the garden's length and were turning to go back again with nothing spoken yet, she asked, 'What's the matter?'

With a promptness that betrayed how much she had been wanting to say something but her voice, like Frevisse's, kept cloister-low, Dame Claire burst out, 'I don't know. Too much. Nothing. I don't know.'

Overt uncertainty was rarely Dame Claire's way. The surprise of it nearly brought Frevisse to a halt, but Dame Claire went on walking, saying, 'It's Lady Blaunche. I don't know what to do.'

'There's something more wrong with her than you thought?'

'What's worst wrong with her she's doing to herself,' Dame Claire said sharply; and then, unhappily, 'No, that's not fair. Some of it is truly her body's unbalanced humours and I'm trying to do what can be done for that. But she's not helping. She's . . .' Dame Claire broke off and started again, annoyance and pity equally mixed, 'There I am, still wanting to be unkind about her when how she presently is isn't even all her own doing. Childbearing simply isn't kind to her and she's unkind because of it.'

'I doubt,' Frevisse murmured, 'she's a mild lady at the best of times.'

'I gather not,' Dame Claire agreed, grimly enough that Frevisse looked sideways at her, again surprised. Very rarely did anything come between Dame Claire and her care for someone she was tending, their needs outweighing all else with her, including her own feelings toward them.

'You'll be able to help her, though?'

Dame Claire drew and let out a long breath before she answered, very quietly, 'I don't know.'

Frevisse stopped and turned toward her, beginning to be alarmed. 'You don't know?'

Dame Claire faced her in turn. 'It's as with a bone or muscle kept twisted out of their right way too long. They're all the harder to draw back to where they should be and harder to keep there once they are. Lady Blaunche's humours have been awry for a long while, not just with this childing but with her others, too, and that her childings have come so near together makes it the worse. There's hardly been chance for her body to right itself between them. For a great many women it doesn't matter. For her, it's otherwise.'

'But surely there's something—'

'Surely there is. But it will take time.'

The flat way she said 'time' told Frevisse she meant more than a little of it and carefully, afraid she would not like the answer, Frevisse asked, 'Longer than Lent?'

'Very possibly.'

Dame Claire did not sound as if she liked her answer any better than Frevisse did, and in a silence now brooding on Frevisse's side as well as Dame Claire's, they walked on.

Since becoming a nun Frevisse had never been anywhere but in St Frideswide's for either Christmas or Easter, the times of each year when heart and mind should be most fully given over to the mystery and joy of, first, Christ's coming into the world and then his triumph over it. To be somewhere else, to be unable to weave herself into the deep patterning of prayers and praise that brought her into the very heart of the mystery, the core of its joy . . .

'Nor does it help,' Dame Claire went on, 'that everything and nearly everyone around her seems bent on making everything worse. Did you know she and her husband quarreled last night?'

'No.'

Nor did Frevisse much want to, but Dame Claire went on, some-what grimly, 'Mistress Avys has taken to telling me everything there's ever been wrong with her lady, which is useful only to a point. Then it becomes more trouble than help and I surely don't need to hear what she and her husband were angry over at each other in their bed. Why can't people remember there are ears on the other side of doors? And there'll be another quarrel tonight if Master Fenner hears what she told Katherine this morning after he and Benedict quarreled.'

'He's quarreled with Benedict, too?'

'Most assuredly.'

The garden was far longer than it was wide but they had reached its end and turned to pass through the arbor, able to glimpse through the barren branches that Katherine and Drew were already well back toward the gate by the garden's other path, not hurrying, merely match-ing each other's pace without apparent need to think about it, their heads turned toward each other, Katherine's tilted a little up toward his, both of them smiling as they talked. Dame Claire made a small nod toward them. 'It looks as if Lady Blaunche's hope there is going to be lost, too. After Master Fenner and Benedict went at it this morning . . .'

'Over what?'

'This Allesley business. What else? I don't know what set them off. The other women and I were with Lady Blaunche in her bedchamber and they were in the parlor and we didn't hear what started them, only from where they were too angry to keep their voices down. First it was Benedict shouting that Master Fenner was a fool not to keep Katherine's wealth in Fenner hands instead of giving it over to people who didn't deserve the luck. Master Fenner shouted back that no matter what Benedict thought and come what may, he was to keep his mouth shut while the dealings with the Allesleys went on or he'd find himself out the door for once and all and not a penny with him to see him on his way.'

'What did Lady Blaunche do at that?'

'By then she was sobbing and trying to leave her bed and Mistress

Avys and Master Geoffrey were trying to keep her there and I went out to those two fools in the parlor.' Grim as Dame Claire sounded over it now, she must have been more so then. 'They were so busy being angry they didn't even know I was there until I came between them and told them what I thought of them.'

'And that ended it?' Frevisse asked, not doubting it did. Despite that Dame Claire was so small-built a woman, when she was angry she was not someone with whom anyone usually argued.

'It would have for Master Fenner. He backed away, said well enough that he was sorry, and started to make for the door, but . . .' Dame Claire's steps slowed, and although no one else was near enough to hear, dropped her voice even lower than it already was. 'But Benedict said after him – thank mercy too low for anyone but Master Fenner and me to hear him – that the reason Master Fenner wouldn't let him have Katherine was because Master Fenner wanted her for himself.'

Not trying to hide she was startled but quick to Robert's defense, Frevisse said, 'He'd not be so willing to give her up to the Allesleys if that were the way of it.'

'That's my thought, too. But the look on his face . . .' Dame Claire shook her head at memory of it. 'He looked as if he wished the floor would open up under Benedict and take him, and it was as if he could barely get the words out when he said he didn't care what Benedict thought about anything so long as he kept it to himself and kept out of the way until he could keep his manners better than he kept his tongue. Then he left and Benedict started in to see his mother and I told him he couldn't and he went away across the room to gloom to himself, I suppose.'

And had still been glooming at dinner, by the look of him. But he had kept his tongue, at any rate.

'*Then* I went back to Lady Blaunche,' Dame Claire was going on, 'just in time to see her grab Katherine by the wrist . . .'

'Katherine was there?'

'Being readied for the Allesleys, with Lady Blaunche telling that girl Emelye and Mistress Dionisia everything to do as if they had no wits of their own. Emelye may not, come to that. But Lady Blaunche caught hold on Katherine and told her to remember that all she need do is flat refuse to marry an Allesley, and Master Fenner would never force her to it.'

Frevisse shook her head slowly in what she wished was disbelief that while Robert was working to make the best he could out of what was never his fault, his wife was still intent on balking him by any means she could manage. Briefly, she looked toward Katherine and Drew, laughing together, and then up at the parlor window, from where all the garden could be seen by anyone leaning even a little way out, and said, 'If she sees them together thus, she's going to be even more unhappy than she is.'

'Merely unhappy would be a blessing. What she'll be is furious. I can only hope she's kept to her bed the way I ordered.'

'Who's with her now?'

'Master Geoffrey, Mistress Avys and Emelye. For what it's worth, so far as Mistress Avys and Emelye count. Mistress Avys enjoys being upset with Lady Blaunche, I think, and Emelye is too afraid of her – or at least too wary – to be much use. Master Geoffrey is more use than both of them put together and doubled. When all that Mistress Avys has to offer is pity for "my poor lady's plight" – and that's like tossing dry pinecones into a hot fire; all it does is stir Lady Blaunche to greater fretting – Master Geoffrey at least tries to quiet her by reminding her that too much choler is good for neither her nor the child. And just ere dinner, to divert her, he brought out an account roll he said she should work over with him.'

'To give her something else to think on than her wrongs?'

'Even so. Mind you, when she saw it was the accounts for this manor there's all the trouble over, she threw it across the room and swore at him and was reaching for something else to throw – at him, I think – but he caught her hand and pointed out that maybe they could show by plain figures from the account roll that the manor had gained in worth while she held it, and if they did, then the Allesleys would have less grounds for demanding compensation along with its return.'

'Someone should have thought of that before,' Frevisse said.

'I think someone did. Gil had just come to fetch Katherine down to dinner and I was near him and half heard him mutter, ". . . thinks we're all sheeps' heads." My guess would be Master Fenner thought of it long since but knew Lady Blaunche would take nothing of it from him.'

'But she took it from Master Geoffrey.'

'Just now, angry at her husband as she is, she'll take just about anything from anyone else, rather than from him and from Master Geoffrey before anyone else.'

Frevisse cast her a sidewise, questioning look to which Dame Claire shook her head.

'No, I don't think there's anything untoward between her and Master Geoffrey. He flatters her and is pleasant company because that's the surest way to keep his place, from what Mistress Avys has said about how the last clerk of the household lost his, but Master Geoffrey has sense enough to know . . .' Dame Claire broke off and said instead, her voice changed, 'Here comes what could be trouble.'

Frevisse had been walking with her head down but she raised it at Dame Claire's warning in time to see Mistress Dionisia rising to her feet from the bench and Gil and Drew's servant straightening from where they had been leaning against the pentice post to make curtsy and bows to Benedict and Emelye just coming through the gateway. Worse, Katherine and Drew, just finishing another circle of the garden, were approaching the gate with no way to turn aside from the newcomers; and without need to say anything between them, Frevisse and Dame Claire walked a little the faster, to bring them up to the others sooner – before anything could happen, was Frevisse's thought but all that she said aloud, very low, was, 'Sent by Lady Blaunche, do you think?'

As quietly, Dame Claire returned, 'Without even pause for doubt, yes.'

They joined the others just as Benedict was saying in not the most friendly of voices, 'We thought to enjoy the garden, too, while the weather is fair.'

'Of course,' said Katherine pleasantly if somewhat too quickly, and after a gap of silence, the six of them looking at one another, she added, 'We've been fortunate in the weather, haven't we?'

It was generally agreed they had, and Emelye added brightly, 'Though I love the way everything smells so sweetly after rain, don't you?'

It seemed everyone did, and while they were agreeing on it, Katherine began to drift away toward the nearest garden path. Inevitably, Drew drifted with her, and if her intent was to put distance between Drew and Benedict, she was helped by Gil stepping forward at that moment to ask Benedict, 'Am I wanted at the hall, do you know, sir?' because when Benedict turned with a scowl to tell him that he wasn't as far as Benedict knew, Katherine took the chance to turn full away to the path, Drew going with her.

Benedict, turning away from Gil, as quickly took Emelye by the elbow and moved to follow but even more quickly Frevisse said to Dame Claire, 'Shall we walk?' and with more haste than grace shifted the two of them directly into Benedict and Emelye's way, between them and Katherine and Drew. The respite would be brief because, although the garden paths were only wide enough for two to walk side by side at a time, the garden was laid out in the common way, with squared beds with paths all right-angled between them, and if Benedict was set on making trouble, there was nothing to stop him from turning into a crosspath to go around the garden beds and come face-on to Drew and Katherine sooner or later, with no likely way Frevisse could see to stop him, and to Dame Claire's whispered question, 'Is there anything we can do?' she could only shake her head.

It was Drew who had a solution, although it took her a time to see it, thinking at first that at every crossing of the paths he was directing Katherine with small, gracious gestures of his hand to turn leftward or rightward into the crosspath simply for the sake of varying from the straight way he and Katherine had gone from garden's end to garden's end before this. Not until perhaps the fifth or sixth time he turned did she see of a sudden what he was doing and it told her that either Katherine had warned him Benedict might want trouble or he had quickly guessed it for himself. Whichever way it was, he was wending a way that would deliberately keep himself and Benedict apart, because after he and Katherine had turned at a corner of the path, anyone behind them had the choice of following them or turning the other way or going straightly on. If Benedict went straightly on after they had turned, then all Drew and Katherine need do to avoid coming face-to-face with him was at the next crossing of paths turn away, putting more distance between them and him. If Benedict turned the opposite way to theirs, then they need merely slow their pace and wait to see which way he turned at his next crosspath, to know which way to turn farther away from him. And if Benedict simply followed them, then Frevisse and Dame Claire were there, forever a discreet half-dozen paces behind Drew and Katherine and constantly in his way. Benedict could only break the pattern by walking more quickly and that he could not do because of Emelye, talking happily away at his side, keeping him to the same strolling pace as

Drew and Katherine, Frevisse and Dame Claire despite how he turned one way and then another, trying to come around face-to-face with Drew again but failing every time.

And then across the several garden beds that were come between them, just before she and Dame Claire turned away after Drew and Katherine yet again, Frevisse saw him pull up short, his eyes widening with the understanding that maybe he was not being thwarted by chance. He was not fully certain of it yet, she guessed, and for a while longer he went on trying to change the pattern to his favor, but as he found that he could not except by resorting to an ungraciousness that would put him openly in the wrong, his brows came down in a scowling stare at Drew's back, his face darkening out of ill temper toward plain anger.

And what would come of that when he was no longer trapped by manners and the garden's paths, Frevisse did not look forward to seeing.

Chapter 11

Rescue came with one of Robert's servants, sent to bid Katherine and Drew back to the hall. They were not far from the gateway when they saw him coming and met him there, Mistress Dionisia, Gil and the Allesley servant near to hear, too, as the man gave his message and Drew asked, 'They're done for today?'

'Yes, sir.'

'And all's well?' Katherine asked as if she would have held back from it if she could.

'No shouting that I heard,' the man said cheerfully.

Benedict, coming up then with Emelye a little shortbreathed from haste beside him, muttered something, low enough he could be ignored, but then as the others moved to leave the garden, he started a purposeful move toward Drew. From the corner of her eye Frevisse saw that Gil had expected as much and was moving to cut him off with a look on his face that boded no good to Benedict and without thinking she veered from Dame Claire and across Benedict's way, to his other side from Emelye, clumsy with her skirts so that he had to falter his stride first for them and then to bow to her while she said, 'For change, why don't I walk with you awhile, Master Benedict? And Emelye, you can keep Dame Claire company.'

Awkwardly, Benedict said, 'Yes. If you like,' as Gil fell back to join Mistress Dionisia and Drew's man, and Dame Claire, only a little behind Frevisse's purpose, drew Emelye ahead to walk with her behind Katherine and Drew going out the gate.

To leave Benedict less time to sort out what had happened and despite the weather never having been among the things of which she

123

much cared to spend time talking, Frevisse said to him, 'Will the weather hold, do you think, or is there going to be more rain?'

Benedict, perforce, joined her in trying to find something worth the saying about how there had been rain yesterday and there might be more tomorrow or that, possibly, there might not, most of the way back to the manor yard, until Frevisse took pity on his effort and asked out of memory of something half-heard in other talk, 'I understand you're to go into someone else's household after Easter.'

Benedict's sullen countenance changed, brightening much the way one of the much-discussed rainy days did when clouds parted to the sun. 'Ned Verney's,' he said. 'He's our northward neighbor here. I had chance at Sir Walter's but I'd rather serve Ned, all taken in all. It's only for two years, until I come of age and into my own, but better with Ned than somewhere else.'

'You don't mind he's helped bring on this arbitration?' she asked, knowing she should not but wanting to know.

Benedict's face predictably darkened but not at Ned Verney. 'It's not that much his doing. Robert is the one who's afraid to fight the Allesleys for what's ours. When Ned saw he couldn't change him, all he did was help him out before he made a worse fool of himself over it.'

That was not the way Frevisse had heard of the business from Katherine and Mistress Dionisia, nor did it sound like Robert as she knew him but more like Lady Blaunche's displeasure talking; but there was no doubting Benedict believed it, which was pity because it would have been better every way if he had been on Robert's side instead of his mother's and to turn him before he goaded himself back into worse humour, she asked, 'How soon after Easter do you go to him?'

His willing talk about that kept them until they passed under the gatehouse arch and into the manor yard where horses and men were already waiting for the arbiters coming down the steps from the hall, with above them Robert, Sir Lewis and Ned Verney coming out the door.

'There's Ned,' Benedict said. 'With Robert,' he added darkly.

For the first time Frevisse gave Ned Verney a long look. He was a match for Robert in age and build, with the look of a man confident of himself and his place, standing in talk with Robert and Sir Lewis at the head of the stairs while the arbiters went to their horses. To Frevisse's relief, as she and Benedict, now sullenly silent, followed Drew, Katherine, Dame Claire and Emelye around the edge of the yard. circling wide from the waiting horses and riders, the talk among the three men looked to be serious but not grim, and when they descended to meet Katherine and Drew just reaching the stairfoot there were smiles and pleasantries all around before Robert, looking past Katherine, saw first Emelye, which puzzled him, and then Benedict. Anger mixed with worry crossed Robert's face in a fleeting frown but Frevisse had been delaying Benedict as best she might by lagging her steps, and there was time for courteous farewells between Robert and Drew and chance for Drew to thank Katherine for her company and her to thank him for his, with a smile that Drew more than willingly matched. By the time Benedict, sullen again, joined them, she was making courteous farewell to Sir Lewis and Master Verney in their turn.

Frevisse, with nothing more she could do, faded aside to join Dame Claire standing a little apart with Emelye, thinking how much at sorry odds Benedict was with everyone else's mutual courtesies, returning only a curt bow of the head and no word at all to Sir Lewis' good-day to him and giving Drew even less – only a glare to the other's farewell. Both men ignored his discourtesy, turning away to their horses, but Master Verney, coming after them toward his own horse, gave Benedict a clenched-fist shove to the shoulder in passing that might have been from friendliness except it was hard enough to sway Benedict backward a step, almost off his balance. It took Benedict by surprise but he caught himself without saying anything and stood, unpleasant-faced, until the Allesleys and Master Verney and everyone else were riding out the gateway in the clatter of hoofs and jingle of harness and Katherine and Emelye, followed by Mistress Dionisia, started for the stairs. He moved then to follow them but Robert caught hold of him by an upper arm and said with low-voiced anger, 'You wait.'

Benedict twisted slightly, trying to break loose without being plain about it, but could not and stood still, glaring at Robert glaring back at him. Above them on the stairs, Katherine and Emelye looked briefly back but Mistress Dionisia bustled them inside and Robert, hand still clenched around Benedict's arm, demanded, 'What do you think you gain by acting the cur the way you did just now?'

Benedict tried again to pull loose and go on past him. Robert, control of his anger visibly slipping, wrenched him back.

'More to the point, what are you doing here at all after I told you not to be anywhere around Drew Allesley if you couldn't put a fair face on?'

Around the now uncrowded yard there were still too many manor folk to see what was happening, and Gil took a step forward with the look of meaning to come between them, then stopped, thinking better of it. Dame Claire, with different instinct, made to draw back and leave, but Frevisse, caught like Gil between wanting to stop them and knowing she could not, held where she was. And now Benedict, letting go hold on his own anger, said fiercely, twisting loose of Robert's hold, 'I don't have to do what you say. Without my mother, you're not anything!' He made to turn away, adding, 'I'm going for a ride. It stinks here.'

But Robert grabbed him by the arm again, shoved him backward hard against the hall's stone wall, and said, close into his face, 'Don't *ever* try to bring your mother in between us. Nor are you going for any ride. Until everything is settled, you're staying where I can see what you do. And if ever you're as rude again as you were just now to Sir Lewis and his son, you'll spend the while until this is finished in your room under guard. Understand me?' Not bothering with Benedict's answer, whatever it would have been, he let go his arm and stepped back from him, adding coldly, 'For that matter, go to your room now and stay there, because all you'll do if you go near your mother is trouble her, and if you do, God help you because I'll have your hide for it.'

Benedict lurched forward from the wall, meaning to go for him, and Robert braced to meet him, but Gil said, low and urgently, 'The younglings are watching.'

To both their credit, Robert and Benedict stopped and looked toward the nursery window across the yard, and Frevisse, looking, too, saw Robin chin-high to the windowsill waving his arms mightily above his head and Tacine in the nursery maid's arms flapping both hands in a floppy wave and John who must have scrambled up on something to be leaning that far out but with his tunic's back firmly gripped by Nurse. Robert raised a hand toward them, managed a wave, and so did Benedict, making Frevisse think the better of him. And when Robin called, 'Come play with us, Father!' and Robert called back, 'Not just yet, small bits,' Benedict said toward the cobble-stones at his feet, 'I'll go,' added at a mutter, 'And to my room afterwards,' then looked at Robert, defying him to refuse.

Robert looked back at him, the silence tight between them until whatever he saw in Benedict's face satisfied him and he nodded curt permission. Benedict nodded curtly back, called to the children, 'It's to be me, instead,' and went, to cheers from the children who promptly disappeared from the window.

Robert, his smile dead the instant they were from sight, his stare flat at Benedict's back, said to Gil, 'See to it everyone, beginning with the stablemen, knows he's not to leave the manor. By horse or other-wise.'

With a grim nod, Gil headed across the yard the other way from Benedict, toward the stables, with everyone else in sight suddenly on their way to somewhere else, too, likely on business they should have been about before now, except for Dame Claire and Frevisse, caught unsure of which was their best way to go, before Robert looked to Frevisse and said with deep-cut pain rather than any anger, 'Blessed St Mark. What am I going to do?'

Without thought, Frevisse answered, 'Come to the chapel with Dame Claire and me.' And to Robert's momentarily blank stare, added, 'There'll be no one else there.'

To that he nodded, and though she and Dame Claire had said nothing to each other about going to the chapel, Dame Claire said nothing now, either, simply came with them as they crossed the yard and into the chapel's cool silence. where Robert went forward and sank onto his knees in front of the altar, bending his head over his tightly clasped hands. Behind him, Frevisse and Dame Claire exchanged brief looks, then went to kneel a little to one side and behind him, making no attempt at any Office, only silently praying as suited them each. Or Dame Claire did, Frevisse supposed. For herself, she was too much heeding the tense curve of Robert's back and the rushed whisper of his praying. The words were too low for hearing but the pleading and pain in them was clear enough and never bettered, only the outpouring broke down at last into shorter and shorter rushes until it finally altogether ceased, leaving him in bowed stillness.

Even then, Frevisse waited until at last he drew a deep, ragged breath and straightened before she said quietly to him, 'Robert.' And when he looked at her, blind-eyed with uneased pain, she said, 'Come away and sit,' and rose to her feet.

He stood up heavily, as if years older than he was, and followed her aside to the chapel's single long-backed bench, brought out for the manor's lord and lady to sit when they came to service and otherwise kept out of the way against one wall. Because Frevisse sat, so did he, and when he was seated, said toward the floor, his clasped hands clamped between his knees, 'My head is one huge ache. All day, ever since this morning, I've tried to watch every word out of my mouth, be careful of everything I said, and now I've gone and ruined it all at Benedict in front of Lord knows how many people.'

More than that, he was not used to giving way to anger at all, toward Benedict or anyone else, Frevisse guessed, or he would not be in such after-pain, and she offered, 'Not all the blame of it is yours.'

'Enough of it is.' He jerked his hands up and scrubbed at his face as if to drive something out of or something into his aching head, dropped them back into his lap, limp now, and said, 'This making peace with Sir Lewis was supposed to better things, save us from trouble to come. All it's done so far is make everything go from bad to worse. *Everything*.'

'Without you dealt with Sir Lewis, think what would come. Worse than all this, from what I've heard.'

Robert cast back his head, looked up and said at the roof beams, 'Yes,' but not as if it comforted him any.

'There would have been people hurt who had no part in the rights and wrongs of the Allesley matter at all,' Frevisse persisted.

'Yes,' Robert granted, still at the roof beams, and added with a forced calm that betrayed he was not calm at all, 'I just wish that that certainty was enough to stop what's hurting now.'

But he knew as surely as Frevisse did that present pain could only be lived through to its end, with only the hope that better would come afterward; and to give him something of that better for comfort, she said, 'If nothing else, Katherine and Master Drew were pleased and pleasant with each other's company the while they were together this afternoon. That at least may go to the good.'

Finally, for the first time since they had sat down together, Robert brought his gaze down and around to stare at her with what looked too much like naked, heart-deep despair for a blank half-moment before saying, 'Yes. I thought as much. Watching them cross the yard just now.' He stood abruptly up. 'I'll leave you to your prayers, my lady. By your leave.'

But he did not wait to have it, simply left. And left Frevisse afraid, without being certain of what.

Chapter 12

There was no more sight of Benedict that day or evening, and Lady Blaunche kept to her room the while, with Dame Claire in attendance after returning from the chapel, and Master Geoffrey, Mistress Avys and Emelye for company. Even the children she saw only briefly and then left them to Robert who, between leaving the chapel and when Frevisse saw him next, at supper served simply in the solar, had rid himself of – or, more likely, buried – his anger and pain. He was simply Robert again and openly glad of his children's company in the parlor for the evening, as ready for play as they were.

Katherine, changed into an everyday dress and her hair braided back, would have joined them, but Mistress Dionisia declared she was too pale, had had too tiring a day, should sit quietly, and looked somewhat surprised when Katherine agreed with her and withdrew to a corner, to sit on piled cushions and read.

Frevisse tried to read, too, psalter in hand, but found it difficult to hold to the words while Robert and the children played a loud game requiring much climbing on, over and under the settle and on, over and under Robert as well, bringing them all to hot, red faces and laughter until Master Geoffrey brought word from Lady Blaunche they had to stop, she couldn't bear the noise. Silence fell with a rock's grace, along with the children's faces, but when Master Geoffrey was gone back into the bedchamber, Robert leaned toward them and said in a mock whisper, 'Ah, well, small bits, we can always go clean the nursery.'

Against expectation, the children brightened back into laughter, immediately ready to go, and Katherine set her book aside and started to rise, but Robert said, 'No. Stay. Dame Frevisse, will you help me see them to their room?'

'Assuredly,' she said, and though she found it was no easy matter to manage eager children down the steep curve of the stairs, even with Robert carrying Tacine, they made it safely enough and she was spared her next fear – that she would be expected to help with them in the nursery – by Robert bidding them tell her good night in her bedchamber and going on with them himself into the nursery where Nurse and Anabilla were presumably waiting to even the odds.

On her own part, Frevisse stayed where she was, thinking she would prefer the bedchamber's quiet to going back to the parlor; but the quiet was a long while coming because whatever 'clean the nursery' meant, it entailed much shouting, laughter and thumping that must have had very little to do with settling down to sleep. When quiet finally did come, she thought Robert would be back but instead heard him leave by the stairs to the yard, not much before Dame Claire joined her.

Together, talking about nothing else, they went to say Compline in the chapel and the rest of the evening went much like the evening before and the next morning began the same as yesterday's, though it was the nursery maid Anabilla who was just out of bed and readying for the day when Frevisse and Dame Claire returned after saying Prime in the gray light of the overcast almost-dawn. She was a shy, freckled girl who ducked her head and whispered when spoken to, murmured them good day, and slipped quickly away to the nursery where sounds of merriment said the children were up, as early a-stir as the rest of the manor, it seemed, because a servant shortly came to the other door with Frevisse and Dame Claire's breakfast.

Despite how Lenten-spare it was – yesterday's bread and some warmed, lightly spiced wine – it was welcome. Fasting at its best brought not greed for more food but grateful pleasure in what there was, and they made no haste with it, were soaking the last of their crusts in the wine when Emelye scratched at the tower door, entered at Dame Claire's bidding, made quick, low curtsy to them, and said, 'Please you, my ladies, where's Nurse?'

'With the children,' Dame Claire said with a nod toward the nursery. Emelye curtsied her thanks and hurried out by the room's other door, only to hurry back soon, curtsy to them again, and say to Dame Claire. 'Can I tell Lady Blaunche you'll be there soon? She's asking for you.'

Dame Claire held up a curve of bread crust and her cup. 'Tell her I'll be there directly I've finished this.'

Emelye bit her lip and Frevisse realized that her haste was from more than duty; her eyes were large with fright as she said, 'Yes, my lady. But soon, please,' curtsied again and more fled than merely left.

'Oh my,' Dame Claire said but made no greater haste toward finishing her bread or wine.

If anything, she moved the more slowly at it, bringing Frevisse to ask, on the chance she wanted to talk of it, 'Nothing is the better with her?'

'Nor will be, no matter what I do, I'm afraid, until she decides herself to make it better. I think someone told her sometime that women *feel* rather than think, and she's been intent on *feeling* as much as "womanly" possible ever since.' That was an unusual amount of bitterness to come from Dame Claire, and Frevisse had no answer to it, could only sit watching her stare at her bread crust still soaking in the wine without noticing it was falling into soaked bits as she said on, 'Her humours are badly awry. There's no doubting that. But she makes it the worse by giving in to it so completely. I wonder if Master Fenner would send for a potion of poppy if I asked? Some could surely be had from Coventry in no more than a day or two.'

Frevisse suspected Robert would send for essence of the sultan's beard if it held out promise of quieting his wife the while he was dealing with the Allesleys but before she could say so, Dame Claire sighed, 'Ah well. In the meanwhile there's today to be dealt with.' She noticed her crust, ate what she could of it and drank the rest with her wine, finishing as Frevisse did, just as there was a rap at the stairway door followed immediately by Robert's two small sons pushing each other into the room.

Out of sight behind them, Nurse said crisply, 'Master Robin, John, you know better than that. Come out and go in properly.'

They promptly pushed each other out of the room, pulled the door closed and knocked at it again. With great seriousness, in honor of their effort, Frevisse said, 'Come in,' and with equal seriousness Robin did, John solemnly at his heels. They both bowed to her and Frevisse bent her head to them in return, saying, 'Sirs.'

Grinning at their success, they came farther in, clearing way for Tacine who tried a curtsy, spreading her baby skirts as if they were a lady's gown, wobbly on her short legs but with Nurse's hand to the small of her back to steady her, followed by an approving, 'That's well done, all of you. Now all of you say, "Good day, my ladies." '

They did and Frevisse and Dame Claire gravely returned the greeting before Nurse, seemingly taking them in charge along with the children, said, 'Would you be good enough to see us all up the stairs to the parlor, please? If you'll do the boys, I'll come with Tacine, please you.'

It made no difference to Dame Claire who had been going up anyway but Frevisse only reluctantly held out her hand to Robin and together, Dame Claire with John and Nurse following with Tacine, they went into the solar where two servants were busy polishing and shifting furniture. The children would have stopped to watch but Nurse said, 'Your lady mother is waiting,' and the boys pulled loose from holding hands to take the stairs at a scurry and scramble ahead of everyone.

Dame Claire and Frevisse and Nurse with Tacine followed at a more reasonable pace, Frevisse first, pausing in the parlor doorway to set John firmly back on his feet after a stumble over the sill, only seeing after she had straightened and followed him into the room that Katherine, Master Geoffrey and Mistress Dionisia were there, standing oddly rigid and scattered around the room, a warning to her that something was badly awry. And the next moment she knew what it was, as Lady Blaunche's voice rose, shrill with anger, beyond the bedchamber door, 'And today? What are you meaning to do today? Yesterday you humiliated Benedict in front of everyone. Today—'

'No one humiliated Benedict but himself.' Except it could only be Robert lashing back at her, Frevisse would not have known his voice, it was so raw with anger, the last dregs of his patience all too obviously gone. 'And no one could have done it as thoroughly as he did, save for maybe you, sending him out there to it.'

He should be stopped, Frevisse thought. They both should be, before they did worse to each other than they probably already had. But there was no one to do it and Lady Blaunche was flailing on, 'I sent him out there to watch out for Katherine which was more than you were doing!'

'Watch out for Katherine? What did you think was going to happen to her in our own garden with two nuns, her woman and Gil to keep watch?'

'That Allesley—'

'Is someone who'll be far the better for her than what *you* would have wished on her!'

133

'Benedict—'

'Would still be thinking of her more as a sister than a wife if you'd not put other into his head.'

'And why not? Is it any the worse than what you're doing? Selling her—'

'Using her to pay off the wrongs you've done,' Robert snarled back. 'That's what I'm doing. Unlike you who only want to use her to make another wrong. Look to yourself for the wrong of it, not to me.'

'Not to you? *Not to you?* You're the one too coward to face down Sir Lewis! You're the one . . .'

The bedchamber door flung open and Robert came out, furious-faced, as Lady Blaunche shrilled after him, '. . . too coward to keep what's rightly mine! I've held that manor for a score of years and now you . . .'

Midway between bedchamber and stairs Robert spun around and shouted back at her, 'That's a score of years longer than ever you should have. Why can't you understand that?'

Lady Blaunche in an amber-colored dressing gown flung into the bedchamber doorway, bracing herself against the frame as she cried, 'What I understand is that you're helping the Allesleys to rob me! Why don't you just give them everything we have at once and leave us all to starve and be done with it?'

'Because when I let myself be driven into marrying you, my lady wife' – he made the name ugly – 'our marriage vows bound me to care for you while we both lived, whether I liked it or not. And just now I don't like it at all.'

'You *wanted* to marry me! You know you did!'

'What I wanted,' Robert said coldly, 'was not to spend the rest of my life cleaning pigsties. That was the only other choice Sir Walter offered me.' He paused, then added deliberately, viciously, 'I should have chosen the pigsties.'

He might as well have struck her with his fist, for the cruelty of it. Frozen, Lady Blaunche stood staring at him openmouthed, then tried to breathe and could not, gasped for air, gasped again on a sob, and turned away, back into her bedchamber, one hand pressed to her throat, the other blindly groping for something, anyone to hold to, and Mistress Avys was there, come hurriedly to put an arm around her waist and catch her outstretched hand, leading her away toward the bed as Dame Claire passed Robert to follow them into the bedchamber, slamming the door behind her.

Robert, for his part, turned his back on the slammed door, his face cold, blank of even anger, his stare past everyone to the far wall that he did not look like he was seeing, and no one else moved or made sound before, after a moment, his gaze dropped and he took in that his children were there, staring at him, stricken, and his coldness cracked and was gone and he went down on one knee, holding his arms out to them, saying, 'Come here, my hearts.'

Robin and John hung back, uncertain, but Tacine squirmed free of Nurse to the floor and came at him in a toddling rush that carried her full into his arms and the instant after that her brothers came, too, and Robert crushed them all to him, his face buried against Tacine's warm, small neck, his hands curved to the back of Robin and John's smooth heads as they burrowed against him.

Only finally did he gently untangle from them, setting first John and then Robin back from him, then working loose Tacine's throttling hold from around his neck, saying while he did, 'There. That sets the day off to a better start.' He kissed Tacine's cheek and, standing up, ruffled the boys' hair. 'You be good to your mother this morning when you see her. I wasn't and she's feeling badly. Yes?'

Three heads made solemn nods.

'Good, then.' He touched each of them on a cheek, smiling. 'I'll see you tonight.'

Nurse came forward to take them back into her keeping, and Robert turned to Frevisse with the smile drained from him. 'I'm most sorry,' he said, 'for all of this.'

He was come back from the far, cold, hating place he had been and in pain, and Frevisse answered, letting him see how much she meant it, 'I'm sorry she's so aggrieved by what you have to do.'

Robert nodded wordlessly, made to leave, then turned back, to Katherine this time, and said, his voice tight to strangling on the words, 'You know that if you mislike anything about this marriage we're making for you, you need only to say and it will never happen.'

Gowned and groomed as she had been yesterday, ready to be displayed again, Katherine went on standing rigidly straight, the way she had been ever since Frevisse had come into the room, her hands clutched together below her breasts, staring at Robert a long moment before she said, no life to the words, 'You need this marriage. I'll make it.'

'Katherine,' Robert began but stopped, stood staring back at her with a look no more readable than hers, tried again, 'Katherine . . .' gave it up, turned away, and disappeared down the stairs.

The difficulty there might have been after that of sorting the morning into some semblance of the ordinary was passed over by Nurse saying briskly to Frevisse, 'You were going to tell the children a story, I think?'

More readily than she would have thought possible a half-hour ago, Frevisse agreed, 'A story. Yes.'

Mistress Dionisia had closed on Katherine, was leading her away to the settle at the far end of the room, talking to her in a soothing rush too low to be heard. Katherine, no longer rigid, was clinging to her hand and shaking her head against whatever was being said to her. Frevisse, distracted by that and stalling while trying to think of a story she could tell, said, 'Where shall we sit?'

'Here,' said John, pulling away from Nurse to run for the window seat and scramble up with clear intent to unlatch and open the shutter. Master Geoffrey said, 'John, no,' and went to stop him, overtaking him as he reached up for the latch and taking firm grip on the back of his loose tunic with one hand while unfastening and folding the shutter open with the other, saying over his shoulder to Frevisse at the same time, 'He loves to lean out of windows,' and to John, 'Stop squirming, child. Do you want Dame Frevisse to tell you a story or not?'

'Story,' said Tacine and, deftly freeing herself from Nurse's hand, she bustled forward to demand of Master Geoffrey, just turned from setting her brother down on the window seat's cushions, 'Up.'

With a smile over her head at Frevisse, he lifted Tacine and put her beside her brother, and when Nurse patted Robin on the back and said, 'You, too,' he shot forward to scramble up on Frevisse's other side as she sat down beside Tacine who promptly crawled into her lap, squirmed around to make herself comfortable in the curve of her arm, and said again contentedly, 'Story,' as John scooted to take her place at Frevisse's side.

Still with no story in mind, Frevisse looked somewhat desperately to Nurse but she was gone to join Katherine and Mistress Dionisia on the settle, the girl sitting between the two women with head bowed and hands clasped tightly together in her lap, Mistress Dionisia still talking low-voiced to her and Nurse resting a hand on her arm.

'Story,' John said, pushing his hard little head against Frevisse's shoulder, bringing her back to her more immediate problem, but Master Geoffrey must have rightly read her look because he said helpfully, 'St Frideswide's tale?'

With relief, Frevisse said, 'Yes. Thank you,' and in the certainty that sooner begun was sooner done, started, in the time-honored way, 'That other year, when things weren't as they are now,' and went on with the story of the Saxon princess who wanted only to serve God, and when a prince tried to carry her off for himself, she fled and hid, 'in the marshes near where Oxford is today but all was wild then,' for three years, while he went on searching for her until God struck him blind. Only when he swore to trouble her no more was he cured, 'given back his sight to see how beautiful the world was to those not blinded by their own wishes,' and St Frideswide lived on to found a nunnery where she had hidden so long, 'and there she lived out her days in prayers and happiness,' Frevisse finished and waited while the children seemingly thought on that for a moment, before Robin looked up with a frown and said,

'She wanted to? Close herself up in a nunnery?'

'Yes.'

'Instead of marrying a prince?'

'She'd rather marry the prince of Heaven,' Frevisse said.

That gave them another momentary pause for thought, until Robin gave a firm nod, satisfied, and said, 'Good.'

Frevisse's fear now was that they would want another story from her, but they proved to be ungreedy. While Robin added, 'Thank you,' John squirmed around to slide from the seat to the floor and ordered his brother and sister, 'Come play,' and, obedient or willing, they went with him away to their toys in the far corner of the room.

Frevisse was willing for Master Geoffrey to betake himself away, too, but he set to talk about the weather that left her small choice but to agree it did indeed look lowering this morning. In truth, after the past few days of clear skies, today had the feel of rain-to-come in the air and they had worked up to sharing their belief that the weather could well be shaping to a storm before the day was out and were beginning to speculate on whether it would wait until afternoon or come this morning, when Tacine across the room pulled back from Robin and John, a rag doll clutched to her breast, and cried out angrily, 'No!'

'Children, hush. Your mother,' Nurse said from where she still sat with Katherine and Mistress Dionisia.

Hushed but unswerving, Tacine repeated, 'No. You can't,' at her brothers and scrambled to her feet.

'Can,' said John.

And from Robin, 'Master Geoffrey said so.'

'You go ask Master Geoffrey,' Nurse said firmly, 'and mind you keep your voices down while you do.'

They came to him in a rush, Tacine still hugging her doll, Robin with a boy-sized wooden sword, John saying eagerly even before they reached the window seat, 'She said Robin could kill Meggy and now she won't let him.'

'Not,' Tacine said firmly.

'You said!'

'No!'

Before John could answer that flat refusal, Master Geoffrey looked to Robin. 'Tell me the start of it.'

'We're sort of playing at doctors, 'cause it's quiet. Only being just sick is nothing and I asked if we could stab her doll and then make her well.'

'And she said we could,' John put in.

'No.'

'Did!'

'No!'

Tacine might not have many words, but she had certainty. Master Geoffrey held up a hand, looked to Tacine's stubborn face, looked at indignant John, returned his look to Robin and asked, 'Did she?'

'Yes, but then John said stabbing wasn't anything. He wanted to cleave her from crown to crotch.'

'Master John,' said Nurse sternly. 'That's not a proper thing or even possible.'

'It is!' he exclaimed, supported by Robin's, 'Master Geoffrey told us.'

Tacine nodded vigorously that he had but added, holding her doll closer, 'Can't!'

'Didn't you?' Robin demanded of the clerk.

'According to the chronicler Master Froissart, it has been done,' Master Geoffrey said judiciously, with an eye to Nurse who gave a small nod that since he was quieting the children, he could go on.

'Did you ever *see* someone cleave someone?' Robin asked, leaning against the clerk's knee.

His brother and sister, equally ready to trade quarreling for a story, sank cross-legged to the floor as Master Geoffrey said, 'I'm pleased to say not. I doubt few have. It would take a mighty sword as well as a mighty man to cut through bone and armor both like that.'

'But you saw Lord Talbot,' John said. '*He* could have.'

'He very likely could,' Master Geoffrey agreed, 'but I never saw him fight.'

'You said . . .' John started in protest.

'I said I saw him in battle, remember, Master John. But it was after he had sworn never to bear arms against the French again so I did not see him fight.'

'And his squires and knights were all around him and never let happen any foe come near enough to strike at him,' Robin said as if repeating a much-loved tale.

'Never a one,' Master Geoffrey said, and John and Tacine happily together chanted, 'Never a one!'

Satisfied and quarrel forgotten, the children returned to their play and Frevisse for sake of conversation that wasn't about the weather asked, 'You were in France, Master Geoffrey?'

'In my regretted youth, yes.' Master Geoffrey smiled. 'I started as an Oxford scholar with some thought of entering the law but was more given to street brawling than studies, I fear, to the point where my tutor told me there was no longer place for me and my hot blood there. I'd sense enough to know my hot blood would be no more welcome back home in Gloucester and joined the muster the Duke of Bedford was gathering to go back to France in 1434.'

'In time for the disaster with Burgundy,' Frevisse said. When the Duke of Burgundy had abandoned his long alliance with England in favor of allying with the king of France, and the French war had gone into the worst squall of fighting there had been in years.

'Even so. By the time my indenture was done, I'd seen enough of fighting that I no longer tended so readily to anger before thought and all I wanted was to go back to Oxford and be the most peaceable of scholars. I did and here I—'

The bedchamber door flew open and Emelye fled into the parlor, weeping. Frevisse stayed where she was but the other three women and Master Geoffrey all sprang to their feet. Katherine even starting toward the girl, but Mistress Avys came out the door on Emelye's heels, said, 'Emelye,' and the girl spun around and fell, weeping harder, into her arms. Patting her on the back, Mistress Avys said over her shoulder to the rest of them, 'Lady Blaunche.' Not that they needed even that much explanation, especially with Dame Claire now in the bedchamber doorway, saying past the two of them with more irk than anything, 'Dame Frevisse, would you come in, please?' Master Geoffrey took a questioning step forward and Dame Claire nodded at him. 'Yes. You, too. Please.'

Very rarely had Frevisse seen Dame Claire reach her patience's end but there was no doubting she was somewhere near it this time and as Mistress Avys led Emelye aside, still patting and talking to her, Frevisse followed Master Geoffrey warily into the bedchamber. Dame Claire, waiting to shut the door behind her, said, low and hurried, 'She's worked herself to such a pitch that all she wants to be is upset. See what you can do. Pray with her maybe. Or for her. Or . . .'

With a courage that had probably served him well in France – not to mention in his Oxford street brawls – Master Geoffrey was crossing directly toward the bed, and from beyond the bedcurtains drawn across its foot, Lady Blaunche cried out to him, 'They're all useless! All they do is cluck the same things over and over at me like stupid hens. It's not going to be all right and I'm sick of everyone saying it is!'

'Or at her,' Dame Claire finished grimly. 'If you can quiet her even a little while I mix a stronger potion . . .'

Frevisse nodded tersely. She did not want to be here but since she was and was needed, despite how little good she thought she could do, she followed Master Geoffrey toward the bed.

The room's one window, facing probably toward the garden and orchard, was still shuttered, keeping the enclosed air stale with sickroom smells and leaving only lamplight by which to see Lady Blaunche sitting up bolt-straight among the bed-shadows, Master Geoffrey now holding her by both hands, saying to her with warm concern, 'My lady. don't do this to yourself. Whatever happens, whatever comes of it, there are your children to think on. Remember how they need you.'

'My children.' Lady Blaunche flung herself backward onto her pillows, returning to angry tears. 'My children! He's ruined everything for them, too. He's ruined it all. Why don't any of you see that?'

'My lady, what we see is that you're making yourself ill to no good purpose,' Master Geoffrey said, taking her hands again.

This time she clung to him, sobbing, 'But that's just it! There's no good purpose left to anything!'

'My lady . . .'

It did not help that he was hardly as old as Robert. An older man would have maybe had more authority with her. As it was the best he looked likely to manage was pity and Frevisse suspected that Lady Blaunche had already had pity in full measure and running over from her women to no use except to make her want more. Indeed, she now let go one hand from Master Geoffrey and reached out to Frevisse, pleading, 'Dear Dame Frevisse, you understand, don't you?'

Staying where she was, beyond reach, her own hands firmly tucked into her opposite sleeves, Frevisse said calmly, 'Understand what?'

'That I've lost Robert! That I've lost everything and there's nothing left!'

Frevisse gave up her silent prayer for humility and patience – Lady Blaunche was trying for neither, that was certain – and instead said, 'You can hardly say in truth that you've lost Master Fenner. You're still married to him, you're bearing his child. Nor have you even nearly lost everything, only one manor that wasn't yours to have anyway.'

Dame Claire across the room, busy with mixing something into a goblet, looked sharply around at her and Master Geoffrey beside the bed turned his head to stare, while Lady Blaunche on her pillows went rigid, momentarily wordless. Taking advantage of that, Frevisse said to her, unrelenting, 'Master Fenner is dealing with the Allesleys because he loves you more than he loves mere acres. He's doing it because he doesn't want to see you and your children in danger.'

Lady Blaunche shifted to sit violently up against her pillows. 'But the lands are mine!'

'What matters more?' Frevisse returned sharply. 'Land or keeping your children safe?'

Lady Blaunche struck the bedclothes with her fists. 'But he ought to fight the Allesleys! He ought to make them leave me the lands!'

Was she that far from reason, to wish that on her husband? Or was she maybe tiring of all the tears that were doing her no good and ready to be convinced out of it, if only someone would? Not much caring which it was, Frevisse said, 'And risk what might happen to you and the children if he loses? He loves you all far too much for that.'

141

'He doesn't love me,' Lady Blaunche said with despairing bitterness, sinking down again into pity. 'Not anymore.'

'My lady,' Master Geoffrey began, 'you can't . . .'

Lady Blaunche pushed him a little aside, reaching past him with both hands toward Frevisse, who this time gave way and moved into her reach, putting out her own hands for Lady Blaunche to grasp with strength surprising in so 'ailing' a woman. Master Geoffrey, flushing an uncomfortable red, shifted farther aside while Lady Blaunche, her mouth trembling, drew Frevisse close and half-whispered in her ear, 'It's that I'm older than he is. That makes it harder for him to love me.'

Firmly, praying she was right, Frevisse said, 'He loves you.'

'But not as much as I love him,' Lady Blaunche moaned, 'and I'm so afraid of losing him. Look at me. I'm old!' She fell back and rolled over to bury her face in a pillow. '*Old!*'

'My lady.' Master Geoffrey dared to reach out and lay a hand on her shoulder. 'You're bearing his child and are beautiful with it, as you're always beautiful when you're with child. Have no fears there.'

Setting her own doubts aside, Frevisse said, 'And he understands how it is with you this while. He knows all isn't well with you but that it's because you're childing and it will pass.'

Lady Blaunche hiccuped on a sob, rolled over and asked, tear-eyed but willing to be hopeful, 'You think so?' She sat up and reached out for each of them to give her a hand to hold. 'He knows it's not my fault, doesn't he? That I can't help being this way when I'm childing?'

'Of course he knows,' Master Geoffrey said. 'He knows and we pray he understands.'

Lady Blaunche let go of Master Geoffrey's hand to take hold of both of Frevisse's again. 'It's that I've always loved him so much more than he loves me, you see. I wanted him from when I first laid eyes on him.' With a heavy tug she pulled Frevisse closer and said, her voice dropped to almost a whisper and strained with distress, 'But Dame Claire says there mustn't be any more children between us, that I have to keep from him . . .' She broke off, fighting new tears, then choked out, 'Have you ever loved someone like that? Loved him so much you thought you'd die without him? Is it because you lost him that you became a nun?'

'I became a nun,' Frevisse answered, more from impatience than because she cared if Lady Blaunche knew, 'because God was my first and best choice. Not,' she added tartly, 'because he was all I had left.'

Even as she said it, she saw that what had been a simple choice for her was one Lady Blaunche could come nowhere near to understanding. Instead, self-pitying tears swelled in Lady Blaunche's eyes again and she pressed her hands to her face, moaning, 'I wish I'd become a nun. Dear God and St Anne, I wish I had!'

'I once thought of becoming a monk,' Master Geoffrey put in.

It was an expert effort to divert Lady Blaunche, Frevisse saw at once, because Lady Blaunche immediately uncovered her face and turned her head toward him. 'You did, didn't you? I remember you saying so once but not why. Was it for a lost love?'

'I've never been fortunate enough to have a love, let be unfortunate enough to lose her. No, it was near the end of my time at Oxford – my second time at Oxford,' he said with a smile that Lady Blaunche damply matched, showing that his Oxford time was something of a jest between them, 'but happily by then I'd grown wits enough to know that taking up the cloistered life is no little matter and that I was thinking of it more because I was a-feared over what would come to me in the world than because I desired to give myself up to God. So for God's sake and my own, I took courage instead of vows and here I am, most content in your service, my lady.'

He took her near hand, raised and kissed it, and Frevisse saw that there was what Lady Blaunche wanted – to be flattered and made much of, even if only by someone whose place here depended on how well he pleased her. But even more than that, what she wanted was to have her own way, and Robert for maybe the first time in their marriage was not giving it to her. *That*, more than childing and unbalanced humours, was what presently drove her and Frevisse was grateful Dame Claire came then with what she had been mixing and that Lady Blaunche was now sufficiently calmed to do as she was told and drank at Dame Claire's bidding.

She was handing the goblet back when a burst of children's laughter from the parlor made her start. 'I'll quiet them,' Master Geoffrey said, making start for the door.

Lady Blaunche drew herself more straightly up in the bed, and said, 'Yes. No. That's Benedict I hear, isn't it? I want to see him. Bid him come to me.'

Master Geoffrey obeyed, quickly going to open the door a narrow way and say out in a hushed voice, 'Master Benedict, your lady mother is asking for you.'

The laughter cut off except for a final helpless giggle that might have been from John being tickled, and after a pause Master Geoffrey stepped back, opening the door wider for Benedict to come cautiously in. He was flushed and his hair a little tousled and there was still something of the delight in play with his halfling brothers and sister about him, but it left him rapidly as, plainly trying to look like he wanted to be there and equally plainly wishing he was not, he crossed to his mother, took her out-held hands in his, kissed her cheek and asked, 'How is it with you, Mother?'

Lady Blaunche faded back onto her pillows, still holding to one of his hands, answering him faint-voiced, 'None so bad as it was, now you're here. Almost everyone is being very kind but I . . .'

From the solar below them there was a sudden thrum of men's voices and Lady Blaunche stiffened, outrage tightening in her. Benedict as guiltily as if it were his fault, said, 'The Allesleys have come. I was on my way to tell you.'

Lady Blaunche sat straight up again, listening viciously. 'And Ned and those treacherous arbiters, too? They're all there?'

'Yes,' Benedict said. 'Of course.'

Lady Blaunche shifted her grip from his hand to his wrist. 'You go, too. You join them. I want you to be there for what they're doing.'

'Robert said I wasn't—'

'Don't you listen to him. It's you he's ruining as well as me. We'll make him do it to your face. If he wants to play the coward and we can't stop him, at least we won't let him do it behind your back.'

'Lady Blaunche . . .' Frevisse started since no one else looked likely to protest, but Lady Blaunche gave her no heed at all, went on with all her will brought to bear on Benedict, ordering at him, 'You go down there now. You walk into the solar as if you belong there and make them face you while they do this thing.'

'Robert said . . .' Benedict tried again.

'Don't you *listen* to him,' Lady Blaunche repeated fiercely, shaking his arm. 'If you walk in there now as if you belong there, Robert won't send you away. It would look too ill if he did. He won't.'

'He said . . .'

'You *go*,' Lady Blaunche ordered and shoved his arm away from her. '*Go*.'

Benedict went – not happily; Frevisse gave him that – but he went, with a bow to his mother and a quick kiss to her cheek, and Lady Blaunche smiled bitterly after him through her tears.

Chapter 13

The morning's promise of changed weather had built up through the early afternoon into a great black threat of storm, with the first growl of thunder an hour ago setting the servants to shuttering the hall windows while the cloud-brought twilight thickened; and when the storm had broken into pouring rain and fierce wind, Robert had said that everyone – Ned, Allesleys and arbiters alike – was welcome to stay not only to supper but the night since darkness was likely to have come on and the roads be treacherous with mud and flooding before the rain was done. No one had refused his offer and soon thereafter agreed to be done with their work for the day and now, papers and purpose all put away, they were scattered around the solar in comfortable talk, with Robert and Sir Lewis a little apart from the rest, standing at the window, one of the few in the manor with glass, watching the rain-lashed orchard and wind-roiled, low-running clouds without much to say to one another but surprisingly easy in their silence together.

Yesterday they and the arbiters had been feeling their way, both sides trying to judge how reasonable or unreasonable, difficult or undifficult the other side was going to be. What they had found, to their rather disbelief, was that no one on either side was looking to make great trouble and today, from there, they had gone straight into the matter's rights and wrongs, far simpler a task than it might have been because Robert was willing to grant most of the right lay on Sir Lewis' side and most of the wrong on his. That had let the talk come down to debate on whether returning the manor would be enough or whether compensation must needs be made, too. It had helped very little that he had been able to show the manor had gained in worth these past years. Circle and delay though he might, he had been unable to break clear of the straight fact that Sir Lewis meant to have compensation and wanted it to be Katherine.

Worse, Robert had no strong reason he could show for not agreeing to what was so undeniably reasonable; and yet, despite that, he had more than once found himself thinking that he and Sir Lewis could have settled everything between them long since if they had been left to themselves at the outset, could even have been friends.

If not for Blaunche.

If not for Benedict.

The thought slid unwanted into Robert's mind, along with too much of the anger he had been keeping buried all day, beginning with when he had left Blaunche this morning. He had buried it then because it was not something he could afford today, then had to bury it deeper when it wanted to break out at Benedict come into the morning's meeting uninvited, then spent the rest of the day holding it down and only partly because of Benedict. He had to blame himself as well, because like the fool he must essentially be, he had sent Benedict to Blaunche this morning with some thought that it would be a comfort to her to have his company. If nothing else, they could be bitter at him together, but Blaunche, as he should have known she would, had taken the chance to turn the boy into a weapon against him yet again.

Not that Benedict had done much or even said much through the day. But he had been a black-browed presence at the council table, glowering at everybody and everything and at Robert most of all, hardly speaking even when spoken to, until finally everyone had simply left him to his sullen glaring. Robert had tried a while ago, at the end of the day's talks, to be rid of him, telling him, aside, he was to go back upstairs and stay there. Benedict had gone, but he had not stayed. When Drew had asked with due courtesy if he might keep company with Mistress Katherine this while until supper, there had been no courteous reason to refuse him and Robert had sent Gil to ask if Katherine would come down. She had, attended by Mistress Dionisia as was right and with Emelye for good measure. But Benedict had come back with them and was now standing with Katherine and Drew across the solar, supposedly companioning Emelye but with displeasure raw on his face and in every movement. The only hope Robert had was that he seemed to be saying very little, probably because Ned, after trading a look with Robert, had drifted aside from talk with Master Durant to join them, putting himself between Benedict and Drew.

Sir Lewis, his gaze following Robert's across the room but with different thought, said, 'They make a goodly couple.'

'They do,' Robert agreed, knowing he meant Katherine and Drew and managing to sound as if he were glad of it instead of curdled halfway to ill with certainty that tomorrow he would have to give way, would have to sign her over to the Allesleys to make the peace everyone wanted. He tried to hold to the thought that when it was done, it would make an end in more ways than one, and after all Katherine had said she was willing and plainly had no aversion to young Drew. Let agreement be made and the quarrel would be settled and by not much after Easter she'd be gone, he'd not have to see her, ache for her ever again, and that he should be glad it could all be as simple as that. Glad. Not half sick with a grieving made all the worse because he must not – *must not* – in any way show it.

Beside him Sir Lewis said, 'I confess I'm surprised you hadn't married her to Master Benedict long before this.'

Surprised at how easily even he kept his voice, Robert answered, 'It would have suited neither of them, I'm afraid.'

'You'd let that influence you?' Sir Lewis asked, with interest more than disbelief.

'I would,' Robert said simply.

Even before his own feeling for Katherine had arisen and without ever saying clearly to himself why not, he had known he would never marry her to Benedict. Only now, unsettled through these past days to find how thoroughly Benedict was his mother's, had he realized it was more because of Blaunche than because of Benedict. She was not someone he would wish on anyone, as mother-in-law or otherwise, and although when he had first put it to himself so bluntly, it had hurt, the hurt had changed nothing. Naked truth was still truth.

'What then if she had objected to Drew after they met?' Sir Lewis asked. 'Or you had found objection to him. Would you have refused their marriage?'

'Yes,' Robert said, again simply but watching to see how Sir Lewis would react.

Sir Lewis rumbled a laugh. 'And so would I if Drew had objected to her. But what would we have done for a settlement then, in place of the marriage?'

Robert smiled. 'Talked longer.'

'And been called fools by everyone who couldn't see why we weren't taking the short way to the end.'

'Better the long way around and no one in pain at the end of it.'

Sir Lewis sobered. 'As to that, how badly off is this going to leave you when all's said and done?'

That Sir Lewis even thought to ask paused Robert, made him want to make his answer as right as possible, so that it was a moment before he was able to say evenly, 'I'll be no worse off than if the wrong had never been done and I'd never had the lands at all.'

'You'll be out, too, what you could have had for Mistress Katherine's marriage.'

'I will,' Robert agreed.

'You would have been able to get a good price for it.'

'I would have. Now I won't. That's all.'

It was Sir Lewis paused then, before saying soberly, 'There's not many could stand so aside from it as that.'

'Then there's many who would double their losses by paying out to lawyers by the dozen,' Robert returned, and Sir Lewis laughed aloud and again Robert thought how very easy it would be to be friends with him.

They were called to supper then, and at Robert's nod, Gil went upstairs to ask Dame Frevisse and the other nun to it. If Blaunche felt hard done by, left only to Mistress Avys' company, so be it, Robert thought sorely. She could have had Benedict with her if she hadn't chosen to make trouble instead.

While everyone was sorting themselves to their places, Gil returned with Dame Frevisse and Dame Claire and saw them to the place they had had before, at the near end of a lower table. Robert briefly wished for Dame Frevisse's company for himself at the high table; her cool, sometimes tart reasoning at things was surprisingly comforting more often than not; but tonight the best he could hope for was chance to talk with her afterwards and his worry went away to how well the cook had managed with over a score of unexpected men to feed.

There at least he proved to have small need for concern. Despite it must have been chaos in the kitchen for a while and there was only one remove instead of a more formal several, the food was plentiful, with a thick soup of onions, bread and wine and the saltfish that followed well-disguised under a ginger sauce, with greens of some sort (from the kitchen garden already, or from along a handy hedgerow? Robert wondered) with vinegar to dress them, and at the end ginger cakes still warm from the ovens.

They started the meal in torchlit twilight, but by its end the storm and its thunder were growling away into the distance, and when they rose from the high table, the hall loud with the scrape of benches being shoved back and men's voices rising, servants were beginning to set some of the window-tall shutters open to let out the torch smoke. Sir Lewis half-questioningly suggested there was no need after all for him and his men to stay the night, but Robert nodded to the blue-black twilight with, 'Dark is coming on early and the roads will still be foul.' He smiled and added, 'Besides, by now my steward has found bedding and places to sleep for everyone. You wouldn't want him to have gone to the trouble for naught, would you?'

Sir Lewis snorted. 'If he's being turned out of his own bed by our staying, he might not mind our going.'

'He's keeping his bed,' Ned said from Sir Lewis' other side. 'It's his servant is being turned out for me to have his.'

They made jesting talk about who would be sleeping where, moving back toward the solar while they did. Robert thought briefly of excusing himself to go aside to speak to Dame Frevisse but she and Dame Claire were still below the dais, beyond a clot of arbiters and he let the chance go, standing aside to let Sir Lewis pass from the hall ahead of him into the solar where the shutters had been closed across the window now that with the dark there was nothing to see. The fire and lamps had been lighted during supper, making the room welcoming. Later it would be Sir Lewis's, Drew's, and the arbiters' bedchamber but for now it was where they would spend the evening in company, and he and Ned and Sir Lewis drifted, still talking, toward the fireplace, followed by Katherine with Drew on her one side and Benedict on the other, Emelye trailing a little behind and Mistress Dionisia not far off. Robert wondered what chance there was that Benedict would leave quietly if told to go. The trick would be to tell him aside, no one else hearing, so as not to shame him worse than he already thought he was, but soon, before he found a way to make trouble . . .

'Benedict, stop it!' Katherine snapped at something Robert had not heard.

'Don't tell me to stop it,' Benedict snapped back at her. 'I'm not who's making a fool of himself here.'

'Benedict, that's enough,' Robert said, more sharply than he knew he should, and Benedict turned on him as if glad to be unleashed, demanding, 'Enough for who? For you? You're the one who's—'

'Benedict,' Robert said more roughly. 'Enough. Leave now.'

'Because you say so? You spend the day fawning on them' – Benedict gestured with contempt around the room at everyone, including the arbiters just drifted through the doorway from the hall – 'and then expect me take orders from you?'

'Benedict, please,' said Katherine, laying a hand on his arm.

Benedict shoved her hand away, turning on her with equal contempt. 'And you. Robert makes like he's the Allesleys' dog and you like you're a bitch in . . .'

That Drew was nearer was the only reason his hand slapped hard into Benedict's face before Robert's did, hard enough to stagger him sideways, and Robert was there the second afterwards, grabbing hold of Benedict's arm as Benedict made to draw his dagger, shoving him farther aside when he would have gone for Drew, ordering at him, 'Stop it, Benedict!'

Red-faced with rage as well as from Drew's blow, pulling against Robert's hold, Benedict yelled, 'He hit me!'

'Half an instant before I would have,' Robert said back, while seeing from the side of his eye that Mistress Dionisia and Dame Frevisse together were moving Katherine and Emelye away toward the wall.

'You were in the wrong, Benedict,' Ned said, coming to his other side, putting hand to his shoulder. 'Let it be.'

'You saw him hit me!' Benedict protested.

'I saw you earn it,' Ned returned.

Benedict jerked away from him and free of Robert, shoving between them, still intent on reaching Drew who, seemingly as ready for daggers-out as he was, moved to meet him. But Sir Lewis thrust into his son's way and Robert, letting go the frayed hold on his anger, caught Benedict by the arm from behind and spun him around, knocked his hand away from his dagger hilt and seized him with both fists by his doublet's front to shake him hard, once, and then again, saying furiously into his face, 'Stop it. You hear me? Stop it!'

Benedict grabbed him by both wrists, trying to twist free and might have – they were not so far apart in size and strength – but Robert's anger, outstripping even Benedict's, made him for at least the moment the stronger, and keeping his hold, he dragged Benedict closer to him, saying between clenched teeth, 'Stop it, you fool, or I'll break your idiot neck.'

Then Ned and Gil and Master Durant were all there, Ned forcing them apart, saying low and rapidly to Robert, 'Let him go. I'll take him,' and, when Robert had loosed Benedict, Ned put himself between them, making Benedict back off a step, talking now at him as Gil and Master Durant drew Robert off, Gil saying, 'Let be, sir. Let be. It's enough for now.'

His rage already going sick and gray inside him, Robert let himself be herded aside, while assuring Gil and Master Durant he was done. Dame Claire had joined Dame Frevisse and Mistress Dionisia around Katherine and Emelye and three of the arbiters were talking to Sir Lewis and Drew, making sure with words that there would be no sudden flare of trouble from there.

And now Ned had Benedict with an arm around his shoulders friendliwise – though likely Benedict would have trouble breaking his grip if he tried – and was steering him toward the door to the hall, Benedict not resisting him, and Robert could have laughed miserably at how quickly the sudden ugliness was over. Over except for what there would be when next he and Benedict had to deal together.

Over except for when next he had to face Blaunche.

Chapter 14

Frevisse had gone through supper with the unease of watching a dogfight about to happen and hoping very much she would be somewhere else when it finally did. That Benedict would be the cause she had little doubt from watching him through the meal, seeing an edge of rancor behind his sullenness that had not been there before, must have grown through the day spent too close to everything he was hating and probably only made the worse by seeing Katherine and Drew together and apparently glad to be. So when finally his anger broke into the open and he looked likely to come to daggers out with Drew, she moved at almost the same moment as Mistress Dionisia to have Katherine and Emelye out of the way; and then it was over, almost as suddenly as it had started, with no more than snarls and snapping and a sudden backing off, like a dogfight where the dogs decided they didn't want it after all, except that Benedict, being guided toward the hallward door by Master Verney, turned to say venomously back at Robert. 'Give her away then, you coward! But if you think I'm ever going to apologize for any—'

'Your apology,' Robert cut him off, 'is the last thing anyone thinks worth the having.'

It was too angrily said. Benedict started a step back toward him but Master Verney said, warning, 'Benedict,' and Frevisse saw by the flinch of Benedict's eyes that he suddenly realized how many men – and Katherine – were looking at him; saw him start to wish that he was out of there and that he did not know how to do it well, so that all he could manage was to draw himself up straight, shake off Master Verney's hand, and leave with what she guessed he meant to be a proud, stalking walk but was only stiff with offended youth.

Master Verney followed him out, leaving behind them an awkward silence that first one man and then another and then the rest set to filling with talk about anything except what had just past, their voices a little too loud, their words a little jumbled. Emelye began to gabble, too, but Mistress Dionisia shushed her and said to her and Katherine both, 'We'll go upstairs now.'

But Katherine said back, 'Not yet,' and, smiling, went forward to join Robert, Sir Lewis and Drew where they were beginning to share regrets and apologies all around. They broke off for Drew to begin offering the same to Katherine who, smiling, thanked him while gracefully making little of the need for it.

Beside Frevisse, Dame Claire murmured, 'I'm away to Lady Blaunche,' and Frevisse nodded, wondering if she should go, too, but Mistress Dionisia was telling Emelye with a pinch on the arm to make it clear, 'Go make talk, too. Help Katherine.'

Rubbing her arm offendedly, Emelye tried, 'But Benedict might need me,' casting her eyes the way he had gone, looking like a sick doe.

Mistress Dionisia, taking none of that from her, said tartly, 'What Master Benedict needs is the flat of a hand hard along the side of his head, and if you mention him again tonight I'll use the brush on more than your hair come bedtime.' But at the same time she looked to Frevisse for help and, less for Emelye's sake than Katherine's, Frevisse gave a nod of understanding and took Emelye by the arm and with her to Robert's other side as Dame Claire slipped away to the parlor stairs. Not that Frevisse envied her going. If the choice was between being with Lady Blaunche and staying here, here was the better. By a very little.

Katherine was telling a story about a quarrel she and Benedict had had when they were younger – something that led to thorns in his shoes and honey in her hair – as if what had just passed was nothing more than that, and before she had done, she had brought even Robert to laughter, leaving little Frevisse need do but follow her lead in keeping the talk in easy ways, until the evening was at last seemingly back to where it should have been, not much before Mistress Avys came at her best silent servant's glide into the room, made her way with downcast eyes to Mistress Dionisia standing aside near the stairway and whispered something in her ear. Mistress Dionisia in her turn came to Katherine and from behind whispered to her, to which Katherine briefly nodded and said a moment later to Robert, Sir

Lewis and Drew, 'I pray your pardon. I'm asked for. By your leave, I'll withdraw?'

They gave their leave with assurances that they regretted doing so, she curtsied to them, they bowed to her, and with a warm smile particularly to Drew, she left, taking Frevisse and Emelye with her, Mistress Dionisia and Mistress Avys following after, out of the solar and up the stairs. Only when they were in the parlor, with Mistress Dionisia closing the stairway door behind them, did Katherine give way, flinging her hands out violently to either side as if to shove unseen things away from her, before grabbing up her too-full skirts and fleeing across the room to the far side of the settle, to turn at bay and declare, pointing a fierce finger at the bedchamber door, 'I won't go in there. Not tonight. I won't!'

Mistress Avys hurried toward her, making hushing gestures and saying, 'No need. She hasn't asked for you. She didn't even have the children brought to her tonight. It was Dame Claire said you might want rescuing. She said to use Lady Blaunche for an excuse.'

Katherine's defiance dropped away into an open, aching wish to believe her. 'Truly?' she asked. And began to cry.

What sleep Frevisse managed that night was broken sometime by another storm, lightning-driven and thunderous, rolling over the rooftops in the darkness and, later, near to dawn, by another one that was still rumbling away into the distance when she arose and went to set back one of the shutters to the coming day.

Dawn was barely at its gray beginning but the morning air to her deep-drawn breath smelled wonderfully of wet earth and young growing things and she leaned on the windowsill, beginning Prime silently without thought of waking Dame Claire to join her. They had not gone to pray in the chapel last night before bed and had agreed then they would not go this morning, either, the manor being so crowded full of men. It was Sunday and there would surely be Mass said in the chapel by the village priest that they could go to with the family and meanwhile Frevisse's private thought was that a little more sleep would do Dame Claire no harm. The brunt of Lady Blaunche's misery had fallen on her yesterday and last night and there would have been worse if Lady Blaunche had come to hear of what had passed between Robert and Benedict but Dame Claire had forestalled that – for everyone's sake as well as Lady Blaunche's – by mixing a three-times-potent dose of valerian and borage into undi-luted wine and insisting that she drink it all swiftly, at almost a single draught.

Even with that, Lady Blaunche had staved off sleep awhile, but when it finally came Dame Claire had assured Mistress Avys that she would sleep the night through. 'And I wish half the morning, too,' she had added to Frevisse later, on their own way to bed, passing through the solar again where the men were still in talk. 'But that's too much to hope for.'

Frevisse's own thought had been that at least Lady Blaunche's drugged sleep would give Robert chance of a good sleep, too. For herself, she surely felt the better for her own rest, disturbed though it had been by the storms; but she was not ready – never ready – for another day of Lady Blaunche's miseries and tried for now to hold her mind only to the simplicity of the spring dawn and Prime's early prayers until behind her the rustle of mattresses told her Dame Claire and Nurse were waking, with the murmur of a prayer from Dame Claire and then Nurse saying with impatient surprise, 'Here. What are you doing there?'

Frevisse swung around, with light enough now from the growing day to see Anabilla, the nurserymaid, sitting up from a huddle of blan-kets on the floor beside Nurse's bed, rubbing her eyes and answering Nurse's question sleepily with, 'Master Fenner told me to.'

'Master Fenner?' Nurse threw back her covers and rose, reaching for her shift hung from the wall rail above her bed. 'What do you mean Master Fenner told you to?' She dropped her shift swiftly over her head and reached for her gown on the same rail. 'He'd not want the children left alone all night. Get up.'

She prodded Anabilla with her foot and the girl shifted out of her blankets and to her feet in one deft movement, away from the foot, protesting the while, 'He did!' She was fully dressed except for her apron folded neatly on top of a nearby stool and her shoes set under it. 'After you'd gone to bed and the children were asleep but I wasn't yet, he came in and said he'd . . .'

Outside, in the yard, a man yelled, harsh with alarm, whirling Frevisse back to the window. Dawn was swelling over the clear sky but much of the yard was still in shadow and in the time it took her to find the man in the darkness at the foot of the stairs down from the hall, Nurse and Anabilla with Dame Claire only a little behind them joined her in looking out. Even then she could not tell what the fellow was yelling for. There was nothing and no one else in sight . . .

Other men came spilling out the hall door above him, most less than half dressed, their shirttails loose, some without their hosen up, but all of them with some weapon in hand, mostly daggers . . .

Unless that was a shape at his feet that, yes, he was pointing at while he yelled too garbled and away from her for her to make out much of what he was saying but . . .

Frevisse pushed away from the window, past the other women and toward and out the door to their own stairs to the yard, meeting Robert coming from the children's room, his hair disheveled, shrugging into his doublet as he came, his belt with its sheathed dagger in his hand. 'What is it?' he demanded of her, starting down the stairs without waiting for answer. 'All I could see was someone yelling.'

'I don't know,' she answered, following. Her unthinking pattern of dressing as soon as she rose from bed had her already gowned and veiled, able to go out, and she did. Catching up her skirts and running well enough she was able to keep close at Robert's back as he shoved in among the men crowded around whatever was the matter and therefore saw almost as soon as he did that it was someone lying sprawled on the cobbles. Saw, in the next moment, that it was Benedict. And that he was dead.

No one lived with their neck that twisted, their head bent that way.

With a moan Robert went down on his knees, belt and dagger dropped, and reached out toward him but stopped because there was so obviously no use. Instead, his hands fell helplessly back into his lap and, his head moving from side to side, trying to refuse belief, he said, low and in pain, 'No. Blessed Jesus, no. Not this.'

Frevisse looked around for someone who would go to him, take him away from here and begin to give the needed orders, but everyone she could see seemed to be servants or Sir Lewis's men for all she could tell of them. That was to be expected; they were who would have been sleeping in the hall, first to hear the outcry, nearest to come. Some were already going back inside to spread word but others were coming out, both from the hall and from around the yard, and she saw first Sir Lewis and Drew at the hall door and then, to her relief, Master Verney crossing the yard, somewhat more dressed than most, with doublet unfastened but strapping on belt and dagger as he came, shoving in among the men until his first sight of Benedict's body brought him to a halt, pain sharp in his face. But he equally saw Benedict was past any help but prayers and went to take Robert by the shoulders, drawing him to his feet and a few steps backward, saying, 'Come away. You don't need to see more here. I'll do what needs doing.'

Dumbly, Robert shook his head, not letting himself be drawn farther off, not looking away from Benedict's body.

'Come away,' Master Verney insisted and looked around, asking, 'Has anyone gone for the priest?'

From the crowd's back someone answered, 'No need for haste there. That's a dead 'un.'

Master Verney cast a sharp look toward the voice. 'You can take your mouth somewhere else.' He picked a man among the others. 'Raulyn. See to Benedict being taken to his room . . .'

From where she stood close aside from Robert, Frevisse said quietly, 'The body should be looked at before it's moved.'

Without pause Master Verney included her in things with which he needed to deal. 'Dame Frevisse, this is no place for you. Lady Blaunche will need . . .'

Robert straightened out of his friend's hold, drew a ragged breath, said, 'Do as she says, Ned. Look to see if there are any wounds on him.'

'His neck is broken . . .' Master Verney started.

'And we want to be sure that's all that happened to him,' said Frevisse.

Master Verney looked to her, back to Robert, opened his mouth, shut it, rethought whatever else he had been going to say and said instead, 'Yes. You're right,' and, forestalling Robert, added, 'No, not you. I'll do it.'

Clearly not liking what he did any more than Frevisse would have if she had had to do it, he knelt and turned Benedict's body over onto its back, careful of head and arm to keep them from flopping, as if that somehow mitigated the ruin there was of what had been a life.

But there was no more wound or blood or torn clothing to the front than on the back. Nor was there any way to tell how long he might have been lying there by how soaking wet his clothing was all around. With the night's rains and the cobbles runneling water, he could have been lying there a half-hour or eight.

'He's only a little stiffened,' Master Verney said, the words thick with the effort to speak evenly. 'He's been dead a few hours maybe.'

Or he might have been unstiffening, for all they could presently tell, Frevisse did not say. There was such variance in how long it took a body to stiffen and unstiffen, depending on so many things difficult to gauge, that it was only sometimes a useful thing.

'He fell,' someone among the men said. 'Fell and broke his neck in the dark and rain. What else?'

'How long was he in the hall last night after you and he left the solar?' Frevisse asked Master Verney.

'We only passed through. I saw him to his room, talked him a little further down, told him he was best to stay there, and went back to the solar.'

'Did he come back to the hall later?' she asked around at the gathered men. There was a general shaking of heads that he had not. 'Or did anyone see him anywhere else he could have been coming from and out the hall door here?' she persisted.

Men looked around at one another but no one answered, except someone offered, 'He could have been seen by someone not here yet.'

'Or he might have fallen going up the stairs,' another voice put in.

Frevisse did not bother with trying to find who was saying what, just asked of all in general, 'You mean he tripped while going up the stairs, managed to fall all the way down, and landed facing away from them, breaking his neck on the way?'

Hesitancy spread out around her, someone finally saying, uncertainly, 'That's not likely, is it?'

She did not answer that. She was too aware that Master Verney was staring up at her from where he still knelt beside Benedict's body, that Robert had not looked away from her since she had asked her first question, and that she had more to ask. But before she could, Lady Blaunche demanded shrilly from the stairs' head, 'What's happened?'

When whatever half-word of something wrong reached her, she must have been dressing to go to Mass because although her hair was still unbound, she was in a bright azure gown rather than her bedrobe; she had to gather her skirts up in both hands as she started down the stairs, demanding, 'Who is it?'

If she noted Sir Lewis and Drew were there, almost at the stairfoot, turned to look up at her like everyone else – if she even knew what they looked like to know them at all – she gave them no heed as they stepped back out of her way along with the men at the stairfoot, the ones who had been blocking her from view of Benedict's body.

By now there was dawnlight enough she knew immediately what she was seeing and it brought her to a sharp halt on the last step, frozen, disbelieving, until all at the same moment Robert began to move toward her and she began to scream and, screaming, let go her skirts and hurled herself forward. Only Sir Lewis' quick grasp of her arm saved her from falling headlong, gave her balance long enough to fling off his hold and stumble off the last step and time for Robert to be in her way, between her and Benedict's body.

She would have shoved blindly past him but he took hold of her by both arms and said at her past her screaming, 'Blaunche, no! You don't want to see!'

She stopped both her screaming and trying to push past him, stood white and rigid in his hold staring at him, just staring, as if she neither knew nor wanted to know who he was, only wanted him out of her way; and Robert abruptly let her go and stepped aside, leaving her to go forward the few paces more and sink, slowly now, onto her knees beside Benedict's body. There was no sound, from her or anyone, save for the whisper of her skirts as they spread out around her as she knelt and in that silence she reached out first to touch her son's hand lying outstretched on the cobbles near her, as if she would not believe he could be anything other than asleep. Then, slowly, she touched his cheek, first with only her fingertips, then her whole hand cupped against it, her warm flesh to his cold. And then, with a moan beginning somewhere deep inside her, she bent and gathered him into her arms as much as she could, holding him to her breast, his head cradled against her neck, her face pressed to his fair, wet hair as she began to rock him . . . rock him . . . moan . . . and rock him . . .

Chapter 15

Mistress Avys came then in a rush down the stairs with Katherine and Mistress Dionisia behind her, closing in around Lady Blaunche in a mingling of tears and outcry as they realized what they were seeing. Dame Claire came next, from the other way, the men parting from in front of her at her crisp words until she was at Robert's side, could see, too, and looked from Benedict's body, still in his mother's arms, to Frevisse who, feeling as white and rigid as Robert looked, moved her head stiffly from side to side, telling her there was no more hope than there looked to be.

But Lady Blaunche at sight of Dame Claire cried out in wordless plea and Dame Claire went forward, knelt, laid hand on Benedict's chest and touched the side of his throat as if looking for heartbeat that too plainly would never be there again, before she said gently to Lady Blaunche, 'He's gone, my lady. Best let them take him now.'

Clutching Benedict's body closer, Lady Blaunche shrank back from her, looked around desperately for help there could not be and, not finding it, turned her face, her eyes shut, to the sky and the rain-washed dawn and cried out with a high-wrought despair, a cry of the death of all the world's hope, of heart breaking and nothing left but pain and pain and more pain after that.

Someone among the onlookers groaned, 'Oh, God,' and it might have been Robert, but he was the only one who dared finally move toward her, a single step, enough that Lady Blaunche's eyes flew open and fixed on him as if on an enemy, as she screamed at him, 'Stay back from us! He's none of yours! Stay back!' Screamed around her at everyone, 'All of you! Stay back! You can't have him!'

Mistress Avys, weeping openly, laid a hand on her arm, trying, 'My lady . . .'

Lady Blaunche twisted away from her touch, making to shield Benedict's body from her as well as from everyone else, crying, 'He's mine! Leave him alone! Leave him alone!' before she collapsed into weeping and bent over him, her hair sliding forward to make a curtain hiding both his face and hers.

Master Verney and Sir Lewis began motioning and quietly ordering the lookers-on to leave and mostly they went willingly, carrying the drift of manor servants come out from kitchen and stable away with them. It was through the outspread of them drawing off that Master Geoffrey came half-running, his clerk's gown unbelted and lifted out of his way to show bare legs and feet as if he had thrown it on after a hasty rousing from bed. Frevisse saw him catch a man's arm and ask something, then freeze in a long look toward the clot of them still at the stairfoot before gathering himself and coming on with less haste but more purpose, ready by the time he reached Lady Blaunche to kneel down on one knee in front of her and say gently to the top of her head, 'My lady, you have to let him go. He died unshriven . . .'

Meaning Benedict's soul had gone out of him unprotected from all the dangers that came after death.

Robert made a protesting move but Frevisse put out a hand to hold him quiet. Whatever was done now would have to come from somewhere other than him as Lady Blaunche jerked upright at Master Geoffrey's words and turned wild eyes on him while he went on steadily, meeting her gaze, '. . . and he should be in the chapel. We can best make prayers over him there, my lady. He'll be safest there.'

He left off then, giving her time to take it in, waiting while first her sobbing lessened, then stopped, and finally, straightening a little, she looked up through her hair to ask, faint-voiced, 'You'll go with him?'

'I'll go with him,' Master Geoffrey assured her. 'I'll take him there and see everything done that needs to be and then you can come to him.' He went so far as to lay a hand over one of hers and say, gently still, 'Please, my lady.'

Lady Blaunche straightened a little more, her hold on Benedict a little lessening. 'I want . . .' she began.

'You *need* to lie down,' Master Geoffrey said. 'For a little while. Only a little while. For the sake of your other child.' He let his eyes briefly drop toward her middle. 'My lady, please. For your other children, too,' he added, and Frevisse and Robert both, belatedly, looked up toward the still-shuttered nursery window where, blessedly, Nurse must be keeping firm hand, St Nicholas be thanked.

'My lady, please,' Master Geoffrey repeated, and now Dame Claire said gently in echo, 'For only a little while. For your baby's sake.'

Lady Blaunche looked up at her half-blindly for a moment before saying uncertainly, 'Yes.' And when Master Geoffrey made to take Benedict's body from her, she let him, then let Mistress Dionisia and Dame Claire help her to her feet, one holding to either elbow and Dame Claire's arm around her waist to steady her as Master Geoffrey carefully laid Benedict's body down and Master Verney came forward with his doublet off and folded into a pillow to put between Benedict's head and the cobbles, as if somehow that would better things.

Maybe it did. At least Lady Blaunche nodded weakly in thanks while she stared down at Benedict's face a moment more before, crying quietly now, she at last let Dame Claire and Mistress Dionisia turn her away toward the stairs. She stumbled a little over her skirts and Mistress Avys made herself useful by crowding beside Mistress Dionisia to lift them aside for her so that it was all three women helped her up the steps, leaving only Katherine who instead of following came a few steps forward and knelt beside Benedict's body, silently there a long moment with bent head and prayer-clasped hands before, with head still bowed, she rose and went after the other women.

Only Frevisse did not go but stayed with Robert and Master Verney, Master Geoffrey, Gil and two other household men who, when Lady Blaunche was gone inside, came forward at Master Verney's nod and, with Gil, took up Benedict's body. As they moved off, slow with their burden, Master Geoffrey said, 'I'll go with them, to see to . . . things.'

Robert, standing staring at where Benedict had lain, made no answer and Frevisse had no authority for any, but Master Verney, without looking away from Robert, nodded that Master Geoffrey should; and when the clerk followed the three men and Benedict's body away toward the chapel, there was silence then in the emptied yard except for somewhere beyond the walls, in the garden probably, a bird was singing gladness to the morning, until finally Robert drew a deep, aching breath, raised his gaze to Master Verney, and asked, 'Father Laurence?'

'I've sent someone for him.'

'The crowner, too.' The king's officer who had to be summoned to any unexpected, ill-done death to determine if there was wrong and, if there was, where it lay and summon in the sheriff. 'He'll have to come.'

'Master Skipton will see to it someone goes for him,' Master Verney said.

'Oh, God.' Robert pressed his hands over his face. 'Why this? Why to Benedict?'

'Why,' Master Verney said, looking to Frevisse, 'all those questions?'

She held silent, gathering her reasons before she answered, very evenly, 'Because they had to be asked.'

'Because you doubt it was a simple fall down the stairs in the dark and rain?' Master Verney pressed.

'Because I think there's a chance that it wasn't, yes.'

'Why think that?' Master Verney pressed again.

Robert was watching her now, too, and as much to him as to Master Verney she answered, 'Because he made enemies yesterday and now he's dead.'

Robert refused that with a shake of his head. 'No. There's no one here would want him dead.'

'Sir Lewis in fear for his son? His son in anger at everything Benedict said, both to him and at Katherine? You for the same reasons? You,' she said to Master Verney, 'for fear he'd ruin the peace you've been so much a part of making?'

'God's mercy, Dame Frevisse!' Robert protested.

Unrelenting, she persisted, 'There's four without even knowing more than I do about him.'

'That doesn't mean he didn't simply fall,' Master Verney returned. 'Going in or coming out,' he added, remembering her earlier questions.

'How simple a fall could it have been?' Frevisse asked. 'He was lying feet toward the stairs, head away, as if he fell coming down, but no one saw him in the hall last night, for him to be coming out from there.'

'He might have gone by the screens passage to somewhere else.'

'Where?' Frevisse asked.

'The kitchen,' Master Verney said, but doubtfully.

'Why?' Frevisse pursued. 'Wouldn't he have had food and drink already brought to his room for the night? Or if not, why wouldn't he send his man for it?' Which brought to mind a belated thought. 'Where is his man?'

'He doesn't have a servant of his own,' Robert said dully. He bent to take up his dropped belt and dagger and began buckling them on with blindly fumbling fingers. 'His mother thought that since I'd been on my own at Benedict's age, no one serving me, it would do him good to be the same.'

Keeping her thoughts on that to herself, Frevisse said, 'Until more questions can be asked and someone says he was in the hall or some-where else that he could have been coming from and down the stairs, we have to think that if he was on the stairs at all and fell, it had to be while going up them.'

Robert looked up from his belt buckle. 'If he was on the stairs at all?' he repeated.

It had to be to the good that he was coming back enough to have caught that, though there was no pleasure for Frevisse in pointing out, 'To fall while going up the stairs and land at the bottom stretched out and facing away from them as he was would be . . .' She paused to choose a word carefully. '. . . difficult.' To the point of being impossible.

'You think he was pushed?' Master Verney asked, frowning. 'That someone pushed him off the stairs?'

'Or that he was never on them.'

There were other ways than by a fall for necks to be broken but she did not have to say so; Master Verney, catching up to her thought, said on a rising note of disbelief, 'You think he was with someone here and they killed him and left him lying in hopes no one would think he was dead from anything but a fall? Is that what you're saying?'

'I'm saying it could have been that way,' Frevisse said stiffly. 'Or that he could have been killed somewhere else and his body dumped here at the stairfoot to make it look like he died of a fall.'

'That would be dangerous,' Master Verney pointed out. 'There'd be the chance of being seen carrying the body, no matter what hour of the night. There's always folk about.'

'Less chance last night than most times,' Robert said. 'There wasn't a torch or lantern stayed lighted in the downpour and wind gusts there were. Except for when there was lightning, the yard was thick dark, black as pitch.'

'How do you know?' Frevisse asked, not fully keeping sharpness out of her voice.

Master Verney gave her a hard look but Robert only answered, 'When I left Sir Lewis and the others at evening's end, I didn't want to see Blaunche again. I went to the children's chamber to sleep instead of my own bed. It was storming again and the yard was dark then. I doubt anyone bothered with trying to keep anything lit last night. I assuredly gave no order for it.'

'Who would be out in that rain to need the light anyway?' Master Verney said.

Pursuing her own way, Frevisse said, 'So moving Benedict's body would have been a gamble but a fairly safe one and maybe one that had to be taken no matter what if the body couldn't be left where it was.'

'But why kill him at all?' Robert asked on a sudden note of anguish. '*Why?*'

'Because it may be more convenient – or safer – for someone if Benedict is dead,' Frevisse offered.

'As you've already said,' Master Verney put in.

'As I've already said,' Frevisse agreed.

'One of us,' Master Verney said bitterly.

'No!' Robert protested. 'None of us!'

'Then whom?' Frevisse asked.

'He fell,' Master Verney said.

'He didn't fall,' Robert said flatly. 'Dame Frevisse has the right of it. Lying like he was, he couldn't have been going up when he fell, and unless you can find someone who says he came back after you took him out of here, he didn't fall while going down, either, and that leaves only that he was killed by someone and probably somewhere else.' He looked at Frevisse out of far older eyes than he had had yesterday. 'Find out who killed him. The way you did with Sir Walter's mother.'

'That isn't a task to ask of her,' Master Verney said. 'It's for the crowner when he comes.'

Robert had not taken his gaze from Frevisse's face nor she from his. 'She'll do it,' he said. 'Won't you? You've started. Don't stop.'

Frevisse doubted she could have, with his will or without it, because this time yesterday Benedict had been alive and now he was dead, and whatever trouble he had been making yesterday, it had been a trouble that would have passed, would have been dealt with and ended sooner or later, one way or another, and he would have gone on with the rest of his life, to other troubles, surely, but to happinesses, too. To his two years in Master Verney's household and marriage and children of his own and maybe, God willing, even old age.

Now he wouldn't.

Now there was nothing left for him, of him, except the hope his soul would find peace and the certainty that through the years when he should have been living his life, his body would be no more than rotting in a grave.

And, yes, the rights and wrongs of the matter were for the crowner to sift out, but, no, she could not let it rest because – she faced it squarely – she was angry. Very angry. And she asked, without directly answering Robert's question, 'Last night, Master Verney, when you left the solar with Benedict, where did you go with him?'

Master Verney sent a look toward Robert who answered only, 'Please, Ned.'

And though he grimaced in displeasure, Master Verney said, 'I took him to his room. It was the best place to have him out of the way, it seemed.'

'You were there with him awhile?'

'I stayed talking with him until he was quieted and I was sure he'd stay there, not go looking to make trouble again. We talked about having him out of here and into my household as soon as this Allesley matter was settled, instead of waiting until after Easter, and that helped enough that I thought he'd do well if I left him for the night and I did. Alive,' he added pointedly.

Frevisse said nothing to that nor bothered with asking either him or Robert how long it had been before he had returned to the solar. It hardly made a difference how long he had been gone. If one knew how, it took only an instant to break a neck. What mattered was where Master Verney had been later, after everyone was to bed, when Benedict's body had been moved, and she was about to ask him when Katherine came suddenly out of the hall doorway above them, her hair pulled free from its loose night-braid and her eyes wide with fear as she cried down the stairs, shrill with panic, 'Robert, help! Lady Blaunche!'

Chapter 16

With fear lurched into his throat, Robert flung himself up the stairs toward Katherine but she had already spun back inside and he only overtook her in the screens passage, to catch her by the arm and demand, 'What is it?'

Face flushed, Katherine said in a desperate rush, 'She's gone mad. We can't stop her. Dame Claire said you were to come,' and would have pulled away from him then but he was quicker than she was, past her and into the hall where her own headlong coming to find him had left a startlement behind her and a clear path among the men that he took at a run, bursting into the solar and across it hardly aware there were men there, too, but he heard Blaunche's screaming before he was to the stairs and hurled himself up their dark spiral, not knowing what he expected to find but finding it soon enough as he burst into the parlor where everything was witness that Blaunche had gone from numb grieving into grief's high rage, with every cushion thrown from settle and window bench, joint stools smashed to pieces against the floor or into a wall, his chair heaved over on its back, the tapestry pulled half down, and Blaunche standing, her back to him, in the midst of it all, briefly out of breath for screaming but looking about her for more to do.

The women, even Dame Claire, were all driven back to the walls, Emelye clutching a torn cushion to her, sobbing uselessly, Mistress Avys crying out, 'My lady, you're childing! Pity the baby! Please!'

'Pity?' Blaunche gasped out at her. 'On the baby? Pity? If it dies before it's ever born, that's pity. You stupid woman. They're all going to die. All my babies. Soon or later, they'll all be . . .' She ran out of breath, dropped to her knees and beat with white-knuckled fists against the floor until she could gasp out, 'They're all going to be dead. Dead. All of them. That's . . . all . . . there . . . is! Like Benedict!'

'My lady . . .' Mistress Avys sobbed, taking a step away from the wall.

Blaunche turned wild eyes on her, stopped her where she was and said, cold with a sudden, horribly false calm, 'I told you . . . to bring them to me. I told you . . . I want . . . to see my children.'

'My lady, I don't think—'

'No, you don't think!' Blaunche stumbled to her feet, back into her rage. 'And you don't know. You've never gone through having children, only to find out that it's all for nothing. That all it comes to is that they die!' Wrenching her skirts aside from her feet with angry hands, she lurched toward the corner where the children's toys were chested and Robert came loose from his frozen horror to follow her, unsure how much he should try to quiet her or whether it was better to let her wear her anger and herself out, until she threw open the toy chest's lid, slamming it back against the wall, and grabbed out the first thing that came to hand, Tacine's doll, and began smashing it down against the chest's edge, screaming, 'Like this!' Gasping with the force of her blows. 'All of it . . . all of it . . . for nothing. For . . . *nothing*.'

She gave over beating it, began wrenching with all her strength to pull off its arm and might have except Robert caught hold of her from behind, wrapped his arms around her to pin her arms to her body – knowing even as he did it that he did it more for Tacine's sake than hers – saying with what he meant to be gentleness, 'Blaunche, no. There's no need. Let be.'

Blaunche dropped the doll and twisted around, breaking his hold and reaching for his throat all in a single swift movement so that only barely in time he jerked backward and caught her by the wrists, pushing her away to arm's length as she tried to come at his face with claw-crooked fingers. Then both nuns were there, Dame Frevisse taking hold of Blaunche from one side, Dame Claire from the other, pulling her arms roughly down, out of his hold, Dame Frevisse saying, 'That's enough, Lady Blaunche! Enough!'

Too blind with her mind's pain to care whom she hurt along with herself so long as it was someone, Blaunche fought against their hold as fiercely as she had fought against Robert and he was trying to find a way to catch hold of her again and help them when unexpectedly Master Geoffrey was there, pushing him aside with, 'Pray, pardon me,' reaching between the nuns to grip Blaunche strongly by the shoulders and brace her to stillness, saying at her, his voice rich with calm and the certainty she would obey him, 'My lady, stop it. My lady, that's enough. Stop.'

And for a wonder she did: went still and stood with head down and breast heaving for half a dozen breaths before slowly she looked up at him through the tangle of her hair.

'Enough for now,' Master Geoffrey said. 'Yes?' And when she did not protest that, he took her by both hands and from the nuns' hold and led her toward the window seat.

Mistress Dionisia, nearest to it, snatched cushions from the floor to put on it before they reached it and moved well aside, leaving Master Geoffrey to sit Blaunche down, then sit down beside her and, still holding her hands, begin to talk to her low and soothingly.

Robert, half-dazed, looked at Dame Frevisse and found her looking back at him with seemingly no more words in her than he had in him. It was Dame Claire, looking at a long scratch on the back of her left hand, who said quietly, for no one except him and Dame Frevisse to hear, 'She must not be let near the children. Not for any reason.'

'No,' Robert agreed and heard his voice hoarse on the word.

'Nor left alone,' Dame Claire said.

'Nor left alone,' Robert echoed, looking back to Blaunche where she sat clinging to Master Geoffrey's hands, head still bowed, still mercifully quiet.

Looking the same way, Dame Claire said, 'She'll be calm for a time now but she's not done. She's worn herself out is all. She'll likely begin again when she can.'

Afraid of exactly that, Robert asked, 'Can't you give her anything to keep her from it?'

'What I have is meant for soothing in the ordinary way of things, not this. I'll try, but if you could send to Coventry, or Northampton maybe, for poppy syrup, that would do the most good, the way she is now.'

'Whoever goes won't be back until late tomorrow with it even at the best,' Robert said, heart sinking.

'Better late tomorrow than not at all,' Dame Claire returned. 'Will you send?'

'Yes.' Of course he would, for that and anything else she asked for, if only it would dull the edge of Blaunche's pain, keep her from rage.

Across the room Mistress Dionisia and Mistress Avys had begun warily to pick up the flung and fallen things – the sewing basket looked to be past rescue and so did most of the joint stools, Robert noted with a corner of his mind – while Emelye had sunk down to the floor in a puddle of skirts and tears in the corner beyond the settle and Katherine was gone to kneel beside her, patting her arm and saying things to her.

'And in the meanwhile keep her from the children,' Dame Claire repeated.

Robert nodded, his throat thick with feelings for which he had no clear words. Too many feelings. Of grief for Benedict. Of fear for . . . and fear *of* . . . Blaunche. And fear and grief and worry for Robin, John and Tacine who would have to be told Benedict was dead and brought to understand it; and he was the one who would have to do it because there was no one else. He would have to tell them that their half brother was dead and help them understand it and find some way to keep from them that their mother was near to mad, in the worst sense of the word . . .

'This will pass,' Dame Claire said. 'Her rage. It will pass and she'll better. This isn't forever.'

Wasn't it? Robert thought. Benedict's death was forever. Why not his mother's grief and rage? But all he said aloud was, 'I pray you pardon me. I'd best go to the children.'

Frevisse stayed standing alone only a few moments longer when Robert had left and Dame Claire gone away to Lady Blaunche, watching Mistress Dionisia and Mistress Avys put the room to rights as best they could be but feeling no urge to help them at it, or Katherine with Emelye, or anyone with Lady Blaunche. What she wanted was to know why Benedict was dead and by whose hand and she left the parlor, taking her thoughts with her, only to find on the shadowed mid-curve of the stairs, out of sight from top or bottom, Robert standing with head and shoulders bowed and one hand braced against the wall, looking as if suddenly he had lost all strength to go on. Guessing he had not heard her soft-soled footfall and not wanting to startle or seem to spy on him, she said quietly, to go unheard by anyone above or below them, 'Robert.'

By the small daylight through a narrow arrow-gap in the wall there, she saw his shoulders lift as he took a steadying breath before he raised his head and turned it to look at her over his right shoulder, his face too much in shadow for her to read it clearly, but there was only weariness in his voice as he said, 'I'm sorry for all of that. I'm sorry you had to be part of it. I'm . . . sorry.'

Carefully, trying for what comfort there could be, Frevisse said, 'Despite what she does, your wife loves you very much I think.'

'With her whole heart,' Robert agreed wearily. 'Her children and I, we're her life.'

'But she's not yours,' Frevisse said before she realized she should not.

But Robert only shook his head, too weary to more than simply agree, saying low and achingly, 'No, she's not. And to make it worse, there was nothing, no reason why I shouldn't have loved her as wholly as she loves me.'

'Except?'

'Except I simply don't. There's no reason why, no great flaw on either side. She simply . . . we simply don't suit each other well. It's nothing more than that and my fault as much as hers.'

'There's no fault, Robert, in what can't be helped.'

'Maybe not. But there's nothing to be done about it, either, except what I've been doing all these years – enduring it. And it's not that I don't love her in some way. For all she's done for me, given me. But, oh God! I wish I wasn't married to her!' His fisted hand flew out and struck against the stairway's stone wall as he cried out, whisper-low but with a pain that had nothing to do with how much he must have hurt his hand, 'At least Katherine will have better . . .' He hit the wall again. '. . . with Drew Allesley. But damn Blaunche for bringing us all to this. And damn whoever was Benedict's death. And damn me!'

'Robert,' Frevisse began, catching hold of his arm before he struck the wall again, and as suddenly back under control as he had been out of it, Robert let his arm fall to his side, out of her hold, and shook his head, refusing anything she might say with, 'No. I know. All that's no use. All we can do is what we're doing. All I can do is what I'm doing, and when it's over and there are no more choices to be made, it will all be right again. As right as it's ever going to be.' And then, 'I have to go to the children.'

'Let me go ahead of you,' Frevisse said quickly. 'Whoever is in the solar will want to be told things. Let me tell them while you go on to your children.'

Robert paused. 'Would you? Thank you, yes, that would help.'

He pressed his back to the stairway's center post, making room for her to crowd past him. It was when she was a step below him that he said in a tightly miserable voice, 'With it all, I haven't even had chance to start mourning him.'

As best she could on the stairs' narrowness, Frevisse turned back to him, said gently without need to think about her answer, 'You've been mourning him every moment since you saw him dead. What you've lacked is time to give way to it and that will come.'

'It will, won't it?' Robert said, bitter with pain past and to come. 'Time and enough. All the rest of my life. Our lives. Blaunche's and mine.'

Because there was nothing but useless agreement to say to that, Frevisse laid a hand briefly on his arm, turned from him and went on down the stairs and into the solar where the Allesleys, arbiters and Master Verney were drawn away to the room's other end, standing around the table making their breakfast from bread and ale and bowls of something probably left over from last night's supper set out there. It would have been well if Robert ate, too, but better if he went straight on to his children without having to deal with anyone else, and as the men looked up, first toward her, then past her, she made a bustle of her going, beginning an excuse on Robert's behalf, distracting them while she heard behind her the door toward the nursery open and close, telling her Robert was safely away as Sir Lewis Allesley said, bringing his glance back to her, 'No, assuredly, we understand perfectly. If we didn't have to be here for the crowner's coming, we'd no more than tell Master Fenner everything over the manor can be settled later and take ourselves off home today.'

'It might be best if we at least went back to the grange and Master Verney's,' suggested one of the arbiters. 'It would put us out of the way and we can be sent for when the crowner comes.' Which could be several days if he was well away elsewhere in the shire or tomorrow if he was near.

'I'd like the chance to speak with Katherine before we go,' Drew put quickly in, but Master Verney was already saying, 'There's no haste about our going, I think,' and Frevisse on his words' heels, lest she have no other chance, asked of them all,

'Did any of you see Master Benedict after he left here with Master Verney last night?'

There was pause then, the men looking among themselves to see what everyone else was going to say, before heads began to shake that, no, none of them had.

She had not supposed so. Among the last places Benedict would have likely come last night was back into the solar but it was better to ask and be sure. What she wanted now was to talk alone with Master Verney and asked him, 'Sir, I must needs do something for Master Fenner. Would you come with me to help?'

'Assuredly, my lady.'

He started toward her and Frevisse started to turn away, but Sir Lewis asked, 'How is it with Lady Blaunche?'

Frevisse paused before facing him again. 'Not well,' she answered because that much they would have guessed from what they must have heard when Lady Blaunche was at her worst.

'Is there anything we can do?' Sir Lewis asked.

Again Frevisse paused, then said, 'Pray.'

Sir Lewis nodded sad understanding to that and she went out, Master Verney holding the door open for her into the hall and following her as she passed among the clots of talking men taking their breakfasts from a hastily set up trestle table in the hall's midst. Talk fell away and heads turned to watch them but no one offered to stop them or ask questions. It was Master Verney, at her side as they neared the hall's far end, who said, 'Have you eaten yet this morning?'

Frevisse came to a halt, realizing she had been ignoring the soft, insistent roiling in her stomach, and said, 'No, I haven't.'

'Allow me,' Master Verney said and went aside to the table, to take up a thick, crusted piece of bread and pour ale into a wooden cup, saying as he brought them back to her. 'No butter or meat, I think?'

'No. Thank you,' she said, truly grateful to be fed because, now that she had been brought to notice, she found she was light-headed as well as empty-stomached, and while fasting was all very well, making oneself ill with it was not. But she walked on while she ate, through the screens passage and out to the head of the stairs to the yard.

As she stopped there, looking down at where Benedict's body had lain, the slow toll of the village church's bell fell clear and heavy on the washed morning air, a single stroke, followed by a long pause, followed by another stroke, counting out the years of

Benedict's life. Starting down the stairs, Frevisse asked, 'How old was he?'

'He turned nineteen the morrow of last St Hilary's,' Master Verney said.

Not even twenty years of life. Not even twenty tolls of his passing bell. Too few, she thought.

As the bell tolled again Master Verney asked, 'For what do you need me, my lady?'

'For your authority. Robert set me to find out Benedict's murderer . . .'

'You'd already set about that before he bid you to it.'

And Master Verney was still not happy about that, but his happiness or unhappiness did not concern her and she only said, 'Yes. And now I need someone with me who'll say I'm bid to it. Someone who can tell me things. Do you think Gil would do well at asking questions I need answered among the servants?'

'As well as anyone,' Master Verney said tersely. 'He has authority as Robert's man and he's liked.'

'Will I find him still with Benedict's body?'

'Very likely.'

That would make it possible to take care of two things at once and when they had crossed the yard to the chapel Gil was indeed still there, along with a priest she presumed was Father Laurence from the village, kneeling in prayer at the altar, and three household servants helping with what needed doing with Benedict's body. It was more usual for the dead to be tended to elsewhere and then brought to sanctuary but Benedict's unshriven death made necessary all the hallowing that could be managed. Or at least so Father Laurence must think or he'd not have allowed trestles and boards to have been brought and set up and Benedict's body to lie there for the men to strip and wash and shroud. It would be dressed for burial, likely, but that could not happen until the crowner had viewed it, so shrouding was all there would be for a while, but just now Gil was overseeing the stripping of the body, with basins of water already set by for the washing, and he looked around when Frevisse and Master Verney came in, to say without other greeting, 'It's for the women to do, I know, but I thought his mother . . .'

He made an uneasy shrug and did not need to finish. There was no possible way Lady Blaunche should have part in this, and her women who would have helped were needed with her and Master Verney said, 'It's better you see to it, yes. Thank you. Gil, Robert has bid Dame Frevisse ask questions about Benedict. About his death. She wants your help with it.'

'About his death?' Gil's unhappy look shifted to Frevisse and deepened toward a frown. 'You were asking questions before, my lady. Like you didn't think it was just a fall.'

'Do you think it was?' Frevisse returned.

Gil frowned more, holding on to his answer before finally saying, 'No. Not the way you were looking at things there in the yard. A fall doesn't make sense. Might have happened but even more might not have, when you come to think about it.'

'Have you found anything about the body that might show what else could have happened? Scrapes? Bruises'? Even a broken bone or bones?'

'Nothing, my lady,' Gil said firmly. 'There's just his neck and it's snapped as neat as doing a dry twig.'

He tried to say it straightly but his mouth wried out of shape and he swallowed thickly, as if keeping down bile.

Frevisse shared his feeling and made no move to look at Benedict's body herself, only said to the men now starting to wash it, 'Nor you? You've seen nothing?'

'Nothing, my lady,' one of them answered and the others bobbed heads in agreement.

'Come outside for a moment, please, Gil. Master Verney.'

She led the way back outside and enough away from the chapel's door that no one could overhear as she said to Gil, 'Will you ask questions for me? For Master Fenner?'

Gil glanced toward Master Verney, who very slightly nodded, before answering, 'Aye.'

'And tell me what you learn before you tell anyone else.'

Gil paused again but without the look to Master Verney before he agreed, 'If that's what Master Fenner wants. What are you wanting me to ask?'

'First, did anyone see Master Benedict anywhere after he left the solar with Master Verney last night? Anyone. Anywhere. And if they did, when? Did any servants go to Benedict's room after the night-food was left there? If they did, was he there and was anyone with him? Understand?'

'You want to know where he was and who he was with last night,' Gil said.

'Yes,' Frevisse answered, relieved that he had wit enough for what she was asking of him. 'I also want to know who was seen moving in the yard last night.'

Gil made a short noise. 'Nobody who didn't have to be, that's sure. Oh.' He gave her a sharper look than he had before. 'And if there's someone who was who can't give a good reason why he was there, he's maybe who did for Master Benedict.'

'Yes.'

Now that he saw the purpose and that there was sense to it, he said with more intent, 'What else, then?'

'Find out if anyone saw to keeping the lanterns lighted in the yard after it started to storm.' Robert had said not but he would not have known for certain after he was to the children's chamber. 'Whoever might have tried to do that might have noticed something. And ask if anyone heard any kind of outcry, whether it seemed to do with this or not.'

'You don't get much outcry with a broken neck,' Gil said glumly, 'and even if there was, there was thunder and rain enough at times to cover a cry if it came then.'

'I know, but asking won't do harm.'

'You care if folk catch on to why I'm asking?'

'I don't see how they can be kept from it.'

'Nor me,' Gil agreed. 'What else?'

There was nothing else she had thought of, but before she could say so, Master Verney said, 'Here's Robert,' and Frevisse turned to see him coming along the yard from the nursery stairway and Master Verney asked as he came near enough, before she could, 'The children?'

'Weeping,' Robert said.

Frevisse thought it would be better for him if he wept, too, but all he looked was gray and somewhere else in his thoughts. 'I've come to be with Benedict a time. Until I'm needed elsewhere.'

'That's good, then,' Gil said in the over-hearty way of someone trying to show sympathy without being soft about it. 'Dame Frevisse says I'm to set to asking questions and it's not right he be left to no one of his own.'

'I'll be here,' Robert said dully, and then, come to sudden remembrance of it, 'Poppy syrup. Dame Claire asked for it. Will you see to telling Master Skipton to send someone to Coventry for it at all speed?'

'Right off,' Gil said.

'Mistress Katherine,' Master Verney put in, and they all looked again along the yard to where she was coming, likewise from the direction of the nursery stairs, head down as she picked her way around the puddles, her skirts lifted awkwardly because she carried a folded cloth over one arm. She had taken time to comb her hair and braid it severely back from her face but had not changed from her plain gown nor, probably, to judge how she matched Robert for gray- ness, had anything to eat, and despite that her face was calm enough as she reached them, her red-rimmed eyes betrayed she had been crying not long before, and Robert asked, not keeping fear from his voice, 'Is anything the worse?'

'She's quieter,' Katherine answered. 'Exhaustion, Dame Claire says. She – Lady Blaunche – sent me with this.' She laid a hand on the folded cloth. 'To shroud him.' She swallowed on tears. 'She said I'm to stay and pray by him because he shouldn't be alone, she says.'

'That's to the good, then,' said Gil, still over-hearty. 'It's what Master Fenner has come for, too.'

'Better you're both here for him,' Master Verney added more quietly, 'and neither of you alone.'

Frevisse silently agreed that for plain kindness' sake, they should neither of them have to be alone just now, but as Robert with no word of his own took the cloth from Katherine and stood aside with a small gesture for her to go ahead of him into the chapel, Frevisse heard in her mind, unbidden, all there had been in his cry of Katherine's name on the stairs a little while ago and had a treacherous thought that on the other hand maybe it was better they not be alone together. There had been something in the way he had said Katherine's name . . .

She cut the thought off. It was something Robert did not deserve, nor Katherine, and she said to Gil as he started to bow before going off on his given business, 'Before anything else, bring food and wine for Master Fenner and Mistress Katherine, please.'

'First thing of all,' he said, his look showing he was beginning to approve of her.

'And when you meet up with the steward, tell him I want to talk with him as soon as may be.'

'Yes, my lady.'

He bowed and left and she realized that the village bell had some-time ceased its tolling of Benedict's years without her noticing and said to Master Verney with a tiredness of heart she hoped she hid, 'Would you show me to Benedict's chamber, please?'

Chapter 17

Frevisse let go by that she would be alone in Benedict's room with a man, against the rules that should govern her. There were times for heeding rules and times for not, she had found, and while following Master Verney to a near doorway, a match for the one to the nursery stairs and her own chamber, she deemed this was a time for not, whatever confession and penance she might have to do for it afterwards.

'These are storerooms here,' he said, nodding toward the doors on either side and starting up the stairs. 'Benedict's room is above.'

'And Master Geoffrey's,' Frevisse said, remembering.

'Even so.'

Both doors were closed and Master Verney had his hand raised to knock at Benedict's before, with the sharpness of bitter remembering, he jerked back, swore under his breath, and opened the door with more violence than needed for anything except to relieve his feelings. Saying nothing because what was there to say, Frevisse followed him in. Master Verney had liked Benedict enough to ask him into his household for two years, been near enough to him to be able to talk him out of the solar last night when possibly no one else could have. Now all that was left was Benedict's body lying in the chapel and the emptiness of a room to which he would never come back.

Frevisse took hard hold on the practical thought that it was not truly an empty room. It was furnished with bed and table, chair, stools, chests, a fireplace on the outer wall, all much the way her own was but more lavishly, as befitted the household's heir, and with the clutter of a young man with only himself to satisfy. A sheathed sword hung by its belt from one bedpost. A boot lay on the floor at the bed's foot, its mate nowhere in sight. Clothing was heaped disorderly on the chest it should probably have been in and other clothing was in a smaller heap on the floor beside the table where a tray with pitcher and cloth-covered plate shared the tabletop with a wooden horse on wheels with one wheel broken off and in two but ready to be mended with gluepot and tools waiting to hand.

Seeing where she was looking, Master Verney said, 'John's. He's ever too hard on his toys and Benedict was ever mending them.'

Frevisse nodded and went on looking. In a corner a cluster of fishing poles leaned against the wall, most of them far too short for Benedict's likely use – had he taken his little half brothers and sister fishing with them or were they something kept from his own childhood, not so long past? – and on a stool beside the bedhead there were two books and a candle stub in a holder. Because books were something she never resisted, she went and picked them up, found one was a leather-bound book of devotions that looked little used and the other a well-worn copy of chivalrous tales.

'Robert gave him that when he and Blaunche married,' Master Verney said. 'A wedding present, he told Benedict. It was the first book anyone had ever given him, I think.'

'And the devotions?'

'From his mother a few Christmases ago.'

It was easy to see which had mattered the most to Benedict but at least he had kept both to hand and with a feeling of fellowship toward Benedict that she had never expected to have, Frevisse put them down exactly where they had been and said, 'The food and drink on the table. Were they there when you came in with Benedict from the solar last night?'

'Yes.'

No servant had come in with them later, then, and that meant that so far as was known, Master Verney had been the last person here with Benedict. She went to lift the cloth, uncovering a thick, folded slice of bread with honey soaked through it and a square-cut piece of ginger cake, and looked in the pitcher and the goblet standing next to it. 'Nothing eaten and only a little of the ale gone. Did he drink it while you were here?'

Master Verney shook his head. 'We talked is all and finally he asked me to leave him alone. He was tired and I think ashamed and disappointed in himself. He wanted to be alone, he said, and I left him sitting on the edge of the bed.'

181

If everything he had told her was the truth, it meant that, so far as was known, Master Verney had been the last person here with Benedict until his murderer came or Benedict went out and was killed elsewhere.

Equally, until she had some thought as to why someone would have killed him, she had to assume, firstly, until she was certain they could not have, that anyone might have done it and, secondly, until she was certain they were not, that anyone could be lying to her. Including Master Verney.

But she kept that to herself as she touched her foot against the little heap of clothing beside the table, then bent to feel of it and said, 'Everything is wet.'

'It was downpouring when we crossed the yard. He changed out of his soaked clothes while we were talking.'

'What did you do?'

'I stood by the door and dripped.'

As would anyone who came into the room last night. There were still puddled places on the floorboards that would tell her nothing, she supposed, for the same reason that there was no use looking for wet clothing to tell who else had been here or met Benedict elsewhere and either killed him at the stairfoot or carried his body there, supposing it had been raining at the time and not between storms. Whatever the way of it had been, with all of last night's rain the murderer would not be the only man in Brinskep Manor with wet clothes today.

Unless the wet clothing belonged to someone who had had no reason to be out in the rain, no reason to be wet.

She should have had Gil ask questions toward learning that, too, would bid him do so when next she saw him. And there was also need, now she thought of it, to find if anyone had taken a message from Benedict to someone. Supposing they arranged to meet in the screens passage, there was chance no one else might have known Benedict was there. When it was late enough, people would be more likely sleeping than wandering and the screens passage was a somewhat possible place for privacy. In which case Benedict lying at the stairfoot dead might have come about by accident after all.

But whomever he had met with would have said something about meeting with him by now. Unless they had immediately seen the danger of being unfairly accused of his murder and held silent. Or they might actually have killed him and were holding silent for even better reason.

But even so, whoever had been messenger between them would have spoken out by now. Or should have. And she would have to go on doubting Benedict had been back to the hall last night and believing that, whatever had happened, it had very possibly happened here. Where there was nothing that told her anything.

'Dame Frevisse?' Master Verney asked.

She came back from her thinking with a start. 'Yes. I'm nearly done.' But she went to look under the bed where there was surprisingly little dust but the missing boot and a small, lidded box shoved against the wall at the head of the bed. Leaving the boot and dust where they were, Frevisse drew out the box, set it on the bed and opened it. Inside, at first look, was nothing much, a mere jumble of things, but Master Verney had crossed the room to join her and now drew a painful breath, reached out and laid his fingertips on a small coil of red-dyed leather. 'Dasher's leash,' he said thickly. 'A greyhound his mother had when Benedict was small. We use to joke they teethed on each other. Benedict grew up and Dasher grew old and here . . .' There were tears on his cheek but there was no shame in crying and he did not bother with wiping them away, instead found and took up something else that looked like nothing much but had mattered enough to Benedict to keep, a two-inch length of chipped flint, neatly crafted into an arrowhead. 'We found this one day along the stream when he was maybe ten years old. I told him how such a thing is supposed to be the tip of a thunderbolt, left behind when lightning strikes down to the ground. I didn't know . . . he'd . . . kept it.'

Master Verney turned sharply and crossed the room away from her, to stand facing the wall. He took the arrowhead with him, clenched in his hand, Frevisse noted but did not say, only closed the box carefully and put it back where it had been under the bed. Every child had such a box or its like, Frevisse suspected. Hers had been very small, hardly larger than her child-hand, because there had been hardly room to spare among her parents' travelling necessities for anything not needed simply to live but she had kept it and its 'treasures' right up to the day she had known, fully and irrevocably, that she would go into a nunnery. That day, with her choice whole and certain in her, she had gone off alone with her box, the last thing she had in all the world that was all her own, the last thing left to her

183

from her parents, and had carefully chosen a place no one would likely ever dig but she could find again if ever she wanted to – knowing even then she never would – and buried it and its 'treasures' as some sort of final parting from everything her life had been until then.

The kind of parting Benedict had been given no chance to make.

The sound of someone coming up the stairs drew her from her thoughts. She straightened from beside the bed and turned to the door as a man paused in the doorway, saw first her, then Master Verney, and said, 'Gil said I was wanted here?' uncertain not about Gil but about why he was wanted.

Master Verney, tucking the arrowhead into his belt pouch and not minding it was plain he had been crying, said, 'Master Fenner has given Dame Frevisse leave to ask questions about Master Benedict's death. She has some for you, Master Skipton, if you please.'

The steward was a small-bodied, black-haired man, brisk and sharp-eyed, and he nodded crisply, used to obeying authority as well as wielding it. 'Whatever is needed, my lady. We – the household – are greatly grieved for his death.'

'He was liked?' Frevisse asked, realizing there were signs of crying to Master Skipton's eyes, too.

'He was.'

The simplicity of the answer as well as its vigor told her something more about Benedict – that what little she had seen of him must have been the worst. And that worst had been the errors of a young man not yet fully formed in judgment and that was something only time could mend in everyone. Time Benedict had not been given. Those who had known him longest, known him best, had thought well enough of him to care deeply he was dead, and that meant they would help the more willingly toward finding his murderer and she said, 'I need you to tell me where everyone slept last night. The Allesleys, the arbiters, Master Verney, all the men that came with them, and the rest of the household.'

Master Skipton drew a deep breath, as if in-gathering his thoughts along with air enough to tell them, and said, 'Sir Lewis and Master Drew and all the arbiters slept in the solar, crowded but private and with no need for them to go out into the rain. Master Verney spent the night in my chamber. His men and the others slept in the hall, except for those who chose to sleep in the stables . . .'

'Some did?'

184

'Two, I think. They had horses the storm made restless, I understand.'

'And the household?'

'Wherever they usually sleep, so far as I know. The kitchen for some. In the hall for others. Some share a chamber on the yard's east side, where my own is, and there are two married couples have rooms of their own there, too.'

'Has there been any talk of anyone not being where they should have been or seen in an unlikely place last night?'

'No.'

'You're certain?'

'Not that's come to my ears but I can ask.'

'Please do,' said Frevisse. 'Was anyone charged with keeping the lanterns lighted in the yard last night?'

'No. They weren't likely to stay lighted for long with the wind there was and who would be out in the storm to need them?'

And whoever had been out, dealing with Benedict's death and body, had preferred the darkness, surely, Frevisse thought and went on, 'After the night-food was brought, did any other servant come here last night, that you know of?'

'No. But I'll ask, if you like.'

'Thank you. Ask, too, if you will, if anyone took a message to Benedict, or from him, last night. And ask if any of the servants noticed that someone who stayed the night where there was no need for them to be out in the rain – in the hall or solar or wherever – had wet clothing this morning.'

Master Skipton's quickened face told Frevisse he understood immediately why she asked that, but all he said was, 'Yes, my lady.'

'And this for both of you,' she said, including Master Verney with a look. 'Did Master Benedict have any. . .' She thought about what word to use. '. . . interest in anyone, a woman or girl, here? Or anywhere,' she added for good measure.

'No,' Master Skipton said. 'None.'

Master Verney was more forthcoming. 'His mother would have heard of it soon enough by way of Mistress Avys and put a stop to it within the hour.'

That closed off the only other course of questioning she had except for, 'One thing more, Master Skipton.' She fixed him with a straight look, to watch as much as hear his answer. 'Did Master Verney stay in your chamber and not leave at any time until the morning?'

Master Skipton's answer was unhesitating. 'Yes.'

'You're certain?'

'Yes.'

'What time did he come to bed?'

'He was there before I was, because I had all the usual evening business of making certain doors were barred and fires covered before I was done for the day as well as making sure as much had been done as could be for our guests, but he left the solar when the Allesleys and arbiters were set to ready to bed.'

'I went back to the hall after leaving Benedict here, dried a little by the fire there, then returned to the solar,' Master Verney said evenly, though he had to know why she was asking where he had been and when last night. 'I thought not to leave Robert to it alone, helped keep up the talk until the evening's end, and left when he did, went from there directly to Master Skipton's room and, yes, stayed there until morning.'

'And Robert?' Frevisse asked evenly.

'Robert?' For the first time Master Verney slightly bridled. 'What about Robert?'

'Where did he go? Do you know?'

'He went with me as far as the yard,' Master Verney said stiffly. 'We parted at the foot of the stairs.' He stopped, the odd look on his face telling her that the same thing was crossing his mind as hers: they had been standing then where Benedict's body was found next morning. But Master Verney steadied and went on, 'He said he was going to see the children, maybe spend the night there. I'd surely not have gone back to Lady Blaunche last night if I'd had choice and was glad he wasn't going to. I wished him good sleeping and went my way to Master Skipton's room.'

'Was it raining then?'

'Not downpouring, just spattering. The end of the storm, before the next one moved in.'

'And you stayed there until morning.'

'Until there was the outcry in the yard after Benedict's body was found, yes,' he said, and Master Skipton nodded in agreement.

There would still have been too many people on the move just then for him to have risked moving Benedict's body between parting from Robert and going to Master Skipton's room. That left only the question of whether Master Skipton was correct that Master Verney had not left during the night, and that hung on how deeply Master Skipton actually slept – deep enough for someone to move about his room without he knew it, or not? – and just now she could think of no way to find that out and stood with bowed head, considering what else she might ask but all that came to mind was, 'Benedict had no enemies you know of who might go to the length of killing him?'

'The greatest enemy he had,' said Master Verney grimly, 'was in some ways his mother. I don't know anyone else.'

'Master Fenner?' she had to ask.

'No!' Master Verney and the steward were both vehement at that, though it was Master Verney who went on, 'What you've seen between them ever since you came here . . . that's not how it's been. Robert never pretended to be Benedict's father or Benedict to be his son, but they were friends. Good friends.'

But so was Master Verney, to both of them; that could color what he said, and she tried Master Skipton, asking, 'Is that how it seemed to you?'

'Master Fenner is a good man and Benedict was a good lad. They liked each other. There was never bad trouble between them until now.'

And then Benedict's loyalty had all turned to his mother, backing her claim to that manor, agreeing with her that he should have Katherine, crossing Robert . . .

Katherine. For whom Robert felt . . . what?

Briefly, before she could shove thought of it away, Frevisse wished she had not heard him cry out Katherine's name on the stairs the way he had . . .

But he would not have set her to find out Benedict's murderer if he was guilty.

Unless he needed to be found out and chose this way because he could not say the words himself.

Unless . . .

All that was pointless wondering. Until she knew more, until she had answers to her other questions from Gil and from Master Skipton, she had as yet no reasonable way to look.

Except at Robert, her mind said again.

Nowhere to look that made any sense, she thought and held to the thought as she thanked Master Skipton for his help given and to come, dismissed him, looked once more around Benedict's room, and told Master Verney she was done here.

Chapter 18

They came out the stairway door into the yard and the bright late morning of a sweet-aired spring day. A general drift of men toward the hall said it must be near to dinnertime but on her own part Frevisse had no urge for food. The fair day was too strongly contrary to all the darkness of Benedict's death and in echo to her own feelings Master Verney let out a deep-taken breath and said, 'We're no further on than we were, are we?'

They were not, though Frevisse held back from saying so, said instead, after a pause, 'You'll go into dinner now?'

'No. Will you?' And when she shook her head, said, 'You're going on with your questions?'

'Yes.'

'The crowner will be here maybe within the day. Yon think you can do better than he will?'

It depended on the crowner, she did not answer. Through the years she had had to do with crowners who ranged from good through a wide band of indifferent to bad, and all she answered now, with the lowered eyes of a humble nun, was, 'Robert asked me to learn what I could.'

'What he asked you to do,' Master Verney corrected sharply, 'was to find Benedict's murderer. You . . .'

What else he might have said was interrupted by Mistress Dionisia making flurried appearance from the nursery stairs' doorway not many yards distant. She hastened toward them, or more likely toward the chapel beyond them, Frevisse supposed, because she pulled up short with surprise at seeing them in her way, then came on at greater speed, gasping out, breathless with her haste, 'Is Master Fenner in the chapel? Do you know where he is?'

'He's there, yes,' Master Verney answered. 'What's toward?'

'Lady Blaunche.' Even breathlessness could not keep the despera-
tion out of Mistress Dionisia's voice. 'She wants the children again.
She's trying to go to them and she mustn't. She's . . .' Fear as well as
barely contained desperation were driving Mistress Dionisia's words.
'She's terrible. She's even ordered Master Geoffrey away from her.
Master Fenner has to come.'

'I'll bring him,' Master Verney said, already turning away toward
the chapel. 'You go back to her and do what you can. You, too, Dame
Frevisse.'

Frevisse would have gone without his order and at another time
would have resented that he gave it but this was not the time for
resenting anything. That Dame Claire had failed to find a way to hold
Lady Blaunche quiet meant the matter could be desperate indeed.

And so it was, she found at the top of the nursery stairs as she
jerked back to keep from bumping into Mistress Dionisia brought to
a sudden stop by Nurse bursting out of the nursery door, saying back,
'You keep them here, Anabilla, no matter what,' at the same time as
Lady Blaunche shrieked out in the other room, 'They're mine! I want
to see them!'

'Not like this,' Dame Claire answered, sounding as desperate as
Mistress Dionisia had in the yard, and Frevisse coming in on Mistress
Dionisia's heels behind Nurse found her struggling – to hold Lady
Blaunche back by main force of a grip on her arms and shoving while
Mistress Avys and Emelye huddled in the tower doorway wringing
their hands and noisily weeping to no purpose but at least blocking
the way of the men crowded and staring behind them.

Wild-haired and wilder-eyed, Lady Blaunche had probably given
them more to stare at when she passed through the solar but, heed-
less of them, she was fighting to break free of Dame Claire, insisting,
furious, 'Mine. They're mine,' while Dame Claire gasped back, 'Lady
Blaunche, listen to me!'

Frevisse made to push past Mistress Dionisia, to go to Dame
Claire's aid, but Nurse was already at Dame Claire's side and into
Lady Blaunche's way, saying with hands on hips, feet braced apart,
and ferocious patience, 'Lady Blaunche, this is *no* way to behave. You
aren't to let the children see you like this. Stop it right this instant.'

For a wonder Lady Blaunche did, went still, still braced against
Dame Claire's hold but staring at Nurse until, all of a sudden, her face

and all its fierceness crumpled, taking her strength with it, and she sank out of Dame Claire's hold to the floor and began to sob as piteously as a heart-rended child. And Nurse, letting go her own fierceness, stood over her and stroked her head, saying, exactly as to a child, 'There, then. That's better. That's better, isn't it, my lady? Tears are best for times like these. You go ahead and cry it out.'

At the same time she gave a look across the room that sent the men in the doorway swiftly out of sight and made Emelye and Mistress Avys gulp to silence on their own tears. Dame Claire used the respite to draw backward to Frevisse who whispered under Nurse's continued crooning to Lady Blaunche, 'Where's Master Geoffrey?'

'She sent him to the chapel to see what was being done with Benedict,' Dame Claire whispered back. 'He'd only just gone when she turned wild with wanting to see the children again. But she shouldn't when she's like this. We don't dare let her.'

The sound of feet taking the stairs in long leaps broke Nurse's spell; as Robert burst into the room, Lady Blaunche lurched to her feet, ready to be wild again, but Nurse flung out a hand at Robert to stop him where he was without taking her eyes from Lady Blaunche and went on saying, 'There. There's no need, my lady. It's only Master Fenner. Bide still now. Bide still.'

Lady Blaunche bided still but, wide-eyed and piteous, begged softly, holding out her hands to him, 'Please?'

Stiff with a wariness he was probably trying not to show, Robert crossed to her, took her out-held hands, and said with the same quieting gentleness as Nurse, 'Please what, my lady?'

Lady Blaunche's mouth trembled. 'The children. Please. May I see them?'

Robert flashed a look to Nurse who gave refusal with a slight sideways movement of her head; but Robert looked back to his wife, into her pleading eyes, then to Nurse again and asked, 'Robin?'

Lady Blaunche gasped and clung more tightly to him, lighting with hope. Nurse hesitated, her gaze flickering from Lady Blaunche to Robert and back again before she gave a single, unwilling nod.

'I'll bring him,' Katherine said from the doorway and Frevisse looked back to see she was there with Master Verney and Master Geoffrey, the two men shifting from her way as she turned back toward the nursery.

'But you must be very quiet,' Nurse insisted at Lady Blaunche firmly. 'If you're not, you'll frighten him. You don't want to do that, do you? So you have to be very quiet with him. You understand?'

Lady Blaunche nodded that she did while taking her hands from Robert and a pace past him, nearer to the doorway, her eyes fixed on it. Across the room Mistress Avys and Emelye were keeping now as still as everyone else, no one wanting to do anything that might set Lady Blaunche off again, everyone hearing a murmuring from the nursery before there was a pause and then Katherine returned, leading Robin by the hand.

At sight of him Lady Blaunche gave a cry and sank to her knees, holding out her arms. He hung slightly back, seeming not to want to be there, and looked for assurance to Robert who nodded encouragingly while Katherine pressed a hand between his shoulder blades, urging him forward. Still reluctant, he went, edging toward his mother, watching her warily, having apparently overheard more than he was meant to, but Lady Blaunche seemed not to notice, beckoned to him with her out-held hands and when he was in reach snatched him to her in a smotheringly close embrace against which Robin neither struggled nor eased before she abruptly set him off from her, her hands lingering on his arms, rubbing up and down them as if to reassure herself he was there, while murmuring to him, far more calm than Frevisse had expected her to be, 'There, little love. You've been crying, haven't you? So have I. We love him, don't we? You and I and John and Tacine. We're all going to miss him terribly, aren't we?' Still crooning, she slid her hands gently up over his shoulders, still stroking, toward his neck, still crooning, until somehow, between one moment and the next, her hands were to his throat, their gentleness gone, her thumbs beginning to press . . .

Robert, Nurse and Frevisse all moved at once, Nurse grabbing Robin away just as he began to cry out with surprise and the start of pain, Robert and Frevisse laying hold on Lady Blaunche from either side, pulling her arms down, pinning them to her side as Nurse swept Robin from the room and Katherine and Master Verney both moved to block the doorway after them while Lady Blaunche began to scream and with the strength of rage flailed free before Dame Claire could join in helping to hold her. She stumbled backward away from Robert grabbing for her again, somehow kicked free of her skirts and fled toward the tower doorway where Mistress Avys and Emelye were no use in stopping her, were shoved aside first by Lady Blaunche, then farther aside by Robert and Frevisse.

It was two men in the solar who blocked Lady Blaunche's going, less by will than because they were standing in her way as she burst into the room and, startled, did not move out of it before Robert overtook her, caught her by one arm, jerked her around and, as she started to collapse toward the floor again, grabbed her up into his arms, cradling her untenderly, crushing her against himself so hard her breath broke from her in a gasp, stopping her words, and he gave her no time to get them back but carried her away up the stairs.

Dame Claire and the other women hurried after him. Frevisse moved aside to let them, wanting nothing to do with helping to settle Lady Blaunche to bed or whatever Robert would do with her, but her sidewise move put her nearly in the way of Drew come from among the still startled men to catch Katherine by the hand, away from the women, saying to her, 'Don't go, my lady. She isn't safe. Keep away from her.'

'I have to go,' Katherine answered, but she was near to tears and let him draw her aside, only casting over her shoulder to Frevisse, 'Go instead of me, please.'

And after all, where else was there to go, Frevisse thought, or what else to do until Master Skipton and Gil brought her some answers? Regretting that, she followed in Master Geoffrey's wake, leaving behind Master Verney whose voice making some manner of explanation to Sir Lewis and the others followed her up the stairs.

In the parlor Robert set Blaunche ungently on her feet and would have gladly pushed her from him but she clutched his doublet's front with both hands, clinging too hard to him, weeping and furious and broken altogether, his hands under her elbows seeming to be all that kept her on her feet as she wailed at him, 'Why did you stop me? Why? Don't you see how better it will be when it's over with? To have it done? To . . .'

'To have Robin dead, too?' Robert asked, furious. 'Because Benedict is dead, you want Robin dead, too? And John and Tacine?'

'Don't you see?' She tugged at his doublet as if to shake sense into him. 'When they're dead, there'll be no more waiting for it to happen. It will be over. No more waiting and being afraid. No more waiting, no more fearing. Just the grieving. Just the grieving, just the grieving . . .'

Robert shoved her roughly away, breaking her hold on him, said to

Master Geoffrey, who happened to be nearest, 'Take her into the bedchamber,' and to Dame Claire, 'Do something with her,' then turned his back and crossed away to the window, not watching them take her, collapsing with tears, away but having to hear Mistress Avys follow after them insisting tearfully to no one in particular, 'She wouldn't have done it. She wouldn't have hurt Robin. She knew we'd stop her. She wouldn't have.'

Distantly, Robert wondered if she believed that or only wanted to.

'Please, sir,' Emelye said almost at his side, and if he had had any strength left with which to be startled, he would have been startled. As it was, the best he could manage was to lean his head toward her, showing he had heard, letting her say, 'Please, sir, might I go pray by Benedict? There's none of us there just now, and . . .'

'Go,' Robert said and when she was gone and he knew, too, that the bedchamber door was safely shut between him and Blaunche, he let go the rigid set of his spine, let his shoulders and back slump, and doubted he would ever have strength to pull himself up straight again, he was so blindingly tired beyond anything he remembered ever being, mind and body both. And here, beyond the window out of which he was almost blindly staring, was everything that had been there yesterday, everything that had been there last week and last month and would likely be there a year from now and the year after that, no matter who was or wasn't alive to see it, and maybe there was comfort in that, though not today, because in his mind he was seeing something there had been once and would never be again – his first sight of sleeping, newborn Robin. And what he was remembering was the upswelling certainty he had had then that nothing could ever matter so much again as keeping that small morsel of life safe.

That same surge of love had come on him with newborn John despite, contrary to Robin, he had been red-faced and squalling through all his first month of life. And again with Tacine who, contrariwise, had lain in his arms staring up at him with her newborn eyes as solemnly as if judging whether or not she approved of him. He expected it would come on him again with the child Blaunche was bearing now – that all-consuming, ever-renewing love. Not all the bother that came with babies and only seemed to worsen as they grew into small children – frightening rashes, scraped knees, clothes outgrown before outworn, last winter's fearsome siege of coughing sickness – had made any difference to his vastness of love for them.

And all Blaunche presently wanted was to end them so she would not have to be afraid of her own pain anymore.

Beside him, Dame Frevisse said quietly, 'Robert. I need to ask you something.'

He turned his head toward her, only vaguely aware of what she had said, only vaguely seeing her as he said, more to something in himself than to her, 'I can't love her anymore. I can't go on pretending that I do. Not even to myself. Let alone to her.' He turned to stare blindly out the window again, saying dull-voiced to the trees or sky or something, 'Whatever happens after this, between us it's finished.'

Part of him expected Dame Frevisse would deny that, would say something meant to be comforting or quieting or even encouraging, God help him. Instead, she said in a voice as level and low as his own, 'I'd keep Katherine away from her, too, from now on.'

Jarred at mention of Katherine, Robert saw her this time as he looked at her and asked, 'What?'

'I'd keep Katherine away from her.' Dame Frevisse repeated it steadily. 'Out of even Lady Blaunche's sight.'

'Why?'

'Because we tend to hate the things we fear.'

'Why would she fear Blaunche, let alone hate her?'

Dame Frevisse paused, searching his face before saying, even more quietly, 'I meant that Lady Blaunche fears Katherine and I doubt it will take much to turn her to hating her, with all that's happened.'

'She wouldn't hurt . . .' Katherine, he had been going to say; but until now he would have said Blaunche would not hurt Robin, either – frighten him maybe with her wildness but not hurt him – and about that he had been direfully wrong. And neither, he found, was he fool enough to ask from where Blaunche's fear of Katherine might come. His own guilt told him that, and if Dame Frevisse had guessed too much about his feelings there, as it seemed she had, then it was that much more likely Blaunche knew too much, too, whether or not she yet admitted anything to herself. When she did admit . . . 'Yes,' he said. 'I'll give order that Katherine should keep away from her.'

And the best way to make surety of Katherine's safety – from him and Blaunche both – was to push through her marriage to Drew Allesley as quickly as might be.

From the bedchamber Blaunche screamed, something crashed and shattered against a wall, and the door was wrenched open for

Mistress Avys and Mistress Dionisia to flee out, Dame Claire following with more dignity but no less speed at their skirt-tails, slamming the door closed behind herself and saying at Robert across the room while Mistress Dionisia led Mistress Avys, collapsing with tears, toward the settle, 'Have you sent for the poppy syrup?'

While Robert groped for some memory of whether he had or not, Dame Frevisse said, 'Gil was to bid Master Skipton send a man. He should be on his way by now.'

'He'd better be. There's no more help she'll take from me, and if she goes any worse than she already is, there'll be nothing for it but to tie her down before she does damage to herself or someone else.'

Mistress Avys let out a wail at that, quickly hushed by Mistress Dionisia, and everything was suddenly more than Robert could go on bearing. He had to be away before anyone suggested he should go in to her because ever seeing Blaunche again was something he never wanted to do and he muttered something to Dame Frevisse and left her so rapidly he was to the stairway door before she overtook him, said at his back as she had said before, 'Robert, I need to ask you something,' so that he had to stop, face her and say stiffly in return, 'My lady?'

'Were you with the children *all* of last night?'

He paused in his answer, held for a moment by the ugliness behind what she was asking, horribly foreseeing how it would be if others came to think he could possibly have killed Benedict, before he answered, meeting her look for look, 'Yes, I was with them *all* night. But there's no way to prove it, is there?'

'No,' she agreed and, surprisingly, half-smiled. 'But I believe you anyway.' Giving him the gift of her trust. The best of all things she could possibly have given him just then. Except for maybe a wife he could love. And Benedict's murderer.

Chapter 19

When Robert had gone and Dame Claire with a shake of her head from where she sat aside on a chair had shown she did not want to talk and Mistress Dionisia was still quieting Mistress Avys with pats on the arm and soothing sounds, Frevisse found herself left with nothing but her thoughts and they, she found, were like Mistress Avys – they wanted patting and soothing and were no comfort to her. All she had learned from all her questioning so far was that no one with any likely interest in having Benedict dead seemed either to have been with him, with chance to kill him, or if they had been with him, had not had chance to move his body when it had to have been moved. Except for Robert, she firmly amended, refusing to avoid it; but everything she knew of him from the past and all she had seen of him since Benedict's death told her he would not have done it.

But if not Robert, then who?

What wasn't she seeing among everything she had found out so far? Or, if she was missing nothing among what she had so far learned, what other questions should she ask? She did not know and that left her with only the hope that either Gil or Master Skipton would bring her something she could use.

Her restless waiting for them would not have let her sit; only her body's prompting that she had been too many hours on her feet brought her to the window seat, where she tried for prayer and quieting of her mind, but neither came before Katherine did, bringing two servants bearing trays with what would pass for today's dinner, the kitchen as upset as everything else, it seemed, able to rise to no better than a fish and vegetable pottage, day-old bread, and dried apple-raisin compote, but Frevisse was glad there would be no need to go down to the hall and eat in company.

'Should I take her something?' Mistress Avys asked with a sniff and a doubtful nod toward the bedchamber door as they gathered to the parlor's small table. 'She's had almost nothing today.'

'If she's quiet,' Dame Claire said, 'best we leave her so.'

Frevisse gave silent agreement to that, nor did anyone else protest. That Lady Blaunche was quiet mattered more to everyone than whether she ate or that she was alone with a man not her husband. She would eat in good time and no wrong was likely to come out of her being with Master Geoffrey, being as she was now. Satisfied of her duty, Mistress Avys went to her own eating with a will. Frevisse on her part took only little and withdrew to the window seat again, noticing that Katherine, too, after dismissing the servants and serving everyone herself, had drawn aside to sit on a floor cushion against a wall with her own food and drink and steadily downcast eyes that invited no one to speak to her. Whatever had passed between her and Drew had not done anything toward gladdening her, it seemed. Nor did she ask after Lady Blaunche or, so far as Frevisse saw, even look toward the shut bedchamber door. But she knew when everyone had finished eating and had risen and was gathering the bowls and cups back to the trays when footsteps on the stairs brought Frevisse to her own feet with a hope that was immediately answered by Master Skipton and Gil entering, one behind the other; but it was Katherine who asked sharply, 'What is it?'

'Nothing, my lady,' Master Skipton hurriedly assured her. 'We've only come to tell Dame Frevisse what she asked about.'

Katherine's look flickered away to Frevisse crossing the room toward them and back to their faces as Mistress Dionisia said, 'Come sit, child. You've been on the move all day,' patting the settle on her other side from where Mistress Avys was now occupying herself with untangling embroidery threads from the ruined sewing basket. Ignoring her and leaving off interest in Master Skipton and Gil, Katherine went wordlessly aside to the floor cushion again, sat, and leaned back to the wall with shut eyes.

Mistress Dionisia watched her worriedly but said nothing, Frevisse noted before giving all her own attention to the steward and Gil, neither of whom looked as if they thought they brought good news, but she asked anyway, 'Anything?'

'Nothing,' Master Skipton said and Gil's grim nod agreed with him.

'Nothing?' Frevisse repeated.

'No one heard any outcry nor saw anybody moving around last night where or when they shouldn't have been,' Gil said. Clearly he and Master Skipton had shared with each other what they had been doing. 'Nor we've not found out when Benedict might have happened at the foot of the stairs.'

'There was one of the Allesley men went to the stables sometime in the night after everyone was settled, belatedly worried over his horse, but he isn't sure of the hour, didn't see anybody, just knows there was no body at the stairfoot then,' Master Skipton said.

'Was there anyone noticed with wet clothing this morning who shouldn't have had?' Frevisse asked with small hope.

'None,' Master Skipton answered. 'And no one took any message anywhere last night, either to Benedict or from him.'

The bedchamber door being silently opened brought everyone's look that way and Katherine straight up, but only Master Geoffrey came out, easing himself backward, watching Lady Blaunche to the last moment where she knelt in prayer at the prie-dieu across the room below the crucifix hung on the wall, her back to them, her head bowed, Frevisse saw past the clerk as he looked around to nod encouragingly at everyone before gentling the door closed.

Mistress Avys, on her feet but held back by Mistress Dionisia's firm grip on her skirts, asked in a carrying whisper, 'How is she? Should I go to her?'

'She's quiet,' Master Geoffrey said low-voiced back. He was pale and his voice dry and strained. 'I'd let her be. She'll call if she needs us.' He sank down on the room's only remaining joint stool. 'Is there anything to drink?'

Katherine made to rise but Gil, already standing, went to the ale pitcher still on the table and poured a cupful and brought it to Master Geoffrey who took it with thanks and drank deeply. A little revived, he noticed how he was being watched by everyone and managed a wearied smile, answering their silent asking, 'There's nothing else to say. She's quiet and, I think, beginning to accept what's happened.'

'Thanks be to the Blessed Virgin,' Mistress Avys murmured and crossed herself as she sank down onto the settle again.

Everyone else echoed her words and gesture, including Master Geoffrey who then looked around, clearly trying to bring himself back from whatever strained places he had had to go with Lady Blaunche, and asked, 'What's toward? Is there anything more about Benedict? Are the Allesleys still here?'

'It's purposed they'll stay until the crowner is done with them,' Master Skipton said. 'Hopefully he'll be here by tonight or early tomorrow.'

'There's no thought of breaking off on agreement with the Allesleys, is there?'

'Not that I've heard.'

Frevisse felt cold run down her spine. Her thought had been that someone had wanted Benedict dead because he was making too much trouble over the agreement with the Allesleys and he was wanted out of the way. What if, instead, his death was meant to delay any signing of any such agreement? What if it was hoped his death would even make such a rift in matters that no agreement would ever be signed at all?

Taken up with that thought, she missed what Master Geoffrey said next but heard Gil say glumly to it, 'Not a thing. Nobody seems to have seen him at all after he left with Master Verney. They went to his room and Master Verney left him there and that's all we have.'

Master Geoffrey went oddly still, staring at Gil but not as if he saw him. Then he blinked, licked his lips and said slowly, the words seeming dragged from him, 'I saw him after that.'

He instantly had Frevisse's and both men's heed, Gil demanding, 'Where?' as she demanded, 'When?'

The force of the questions seemed to unsettle him. He answered unevenly, 'I went . . . I saw him in his room. I went to see him.'

'When?' Frevisse insisted.

'At evening's end, when everyone was settling to bed. I was going to my own but there was light under his chamber door and I knocked and he let me in. We talked.'

'About what? About anyone?' she persisted.

'About how badly he felt for what had happened. He was sorry and uncertain what to do . . . I said maybe if he prayed, if we prayed, in the chapel together . . .'

'You went to the chapel?' Frevisse asked, at the same time berating herself in the back of her mind that she had not somehow found a way to question Master Geoffrey before now. But he had been so taken up, first with Benedict, then with Lady Blaunche's needs, and she hadn't thought . . .

'We did. It wasn't raining then. We went and knelt and prayed together and after a while he said I could go if I wanted, he was better. I left him there.' Master Geoffrey looked around at all their faces – both men and all the women now intent on him. 'I shouldn't have, should I? Someone came and killed him there, didn't they?'

'We don't know,' Frevisse said quickly, not wanting him to go upset past answering her more. 'You didn't hear him come back to his room?'

'No. I went to bed and sleep. The storms woke me but I slept again each time. If he came back, I didn't hear him.'

'Or anyone else on the stairs, maybe looking for him?'

'I didn't hear anything but the storm all night.' On that Master Geoffrey was certain.

But someone could have gone to the chapel for their own praying, found Benedict there, come up behind him and killed him, and no one would have heard or known. Then all the murderer would have needed do was wait until the yard was at its darkest and emptiest and move the body to the stairfoot and hope no more would be suspected than a fall. That he'd laid the body wrong was simply his mischance, probably made because he was hurried.

But last night here people had slept crowded. Anyone coming and going from wherever he had slept should have been noticed.

Except Robert.

The thought sickened her with a pain that both told her how much she did not want him to be the murderer and warned her she must be careful of that want, so it did not blind her.

And then she thought of the other possibility there was, one she had altogether missed until now. Master Geoffrey.

With his room there at the head of the stairs with Benedict's, who besides the clerk had been better able to come to Benedict unseen, better able to have killed him safely, better able to have waited with no danger to himself until the safest time to move Benedict's body with no one to ask him afterwards where he had been or why? And if his clothing was wet, well, there was nothing suspicious there, he'd had to cross the yard to reach his room, hadn't he?

But all that was almost equally true of Robert if he had happened

201

on Benedict in the chapel. And he might well have. He could have gone there to pray himself before ever he went to the nursery but found Benedict alone and . . . killed him.

Why? Out of a sudden giving way to his anger at all the trouble Benedict had been? Or out of fear that Benedict would make more? Or as a way both to be rid of Benedict and to delay the agreement without it seeming to be his fault, thereby delaying Katherine's marriage, having found at this late hour he could not after all bring himself to part with her? How strong his feeling for Katherine was and how deep it ran were things she could only guess but she was afraid of it, because what if it was strong enough, deep enough, for Benedict's life to have been forfeit to it?

Though Master Geoffrey had had chance to kill Benedict, he had had no reason to, while Robert had had both.

The men were meanwhile wondering to each other where Lady Blaunche might decide Benedict should be buried, whether here, which would make the least trouble, or in the Fenner chapel at St Andrew's, Northampton, but their talk and Frevisse's thoughts were broken off by Mistress Avys rising to her feet and crying out, 'Stop it! He's barely shrouded. How can you set to thinking about thrusting him into the ground so soon? What if she hears you?'

They had been speaking too low for that to be even a likelihood and Gil started, 'She can't . . .'

Mistress Avys grabbed up a small cushion and threw it at him, so misaimed it came nowhere near. 'You men! What do you know? She hasn't eaten. She barely slept. She's been crying since yesterday.' Sniffing angrily, she started for the bedchamber door. 'I'm not leaving her alone anymore. I want to see her. I'm going in.'

'Let me go first!' Dame Claire said, rising behind her.

Master Geoffrey, nearer to the door, put himself directly into her way, saying, 'Or better yet, just look quietly. If she's still at prayer, we can leave her awhile longer, surely.'

Mistress Avys paused, caught on trying to make up her mind between them, giving Dame Claire time to reach her and say soothingly, 'He's right. Let's see how she does before anyone goes in.'

Mistress Avys made a doubting sound that Master Geoffrey chose to take for agreement and turned from her to the bedchamber door, edging it slowly open the smallest fingerwidth through which he could peer. And froze, so suddenly and sharply still that Frevisse was already rising to her feet even before he gave a wordless cry, shoved wide the door, and broke across the room toward Lady Blaunche, crumpled to the floor beside the prie-dieu.

Chapter 20

Mistress Avys screamed, shrill above anyone else's outcry, but Gil, Master Skipton and Frevisse all moved more swiftly, reached Lady Blaunche barely after Master Geoffrey, Gil going down on his knees beside the clerk to help turn her carefully over, then crying out himself, his hand coming away bloody in the same moment Master Geoffrey sobbed, 'Merciful God!' and held up a bloodied dagger.

Mistress Avys, clinging to the doorframe, began to scream in earnest but Dame Claire grabbed her and shoved her hard toward Mistress Dionisia, ordering, 'Have her out and keep her out!', before coming to push Frevisse, Master Skipton, and Master Geoffrey aside and kneel beside Gil who was gasping, 'She's stabbed herself. Dear God, look. She's stabbed hereself . . .'

'She's alive,' Dame Claire said. 'Lift her to the bed.' Standing up and out of the way, gesturing to him and Master Skipton to do it because Master Geoffrey, still on his knees, had raised clasped hands and desperate eyes to the crucifix on the wall above the prie-dieu and was crying out prayers that were as surely needed as anything Dame Claire might do because Lady Blaunche might still be alive but there was dreadfully much blood soaked into the rush matting where she had lain, and as the men raised her, Frevisse went around the bed to its far side, jerked the covers away into a heap on the floor against the wall out of the way, leaving only the bottom sheet over the mattress, and was wrapping the bedcurtains out of the way around the bedposts as the men laid Lady Blaunche onto the bed in haste.

Now what she had done was plain to see. A slit in her gown below her left breast showed where she had driven the dagger in, with a wide, long soak of blood, dark on the gown's blue, to show how much she had bled from it; and despite she was alive, she wouldn't be for long, Frevisse judged with a sick sinking of heart, although Dame Claire was ordering at anyone, 'Open the shutters. I want more light,' and rolling up her sleeves without taking her gaze from Lady Blaunche.

With Gil and Master Skipton just stepping back from the bed, and Mistress Dionisia still trying to draw Mistress Avys, wailing and useless, back from the doorway, it was Katherine who ran to pull open the shutters while Frevisse went to shove Mistress Avys fully out of the room with, 'Enough. Go over there and pray,' pointing across the parlor at anywhere so long as it was away, adding, 'Take her,' to Mistress Dionisia, who grimly did as Frevisse, wishing she was going with them, turned back to whatever else Dame Claire might need of her.

But even as she did, Dame Claire said with the despair that always came on her when there was no use in any of her skill, 'Master Geoffrey, bring the crucifix. Quickly! Confess her.'

With a moan, the clerk lurched up from the prie-dieu and fumbled as if blind toward the crucifix on the wall.

'*Quickly*,' Dame Claire cried and Frevisse ran to grab up the dagger, dropped by Master Geoffrey and kicked by someone into the middle of the floor, and flung herself to the bedside where Lady Blaunche had opened her eyes in a wide stare upward, her mouth gaping for air she was not finding. Frevisse held up the dagger by its bloodied blade above her face, where she had to see it, making blade and hilt and handguard into a cross above her, asking at her desperately, 'Do you repent of all your sins and pray to God to receive your immortal soul?'

Lady Blaunche gasped, gasped again, choked with a jerking motion of her head that had to be a nod. And went still.

Mouth still gaped. Eyes still stared. But emptily. She was no longer there.

'The baby,' Dame Claire said and grabbed the dagger from Frevisse so quickly that only barely she let go in time not to be cut but she understood the frantic haste. With Lady Blaunche dead, the baby she was bearing would very soon, if not already, be dead, too, and if it was not baptized before it died, its immortal soul would be doomed to that outermost ring of Hell where souls unsaved but not greatly sinful were left for eternity untormented by anything but the worst torment of all – of never having hope of seeing the face of God. The Church's law and all pity demanded attempt be made, since there was no hope of the unborn's body, to save its soul, and that could only be done by . . .

With swift, brutal force Dame Claire grabbed up the front of Lady Blaunche's gown, thrust the dagger through and ripped the cloth open in a wide gash to Lady Blaunche's knees.

'Water,' she ordered, setting to do the same to the undergown. 'And towels.'

Gil and Master Skipton stayed standing as they were, not yet comprehending anymore than that Lady Blaunche was dead. Even Master Geoffrey, turned back from the wall without the crucifix, made no move. Only Frevisse did, going to the nearby table where pitcher and basin stood and a towel hung, ordering Master Skipton on the way, 'We need more water, more towels. Fetch them.' It was best to have men out of the way for this anyway. 'Gil, guard the door that no one comes in here. Master Geoffrey, pray some more.'

Only when she had towel, basin and pitcher in hand and the men were obeying her did she realize Katherine was standing beside the window, frozen and staring at Lady Blaunche; and Frevisse, frightened for her because what was coming was something she should not see, snapped, 'Katherine, go tend to Mistress Avys so Mistress Dionisia can come in here. We need her.'

Katherine turned a blank stare with horror to her instead of moving.

'Go!' Frevisse ordered more harshly and Katherine did, following Master Skipton and Gil out of the room, and she went on to Dame Claire who paused with dagger poised over Lady Blaunche's bared belly and looked at her with sickened, fearing eyes, to which Frevisse, equally sickened and in fear, said, 'You have to.'

And Dame Claire turned back to Lady Blaunche's body and did.

Made a long, sure-handed slice with the dagger point down the belly just left of the center line, the white flesh parting, opening to show the red flesh underneath. And made another dagger stroke, slicing through that . . .

A bare few minutes – that seemed to go on forever – later, it was over, the thing done.

Mistress Dionisia was there by then, tight-faced with the same effort not to be sick that Frevisse was fighting down but taking up a share of what needed doing, the three of them working together in grim silence, each of them knowing what was needed. There was nothing to be done about the smell of blood and filth except wait until the mattress could be taken away and herbs burned to purify the air, but Mistress Dionisia brought towels from a chest along one wall to sop up and wipe away as much blood as could be. Then Frevisse and Dame Claire lifted Lady Blaunche's body and Mistress Dionisia brought a blanket from a chest at the foot of the bed to spread over the ruined mattress and, when Lady Blaunche was laid down again and straightened, they put more towels over the great wound to take whatever after-seepage there would be, pulled her gown closed over it, and bound another towel tightly around her belly to keep it as together as might be until needle and thread could be brought to stitch it closed and her body altogether cleaned and readied for burial.

By then there was a clutter of voices beyond the closed door to the parlor – Mistress Avys crying out things, men asking questions, Gil gruffly answering and still holding off anyone from coming in. But Robert and the priest must be let in soon, and Mistress Dionisia quickly brought another sheet to cover Lady Blaunche from neck to feet, hiding all that had been done, and then a pillow slip of fine linen that Dame Claire used to wrap up what there had been of the baby as tenderly as if it still lived and laid it – him – for now in the emptied basin that was all the cradle he would ever have.

But he would be buried with his mother and the both of them in consecrated ground because Frevisse and Dame Claire could testify that Lady Blaunche with her last breath had repented of her self-murder and that the baby had moved as Dame Claire lifted him free of his mother's body for Frevisse to baptize with plain water and the necessary words – *In nomine Patri, et Filio, et Spiritui Sancto*. In the name of the Father, and of the Son, and of the Holy Spirit – enough, in such desperate need, for his salvation before he ceased to be alive.

That was all the comfort they would have to offer Robert, Frevisse was afraid.

She could hear his voice among those outside the door now, questioning and frightened, and despite she could not hear the words, she knew there was no mercy in keeping him out any longer. They had made things as well as could be for him to see and she said to Mistress Dionisia, 'Best you let Master Fenner and the priest come in now,' and to Dame Claire, stepped back from the bed after setting the basin beside Lady Blaunche's body, 'Best you sit, before you fall,' with a nod toward the chest at the foot of the bed, and wished she could say more – Dame Claire never took well the losing of someone in her care, whatever the cause – but Mistress Dionisia was opening the door to Robert.

He stood for a moment, not coming in. There was a crowd of people behind him that were probably not so many as they seemed to Frevisse but they somehow drew back from the opened door, suddenly silent and leaving him alone to this, and carefully, maybe wary of what he was going to see, surely wary with pain, he came in, with a look to Mistress Dionisia to shut the door behind him.

'Until Father Laurence comes,' he whispered as if his voice would rise to nothing more, and while she did, stood where he was before, slowly, slowly, he crossed to the bedside and stood looking down at the stillness that had been his wife. Stood looking with the numbness of someone looking at too much grief too suddenly, the numbness of someone taken so great a blow that there was no pain yet, no feeling at all.

But that would not save him even a little when finally the numbness went and the pain came in full force, and carefully, into his silence, Frevisse said, 'She was aware enough, at the very last, to ask forgiveness.'

'So Gil said.' Robert drew a deep, shaken breath. 'The baby?'

'Safe. Baptized. A son, if you want to name him.'

Robert took his eyes from Lady Blaunche's death-smoothed face for the first time, to look at the small, carefully wrapped bundle beside her, and a little blankly said, 'We hadn't talked yet about . . . I'll have to think. I . . .'

That was the moment pain began to awake in him. His eyes widened with it and his breath shortened as he turned to Frevisse to ask on a rising note of dread, 'What am I going to do? What am I going to tell the children? How am I going to bring them to understand?'

'It was despair,' Frevisse said quickly. 'Benedict's death was more than she could bear. She gave way.'

Robert's face hardened. 'Whoever killed Benedict just as surely killed her, killed the baby. Someone . . .'

A cautious rap at the door silenced him and there was a distracted time as Father Laurence came in and Dame Claire went to assure him Lady Blaunche had died in grace and Mistress Avys came held up between Katherine and Emelye, all of them tear-marred but Mistress Avys's screaming worn out to wracking sobs. They circled to the bed's far side and knelt across from Robert, sinking to his knees at Lady Blaunche's near side while Frevisse, nearer the bed's foot, and Dame Claire joined him, with Mistress Dionisia kneeling a little farther off as Father Laurence at the foot of the bed began prayers.

From beyond the open door to the parlor came the heavy sounds of a great many other people going down to their knees, too. Household folk with a right to be there, Frevisse supposed, but Gil had rightly kept anyone else from entering the bedchamber. Only those nearest Lady Blaunche in her life were here, save for her children – her living children and Benedict; but she would be with Benedict soon enough, leaving her living children to their grief because her own grief for their half brother had killed her.

Frevisse realized she was following her thoughts instead of praying and, startled, opened her eyes. Above her the priest was praying, '*Ne recorderis peccata mea, Domine, Dum veneris judicare saeculum per ignem.*' Do not remember my sins, Lord, When you will come to judge the age by fire. And with Dame Claire she responded, '*Dirige, Domine, Deus meus, in conspectu tuo viam meam.*' Guide, Lord, my God, in your sight my way. But she said it only by form. There was nothing of her mind behind it, she realized, a poor way of prayer at the best of times and worse now when there was such deep need.

But even as she thought that, while saying with the others, '*Requiem aeternam,*' she found she was looking at the long, bright swathe of Lady Blaunche's blue gown trailing over the edge of the bed in front of her. There had not been time to undress the body. That was something her women would do with all else that would be needed to ready her for burial; for now, no one had even taken time to gather up her skirt fully out of sight under the sheet and so it was draped there, a graceful richness of fabric.

With a bloodstain in the wrong place.

Frevisse paused, took a backward step in her mind and looked at that thought again as intently as she was now staring at the bloodstain.

It was in the wrong place.

There had already been a great ruining of the gown with blood all down Lady Blaunche's left side from where she had fallen after stabbing herself, and there had been more afterwards with what Dame

Claire had had to do, but all that had been higher on the gown and more on its left side than anywhere. This blood was on the right side, near to the gown's hem.

Nowhere near the death wound or Dame Claire's cutting.

Nor did it have the look of someone having wiped their hands there. That would have made a shallow smear. This was a long, narrow, soaked-in-seeming stain, dark against the gown's blue, as if it had had time to dry.

Frevisse clasped her hands more tightly, resisting what she wanted to do until Father Laurence finished, but the moment he had and they had all echoed the final '*Requiem aeternum*,' she crossed herself with more haste than piety, grabbed for the skirt and turned it back, wanting to see if the blood had soaked through the thick velvet from the inside to out or from out to in.

There was almost no stain on the inside.

So it had come from the outside to in, and for that to be, either something long and narrow and bloody had lain on the skirt or the skirt had lain on it.

'Dame Frevisse?' Dame Claire asked, now standing over her.

Frevisse stood up and turned away, shaking her head, wanting time for thinking. Around the bed the others were rising, too, save for Robert still on his knees, head still bowed. Frevisse gazed down at the back of his head for a moment, then looked around, saw Master Verney with Gil at the doorway, uncertain if he should come in, and Master Geoffrey standing up stiff-kneed from the prie-dieu. But it was Master Skipton she wanted.

'Dame Frevisse,' Dame Claire said, 'we should . . .'

Frevisse shook her head again and left her, going past Master Verney and Gil into the parlor where the steward was directing several maidservants to build up the hearth fire and bring a pot to heat the water for cleansing Lady Blaunche's body, with someone to take word to the laundress that there would shortly be sheets in need of immediate washing. He did not say, *Before the blood set and could never be washed out*, but the tense set of his whole face betrayed he was holding steady and to his duty with an effort that broke a little when he had dismissed the maids and turned to Frevisse. In a shaken voice he said, 'First Master Benedict and now this. It's terrible.'

'Have you been steward here for long?' Frevisse asked without heed for what he was saying.

Surprised enough not to ask why, he answered, 'Fifteen years. And my father and grandfather were stewards here before me.'

It was often that way with smaller manors, sons of a family carrying on an office from one generation into the next, their familiarity with the people and place to everyone's advantage. Frevisse had hoped it was that way here and asked, 'Then you'd know, if anyone does, whether there's any secret way into the tower here. Is there?'

He looked at her as if she had somehow taken leave of her good sense. 'What?'

'A secret way in. Hidden stairs. Some way to come and go unseen.'

'Of course not. Why would there be?' He was catching up now without quite believing she was asking such a thing. 'A stone tower is costly when just built simply. Add something like that . . . Besides, how could it be secret with everyone on the manor watching the place being built?'

'This was built a goodly while ago.'

'A hundred and fifty years. Maybe more. Very likely more.'

'People could have forgotten.'

'They remember whose grandfather kicked a cow and broke his foot three generations back. I think there'd be talk about "that secret way to the lord's parlor." Don't you?'

She did and turned sharply back toward the bedchamber, ignoring Master Skipton beginning to ask, 'Why . . .' because she did not have time to tell him why. There was one more thing she wanted to see, and returning to the bedchamber where Gil still guarded the doorway, she found Robert had risen and moved away from the bed, was now in the middle of the room, standing with head down and shoulders slack, listening to Master Verney and the priest, with Master Geoffrey to hand in case he was needed while at the bed the women, including Dame Claire and a maidservant, were readying to go on with what next needed to be done with Lady Blaunche's body as soon as the men were gone.

Circling past the men and away from the women, Frevisse went to the prie-dieu and found what she had hoped was there – dark on the pale, woven-rush matting that covered the floor, a streak of blood much the same in length and breadth as the stain on Lady Blaunche's skirt.

So Lady Blaunche's skirt had lain on whatever had lain there, and sickly sure that she was guessing rightly, Frevisse knelt on the prie-dieu's cushion, as Lady Blaunche must have done, and looked back over her right shoulder to where her own, far less full, skirts now covered the stain. On the rush matting to the left of her was the greater spread of Lady Blaunche's blood from the wound under her left breast, where she had slumped sideways and down and bled, far from that streak. Just as on her gown that streak had been far from the wound.

Beside her, startling her, Master Verney said, 'She must have braced the dagger's pommel there.' He leaned over to point to a marred place on one leg of the prie-dieu, just under the edge of the slanted top where a prayer book still lay open. It was a rounded dent that looked, as he said, to be made by the rounded pommel of a dagger's hilt pressed heavily into the wood. 'She braced it there, then thrust herself onto it.' He sounded as sick at the thought as Frevisse felt.

Frevisse put out her hand, ran two fingers around the curve of the marred wood. 'Who noticed this?'

'Master Geoffrey.'

'He showed it to you?'

'When I came in.'

'The dagger.' She heard her voice dry with strain, not sounding like her own. 'Whose is it?'

'It's an old one of Robert's. It's kept there.' Master Verney nodded to the chest beside the wall at the head of the bed. 'For need when another isn't to hand, I gather.'

'And anyone and everyone could know it's there.'

Master Verney was openly puzzled. 'Yes,' he said and waited as if expecting more questions but Frevisse had answers enough. Everything was come together into a whole, and when above her, Master Verney said heavily, 'How could she bring herself to such a thing? Even . . .'

'She didn't,' Frevisse said curtly, braced her hands on the prie-dieu and pushed herself sharply up to her feet. With the anger she had first had at Benedict's death scalding in her now, she turned toward where Robert and the priest were still in talk, with Master Geoffrey still standing with them, and raised her voice for everyone in the room to hear her as she said, 'She *didn't* kill herself. She was murdered. By the same man who murdered her son.'

The words rasped into a silence fully come before she had finished saying them, with everyone – the men, the women by the bed, Gil at the door – turned to look at her, but her own look only on Master Geoffrey, watching his eyes widen and the blood drain from his face as he understood what she was saying.

Robert turned his head to stare toward the clerk, then back to Frevisse. 'What?' he asked.

Her gaze still locked to Master Geoffrey's, Frevisse said, coldly now, 'From all I've been able to learn, no one with cause to want Benedict dead had any way to come to him unnoticed last night or chance to put his body at the foot of the stairs except you, Robert. The other man best able to both come to Benedict and move his body is Master Geoffrey.'

'Who had no cause to kill him,' Robert said, but slowly, watching, as everyone was watching now, the slow mount of blood back into the clerk's face and the rapid lift and fall of his heavy breathing, his stare still at Dame Frevisse still staring back at him as she said,

'No cause we know of. No more cause than we know of for him to kill Lady Blaunche. But he did, because she didn't kill herself and there's no one else could have done it except him.'

From the bed Mistress Dionisia said, questioning, 'But we saw her when he left the bedchamber. She was at the prie-dieu, praying.'

'She was dying,' Frevisse said. 'He made sure we saw her there, to believe she was well, but she was dying even as he left her.'

'How can you say,' Master Verney asked carefully, 'that she didn't kill herself?'

'Because no matter how great a despair she might have been in, even despair great enough to thrust herself onto a dagger, she would not then have bothered to reach back and carefully hide the dagger under her skirts. Why would she? What possible reason could she have had for doing that? But that is where it was.' Frevisse pointed toward the narrow bloodstain on the matting. 'There's a stain on her skirt matching that, where her skirt laid over it. Look where it is. And remember how she was lying when we found her.' She turned that demand on the women. 'There's a dent in the prie-dieu where she's supposed to have braced the dagger, and we found her fallen to the left, as if she had been kneeling and crumpled down from there. Why would the dagger be behind her to the right and under her skirts where the blood shows it was? And *you*.' She came fiercely back to Master Geoffrey. 'You found the dagger, showed it to us, before we'd barely begun to grasp that she was hurt, before we'd done more than turn her over, when it would have still been covered by the spread of her skirts. You knew it was there and the only way you could have known that was if you'd put it there.'

Master Geoffrey took a gasping breath and started, 'I had no reason—'

'Don't tell me you had no reason!' Frevisse flared. 'Whyever you did it, you were the only one who *could* have done it. And the only one besides Robert who could have killed Benedict and moved his body. You . . .'

Robert, all his grief-driven fury unleashed, went at Master Geoffrey to grab him by the front of his gown as less than a day before he had grabbed Benedict, and shove him backward, backward, backward, hard thrust after hard thrust, until they came up against the wall, there to jerk him forward and drive him back, cracking his head against the stone, yelling at him, 'Why?' Jerking him forward and driving his head back again, still yelling, 'Why? You bastard-get! *Why?*'

Chapter 21

Three days.

No . . .

Four.

Four days since their deaths.

Standing at the parlor's window, looking out over the orchard, its branches softened with pale, opening blossoms under a gentle sky, Robert made count of the days. Four days since they died. Three since the crowner came and left. Two since their burial. One since Sir Lewis had sent message from the grange that he was going home and there need be no haste in finishing the matter between them, that it could bide until Midsummer if Robert wanted.

Four days.

And all the rest of his life ahead of him. And no desire in him to live it. An ugly stretch of time where grief, he knew, would flatten out under the burden of necessities, the way it had flattened for brief whiles these past four days. Flattened but not left him because it would never leave him, was now as much a part of him as the white scar along his right knee where he had fallen on a broken edge of a board when he was eight years old, on an afternoon that would have long since been lost to memory except for the pain there had been and the scar there was, and that was how his grief would be, with him forever from here onward, through all his days. Grief for what might have been between him and Blaunche but never was and now never would be. Grief for everything lost with Benedict's death – beginning with the chance to have made peace with him.

Grief for all the things there would never be chance for now.

Ned and Gil had pulled him off Geoffrey Hannys before he had managed to kill him, there in the bedchamber four days ago. Robert supposed he was glad of that but he had not been at the time. At the time he had wanted the man as dead as Blaunche and Benedict and the unnamed baby were, but Ned and Gil had dragged him back, Ned saying, 'Let be. We'll see to him. Leave it, Robert!' But when Geoffrey had made a clumsy try for the door then, sidling away along the wall, it had been Ned who had turned to backhand him across the face, driving his head against the wall again; and when Geoffrey had started to slump toward the floor, it had been Ned who gave him a hard shove down, to be sure he made it.

Gil had taken Robert to sit on the chest at the foot of the bed then, and Katherine had brought him wine, and Ned had made him drink it, until finally, still sick and shaken inwardly but outwardly quieted, he had been able to look across to Geoffrey dragging himself up to sit back against the wall, blood at the corner of his mouth, and ask him without the outward rage this time, 'Why?'

Geoffrey had wiped blood from his mouth and held out his hand to show it, saying bitterly, 'Look.'

No one had, except at him, and what he must have seen on all their faces made him drop his hand into this lap, lean his head back tenderly against the wall, and set his gaze disgustedly toward the room's far side rather than to any of them while he said, sullen, 'At evening's end yesterday, I went to Benedict in his room, to tell him how his mother did and see how he was. He was still angry. Mostly at "Master" Fenner.'

Robert had wondered briefly from where the black scorn Geoffrey put into his name came.

'I thought he was angry enough he'd take well to the thought of how much better it would be to have me married to his mother instead.'

Gil had sworn at that and Ned had demanded, incredulous, 'This was something you'd thought on?'

'Of course I'd thought on it.' Geoffrey had been still full of scorn. 'Almost since I'd first come into the household I'd been thinking on it. There was Lady Blaunche, ripe and ready for anything a man could give her, and there he was – "Master" Fenner – tucked into as soft a place as a man could hope for and too stupid to make the most of it. All I needed was time enough to bring her around to seeing how much better I would be to her than he was, and then if it happened he died, I'd be here to hand to be first her comfort and then her next husband.'

'And if Robert didn't "happen" to die one way,' Ned had said in a dangerously level voice, 'you would have seen he "happened" to another?'

'Why not? He wasn't anybody. He'd have had nothing, been nothing, except she married him. Why shouldn't she do as much for me?'

'You said that to Benedict?' Robert had asked and been surprised by how evenly he said it, not realizing until later how numb he was.

Geoffrey's scorn had only deepened. 'Of course I didn't. I started something about how you were failing his mother. He agreed to that readily enough. He said you were a fool who didn't understand anything. I said that at least I could quiet her, could keep her happier than he did and added, as if half-jesting, that it would be better all around if she had married me instead of him. The young idiot . . .' Geoffrey's bitterness had been immense. '. . . he laughed in my face. He said he'd rather quarrel with Master Fenner about anything, anytime, than ever even try to think of me married to his mother. The whelp. He laughed and turned away from me, still laughing. He made me so angry, laughing like I was some sort of jest . . .' Geoffrey put out his hands and made a quick, small twisting gesture, as if he held a neck and to break it was a simple thing; and shrugged, dropping his hands into his lap again. 'I learned about necks in France, for when there was a guard that needed to be quietly dead. I didn't even think about it, just did it, and afterwards sorry was no use, so why bother? Besides, I knew, when I came to think about it, that he would have poisoned his mother against me if he'd lived. This way, with him dead, I could better my chances with Lady Blaunche by "comforting" her in her grief. I waited until everything was quiet, took him out, and dumped him at the foot of the stairs, hoping it would be taken for chance he was dead. It was only later, when questions were being asked, I realized there was chance I could make Master Fenner look guilty of the killing and be rid of him, too, and that was all the better.' Geoffrey touched the sore corner of his mouth where the blood was drying. 'It would have worked, too. It only all went wrong because of her, the stupid bitch.'

With a hand bearing down on Robert's shoulder to keep him from rising, Ned had asked, 'Lady Blaunche?'

'Who else?' Geoffrey had been too lost in angry memory to notice anything besides himself. 'There she was. She'd wanted no one with her but me and we were alone together. I'd quieted her out of crying, was holding her by the hands, flattering her with hope and suchlike, telling her anything I thought she might want to hear, and she was all grateful and warming to me so I told her I loved her and that I wished I was her husband, how different everything would have been if I was. And you know what the bitch did? She looked at me as if I'd never had a wit in my head, as if there was nothing between us and never had been, and said, all scorn, "Ha!" and started to turn her back on me, just like her cur of a son had done. Turned away like I wasn't even worth the looking at. She made me that angry, I hit her.'

Robert had groaned and bowed his head into his hands. If Geoffrey heard him, it had not mattered; the man had been deaf to everything but his own grievance, going on, 'Harder maybe than I meant to. It knocked her sideways. She hit the side of her head there, on the corner of that chest.' He had pointed to the one beside the bed. 'Hard enough it half stunned her. She slumped down without even a sound and left me standing here knowing I'd lost my chance at everything. I'd have no chance with her after that and she'd ruin me for life into the bargain if she had the chance. So I took the dagger . . .'

'How did you know it was there?' Ned asked.

'It was one of those idiot things she was pleased about.' Geoffrey shrilled his voice like an unlikely woman's with, ' "Robert keeps a dagger in the chest by our bed, for better safety, he's that careful for me." As if we all lived in constant peril of attack.' Geoffrey's contempt was open.

'It was my father's,' Robert said thickly. 'The only thing of his I have. That's why I keep it there.'

'Well, she'd gone on about it enough that I knew where it was. She was still so dazed from the blow to her head, she was just lying there, didn't see me take the dagger from the chest, was hardly aware when I dragged her to her feet and over to the prie-dieu. She was even holding on to me while I did, moaning a little. She managed to ask, "What?" like she wasn't sure what had happened, and I said it was the baby, there was something wrong with the baby, she had to pray while I went for Dame Claire, and forced her down to her knees at the prie-dieu like she was praying while she was still trying to understand what I'd said. Then I ran the dagger into her without her ever seeing it was even in my hand. All she felt was the pain when I pulled it out. Her eyes widened at it and she gasped, "The baby," thinking that was what it was, and I grabbed her hands before she could feel at her side, wrapped her fingers around the edges of the prie-dieu and told her to pray while I went for help. She was already past speaking, in pain so bad she could only gasp and nod at what I told her. I knew she wouldn't last long, not with where I'd stabbed her. All I had to do was get out of there while she was still upright. It took hardly an instant to make the dent in the wood and put the dagger under the edge of her skirt.' He cast an angry look at Dame Frevisse. 'Just as you guessed. And I made sure some of you saw her when I came out the door so you could say she was alive when I left her. All I had to do then was wait until someone wanted to go see how she did and be sure I reached her first, to "find" the dagger that proved she'd killed herself. It all went right, except for you,' he had said at Dame Frevisse. 'Except for you, nobody would have thought anything but what I meant them to.'

She had not answered him, and only finally had something of the cold stares and silence all around him begun to pierce his self-concern about his cleverness and wrongs, and he had stiffened, had looked around at all of them, and said angrily, as if anger would make them understand where his reasons had not, 'They asked for what happened to them. Both of them. They shouldn't have made me angry the way they did. They were stupid with pride, the both of them.'

'And what are you,' Dame Frevisse had said back coldly, 'but stupid with even worse pride? They were guilty of scorn because of theirs. You're guilty of murder because of yours. That makes your pride by far more stupid and damning than ever theirs was.'

Geoffrey had opened his mouth to answer, then closed it, confusion briefly on his face before Ned took hold on his arm, wrenched him to his feet, and shoved him out of the room to find somewhere to keep him until the crowner came and took him away.

And now . . .

Robert had carefully done what needed doing through these past four days and held to thoughts of Robin and John and Tacine while he did because they were all that was left to him out of what had been his life.

He had spent as much time as he could with them, had done what he could to help them understand what had happened, had comforted them, had cried with them, been grateful for the comfort that being with them gave. Been grateful, too, that much of the time when he could not be with them, Katherine had been.

But Katherine was among the things he did not want to think on anymore. The settlement with Sir Lewis was postponed, that was all, and all that meant was that he had more days to be gone through until she was safely married and out of his life.

More days of more despair before he could even begin to hope the sharp-edged pain of finally losing her would begin to dull.

A spring wind, fresh with the greening promise of the world, eased through the window, gentle on his face, and only because he was for the moment out of tears did he not cry with weary grief for everything that was and was not and would never be.

'Robert,' Dame Frevisse said behind him with the gentleness of these past days that had at first seemed to him odd, until he had realized that gentleness was a true part of her, seldom seen because she seldom felt there was need to give it. That she was giving it to him told him how much his pain must be showing but he was past being able to hide it and he turned from the window to her and said the one thing to which his mind kept returning. 'They're dead.'

Dame Frevisse's agreement was blessedly simple. 'They're dead. And part of you will never cease to grieve for it.' She paused, then added, 'But you'll go on living nonetheless. Katherine wishes to speak with you, with me to listen while she does.'

From the moment he had turned around, Robert had been aware that Katherine was there, standing a little beyond Dame Frevisse, and had kept his eyes from her. He had been too much aware of Katherine all these four days; knew how much she had taken on herself besides the children; had wanted to comfort her the times he had seen she had been crying but had kept away from her because comforting her belonged to Drew Allesley; had kept away from ever looking directly at her and did not want to now, but Dame Frevisse was there, waiting, and he turned his gaze toward her.

Katherine . . .

Like all the household except for the lowest servants, she was dressed in mourning black. It made her look so very young and she was standing there as if somehow afraid but determined not to be and at the same time in need of being held until the fear went away, that he said more harshly than he meant to, 'Yes?' because she was Drew Allesley's to hold, not his. Not ever his.

Katherine stiffened at his voice and started to draw back but Frevisse took her by the arm, drew her forward, said, 'Tell him,' and moved aside herself, leaving them facing each other. Neither Robert nor Katherine looked happy at that but she had not brought Katherine to this point to let her off it and she said again, crisply, when Katherine held silent, 'Tell him.'

Katherine glanced back at her, asking for help but must have seen that Frevisse was not going to give it because she dropped her gaze to the floor, took a large, uneven breath, and said, to have it over with, 'I was talking with Dame Frevisse. About becoming a nun.'

Because she was looking down, she did not see Robert flinch back from that, his eyes startled with pain; and by the time she looked up at him he had recovered himself so that it was to his cold stare that she had to say, 'I've told her I don't want to marry Drew Allesley. I'm sorry. I don't. We went – Drew and I – we went to Sir Lewis while he was still here and told him . . .'

'You told Sir Lewis *what*?'

Robert's voice rose in what Frevisse heard as pain and disbelief but Katherine maybe heard only as anger because she said on a dry sob and with great desperation, 'We told him we didn't want to marry each other. We . . .'

'But you both . . . you and Drew . . .'

Katherine straightened, lifted her chin, and said to Robert almost angrily, 'There's someone else his father was dealing for. Before me. Someone Drew would rather have, if given a choice. He told me so before we'd been two hours in each other's company, but Sir Lewis changed his mind, decided to be set on having me and my fortune as a way to cost Lady Blaunche for having made so much trouble for so long. You were willing to it, too, and neither Drew nor I saw way out of it, but now that Lady Blaunche is . . .'

Katherine abruptly stopped, afraid she would give pain, but Robert said it for her unflinchingly. 'Now that Blaunche is dead.'

'Yes. Because he likes you and nothing will count with her anymore, Sir Lewis is willing to let go the marriage, he said. When Drew and I told him we didn't want it, he said that. He said . . .' Katherine fumbled to a stop, searching Robert's face for something besides the emptiness with which he was staring at her. Not finding it, she finished quickly, looking at the floor again, 'He said to tell you he'd settle with you without there was a marriage and now I've told you so and beg your pardon if I've offended.'

She made him a curt curtsy and started to draw back, head still bowed. Quelling an urge to impatience at both her and Robert, Frevisse put a hand to the middle of her back, stopping her, and said, 'Tell him the rest. The other thing we talked of.'

Katherine gave her a desperate look.

'The rest,' Frevisse insisted. 'He won't say it. You have to.'

'About your wanting to be a nun,' Robert put in, his voice barren and harsh. 'You want to tell me you want to go back to St Frideswide's with Dame Frevisse when she goes tomorrow because you want to be a nun.'

'No,' Katherine began, startled. 'I don't . . .'

'This afternoon, then? There's still time to put a few miles between you and here if that's what you want so much.'

'Robert,' Frevisse cut in sharply, silencing him, then said to Katherine, equally sharp, 'Say it. What you said to me. Look at him and say it.'

And Katherine did, caught between tears and an anger at Robert's harshness, the words pouring out even more vehemently than they had to Frevisse. 'I only want to be a nun if I can't marry you. That's what I told Dame Frevisse. That I've loved you for this year and more and that I want to marry you or else be a nun. I said I'd tell you when the time was better for it but she said I had to tell you now. That you needed to hear it. She said . . .' Katherine broke off, not able to go on against Robert's frozen stare; bowed her head and said as she sank in a low curtsy, the words smothered by shame and tears, 'But I shouldn't have and I'm sorry and pray your pardon. I . . .'

Robert gave a low cry, closed the few feet between them in a single stride, bent to take hold of her beneath the elbows and raised her up, held her away from him to let her look into his face Where all his heart was naked to be seen. And Katherine after a long moment's look went simply into his arms, that closed around her as if bringing her home.

And Frevisse turned away and left them, with for the first time in too many days a quiet surety that some way now there would be goodness come from all the ill there had been.

Author's Note

The idea that the 1400s in England were a black pit of constant lawlessness and violence is no longer an unquestioned given of scholarship. That Robert and Sir Lewis would choose arbitration over armed conflict is very much in character for their time and place, especially because, at the time of this story, the massive breakdown of royal power that led to the outbreak of the Wars of the Roses in the next decade was only a shadowed possibility. Evidence abounds that in normal times most people – at all levels of society and right through the century – preferred to utilize the well-developed and thoroughly structured system of arbitration to settle disputes. on the very good grounds that arbitration did not tend to leave you dead and cost *far* less than hiring lawyers and going to court – motivations as valid then as now.

The medieval medical theory of bodily 'humours' held (to put it as briefly as mercifully possible) that there are four humours to the body – hot, cold, moist and dry – and if they are in balance, none outweighing the others in influence, then a person is healthy. Likewise, lost health can be restored by putting the humours into balance again and elaborate treatises of the time dealt with how this could be done. What this evidences is a basic grasp of the idea of hormonal imbalance and attempts with insufficient tools to cope with it, as Dame Claire does with Lady Blaunche. But then, even today, hormonal balance is often a difficult thing to manage and it should be understood that the Middle Ages were not a willfully ignorant time. Rather than wallowing in darkness, waiting for the Renaissance to happen, centuries of concentrated effort went into developing tools both of the mind and hand and in accumulating knowledge, some of it rescued out of the abyss left by the fall of Rome, much of it newly discovered, all of it laying the basis for the breakthroughs of the Renaissance, which then – like an ungrateful child – turned on its begetter and scorned it.

As for Caesarean delivery, it was well-known in the Middle Ages, as so amply detailed and illustrated in *Not of Woman Born: Representations of Caesarean Birth in Medieval and Renaissance Culture* by Renate Blumenfeld-Kosinski. As a passing point of interest, the incision was traditionally made along the woman's linea alba, lengthwise to the body, because there was less blood that way, making it easier to find and deliver the baby in time for baptism before it, usually, died. Because the mother was almost invariably dead before this was done, it did not matter that all the belly muscles were severed in the process. Far later, when advances in surgery made it possible to perform C-sections with child and mother surviving, doctors continued to slice vertically rather than crosswise despite it was no longer necessary to do so and that it was understood that an incision side to side, *between* the stomach muscles, would leave them intact. Only eventually, and not many years ago, in the 1970s, did it occur to doctors to change their technique, and not all, I'm informed, have done so yet. One has to ask, when someone talks about the 'barbarous' Middle Ages, what we should term such willful and unnecessary mutilation of a body today.

Among the very many works I accessed in developing the background for this story, of particular note and much use was Christine Carpenter's densely detailed book *Locality and Polity: A Study of Warwickshire Landed Society, 1401–1499*. A scholarly delight.

16/3/02